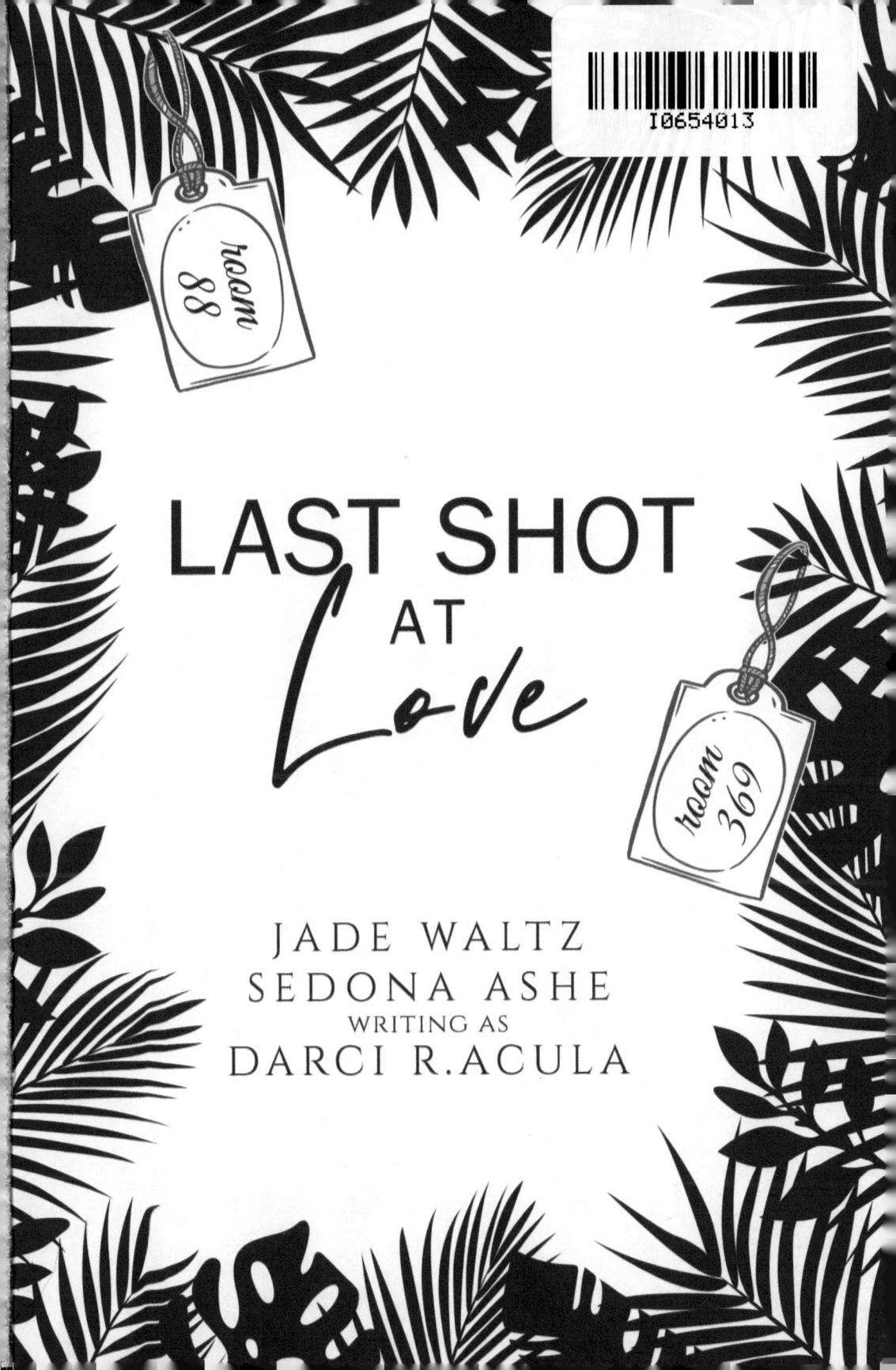

room 88

room 369

LAST SHOT
AT
Love

JADE WALTZ
SEDONA ASHE
WRITING AS
DARCI R.ACULA

CONTENTS

ROOM 369
Jade Waltz

ROOM 88
Darci R. Acula

ROOM
369

JADE WALTZ

Room 369

Jade Waltz

Cover artwork by Gombar Sanja

https://bookcoverforyou.com/

Interior artwork by Cauldron Press

www.cauldronpress.ca

Room 369:

Kael, the feline master chef, ousted from his culinary job...
Grishka, the female orc with a heart as deep as the roots in her lumber yard...

Destiny beckons these two lonely paranormals in the prime of their lives find their fates intertwined at the Last Resort.

When they lock eyes, it's more than mere sparks that dance between them;
it's an inferno of desire that rages through a single, passion-laced night.

Chapter 1

GRISHKA

room 369

The sun was unrelenting today, its rays beaming down mercilessly on the tree plantation nestled deep in the mountains that had been in my family for generations. It baked the earth beneath my boots and cast a glistening sheen of sweat across my muscled forearms. With each swing of my ax, wood split with a satisfying crack, adding to the pile that would soon be transported to the sawmill.

Brushing a hand across my forehead, I pushed away the damp strands of hair, feeling the grit and determination that came with hard work. The distant hum of the sawmill and the clatter of heavy work equipment filled the air, mingling with the occasional calls and laughter of my kin.

My clan—fellow orcs, their mates, and long-time friends —worked beside me, their forms moving rhythmically as we all contributed to the day's labor to make quota.

A sudden buzzing against my wrist broke my concentration, and I cursed under my breath at whoever was trying to contact me while I was at work. Everyone I knew was currently working on the plantation and was aware of the dangers associated with our occupation.

One wrong move could mean a great injury—or worse, death—which was understood by those who had my number.

Growling in frustration, I swung and embedded my ax in a log with a long thunk and glanced down.

My beehive smartwatch displayed an alert that made my heart skip. An email from P-Harmony flashed on the small screen. My eyebrow scrunched in curiosity as well as a hint of skepticism at why they were contacting me after all these months.

I'd half-heartedly signed up for the fated mate matching program, not really expecting anything to come of it. I assumed they were too good to be true, not believing their guarantee that I'd find my destined and leave their program as a happy, matched couple—or clan.

After thirty-five years, I had given up on love, and the last thing I needed was false hopes and a broken heart.

With a sigh, I peeled off my gloves, revealing my callused green skinned hands, and tapped the screen to open the email.

Shock coursed through me like a bolt of lightning. "Matched." The word glared at me from the screen, and my heart skipped a beat. How?

"Grishka?" My brother, Axel, approached, his own ax resting casually on his shoulder. He was a mountain of an orc, even among our kind, with a gaze as sharp as the blade he carried. "Why'd you stop? Is something wrong?"

I glanced up at him, my eyes wide, my chest tight with a mixture of disbelief and a budding hope. "Remember when I told you about that fated mate matching program? How I filled out all those questionnaires, half-joking that they might find me my fated mate? Because let's face it, Axel, it's obvious they aren't around here, or amongst the other clans we trade with."

Axel's expression softened. "You mean to say..."

I nodded, my heart pounding in my chest. "They found someone. A match. For me. After all these years…"

He raised a brow, the lines of his face folding into a familiar, protective concern. "Really? Matched? You mean with the—"

"Yes, the mate program," I cut in, still staring at the words on the screen as if they might vanish if I looked away. "I never thought... I mean, with our kind, it's not like others want to live away from civilization and the exciting city life. I didn't think my fated mate would also be desperate enough to try the program, in hopes to find… me."

Axel huffed a laugh. "Grishka, you're telling me, out of all the males in these mountains, your fated mate is someone from an online program?" His voice was thick with amusement, but his eyes held a glint of something else —maybe hope for me.

A small, tentative smile tugged at my lips. "Seems like

it," I replied, my mind already racing with the possibilities. Could it be true?

Could there be someone destined for me after all this time, after surrendering myself to solitude, putting my concentration on my career, and caring for my family?

"Well, little sister." Axel clapped me on the back, his grin broad and genuine. Looks like you're in for a vacation. Who's the lucky male?"

I blinked, the reality of it all still sinking in. "I... I haven't checked yet." I glanced back down at my honeycomb smartwatch and scanned the email once again, unable to believe this was real... that this was really happening. "It says his name is Kael."

The lines on Axel's forehead deepened as his frown set in. "That doesn't sound like an orc name," he mused, his eyes narrowing slightly. "Did they give you any other information about this mystery Kael?"

I shook my head. "It doesn't matter," I insisted, my voice firm. "The program matches us based on compatibility—like our personalities and needs—not on our names or even our species. That's part of the discovery... the adventure of it all."

Axel's eyebrow arched, a silent, skeptical question in his gaze. He crossed his arms, muscles bulging under his work-worn shirt. "And you're okay with that? With not knowing what species Kael is?"

I nodded, a smile tugging at the corners of my mouth. "That's part of the fun, Axel. I can't know everything going into this, or it would ruin the experience. Besides," I added with a growing smile, "if it's fated, then it's meant to be."

He let out a low grunt. "But how do you know this company is right?" he pressed, his protective brotherly instincts flaring as he stepped closer. "How can you be sure they're not just making this up? Pairing you with someone you're not actually compatible with?"

I met his gaze, my own filled with a confidence I was only beginning to feel. "Because there are too many success stories, too many testimonials from happy couples who were once skeptics like you," I said, my voice firm. "They doubted the process, yet it worked for them."

Axel sighed, the sound conveying a resignation that only a caring brother could have. The tension in his body eased slightly as he combed his fingers through his thick hair. "I guess this means you'll be gone for a few weeks... maybe even a month."

The reality of his words settled over me like the dense humidity in the air. Leaving the mountains, my home, for the exotic resort to meet my fated mate—the thought was both thrilling and terrifying.

"Yeah," I admitted softly. "But I have to meet him. I have to find out if this is real."

Axel studied me for a long moment, his gaze searching my face as if looking for assurance in my decision. Then, slowly, he nodded. "Just... be careful, Grishka. This world... it's not always welcoming to our kind, especially since we're known for being more isolated than other paranormal species. I don't want to see you hurt."

I reached out, squeezing his shoulder. "I will. And who knows?" I said with a wry grin. "Maybe Kael will be more than capable to handle a mountain-raised orc warrior like me."

Axel's chuckle rumbled through the air, and he shook his head. "For his sake, I hope he is."

The playful chaos erupted without warning, as a band of children wielding wooden swords and shields, their laughter as loud and carefree as the river beside our plantation, charged through the work area. The sight was a blend of orcish robustness and the delicate features of humans and other paranormal species, from the smallest toddler gripping a toy ax to the pre-teens with their cloth-wrapped arrows. They were the embodiment of wild, youthful abandon.

I leaned on my axe, a smile spreading across my sweat-glistened face as I watched them. Love for my nieces and nephews swelled in my chest, a warm, comforting presence—but I had no envy for my brother's prolific family life.

They were far too much for me. I loved my nieces and nephews, but I'd let Axel spread his seed upon the world. He and his orc bride... they were like bunhuns, always ensuring she was round and happy. Something I was fine with going without.

I cherished my freedom too dearly, and seeing Axel's brood only affirmed my choice.

"Hey! Away from the machinery! To the nursery rows with you lot!" Axel's commanding voice boomed over the children's ruckus and the noises from the plantation, a mix of affection and authority.

My eldest niece, Visara, a spitfire image of her father, huffed at the command. "But the nursery's not fun, Dad!" she protested, rolling her eyes with the dramatic flair only a young orcish girl could muster.

Axel shot back, "Bored of babysitting, are you? Want to work here instead? Pick up a real ax and contribute like an adult."

She stomped her foot in protest. "That's not fair!"

"That's life, Visara," Axel retorted with a shrug. "Fair doesn't always come into it. Everyone in the clan has their part to do."

Zangerth, Axel's responsible eldest son, intervened, stepping beside his sister. "C'mon, Visara," he urged gently, placing a light hand on her shoulder. "Let's go."

She shrugged it off, her pride wounded, and stormed off towards the nursery, her body language screaming teenage indignation.

"I'm sorry, Dad. We'll keep out of the way from now on," Zangerth promised, his apology sincere.

Axel nodded, the sternness melting into a father's love. "Thank you, Son. I love you."

We watched them race each other back to the nursery, their energy undimmed by the scolding. Axel shook his head, a weary sigh escaping him. "My wife keeps saying this is how all teenage daughters act. She's going to give me gray hair."

I laughed, the sound rich and hearty. "She's only the

first of your dozen," I teased. "You'll be bald by the time the youngest is her age!"

He shot me a glare. "Eat your words, Grishka. Just wait until you have your own."

I clapped him on the shoulder, shaking my head. "You have enough children for the both of us, Brother. I'd rather keep my freedom and be the cool aunt."

Axel's expression shifted, his lips pinched in a line of contemplation. "Things might change once you meet this Kael."

I shook my head. "I highly doubt it," I replied, confidence threading my tone. "I made my preferences clear in the survey, but I'll make sure to mention it again when the moment is right."

His gaze didn't waver. "When are you leaving?"

Glancing across the plantation, I watched as the sun began its descent, painting the sky in hues of orange and pink. The mountains' peaks cast long shadows, signaling the end of another day's hard work. "I'm supposed to report to the resort next Thursday," I said, feeling a pang of something akin to nostalgia settle in the pits of my stomach.

"And when will you return?" His voice held the barest hint of sorrow.

A frown tugged at my lips, the uncertainty of the future casting a shadow in my heart. "Truthfully, I don't know if I will return. At least not right away," I admitted, gathering my thoughts. "That's up to Kael and me to decide... If things even progress to that stage for one, or both, of us to relocate."

Axel looked at me, his eyes softening. The setting sun cast a warm glow on his face, highlighting the lines of worry as he stepped closer. "Just remember, you'll always have a home to come back to," he said, his voice firm, leaving no room for doubt.

"I know, Brother," I whispered, my throat tight. "And I'll never forget that. No matter where this path leads me, this place, this family, will always remain a part of me."

"What do you mean, I am fired?" I demanded, my voice sharp with disbelief.

Sir Ralph, the human male butler, stood before me. His gray hair was impeccably styled, and his glasses perched neatly on his nose, complementing the crisp lines of his suit. He exuded a quiet dignity, but today, his eyes held a hint of regret.

"The madam's new husband doesn't want a male chef, especially a catman, working for the household," he explained, his voice steady despite the unfairness of the situation.

A hiss escaped my bared teeth, my fur bristling with indignation, and my tail flicked back and forth in a display of feline agitation. "After five years of service, she couldn't even tell me herself?" I hissed, the sting of betrayal sharp in my throat. "She can't even tell me to my face, and sends you to do her dirty work?"

"Mr. Chad insisted on handling it," Sir Ralph corrected,

his tone apologetic with a hint of distaste I had never heard from him before. "He knew Lady Annabellelynn would refuse to let you go, and he feared you might convince her to keep you on staff."

I spat out a bitter laugh, the sound echoed in the stainless steel surroundings of the modern kitchen. "Mr. Chad must be jealous of my raw talent," I sneered. "Threatened, perhaps, by having a 'sexy catman' working for the Lady Annabellelynn." I let out a scoff. "It's not my fault human women find my species alluring, nor that I am in my prime —strong, skilled, and single."

Turning away, I swiftly gathered my prized knives, carefully sliding them into my roll bag. My mind raced over the inventory of the kitchen, as I glanced around the kitchen that had been my realm, but I found nothing else that belonged to me. The spices and special ingredients were Lady Annabellelynn's, chosen for her unique palate. The recipes, though—they were mine, a culmination of years honing dishes to her exacting tastes—a feat not easily replicated.

Good luck to whoever dared to replace me.

Untying my apron, I tossed it onto the counter along with my hat. It was a final act of severance, leaving behind a part of myself that had been dedicated to this household.

My recipes, my culinary secrets, they were part of me, and I would take them wherever I went, leaving behind only the memory of flavors that no one else could recreate.

Slinging the knife roll over my shoulder, I turned to face Sir Ralph and extended my paw. "It's been an honor to work alongside you," I said, my voice laced with genuine respect.

With a practiced grace, he reached into his suit jacket and produced an envelope. "This should be the rest you are owed, plus a bonus for the inconvenience of breaking your contract early," he explained, his voice carrying a note of respect.

I accepted the envelope, slipping it into the pocket of my knife roll without looking. The money was a small comfort for the abrupt end to my tenure.

Our handshake was firm, an unspoken understanding passing between us.

"It's been an honor to meet you, Kael. I sincerely hope your next position is your forever home. You will be greatly missed."

"Thank you, Sir Ralph," I replied, patting him on the shoulder. "It's been great, old man. But now, it's time for me to see myself out."

With that, I turned and walked through the kitchen one last time, each step a mixture of nostalgia and defiant resolve. I paused at the doorway, glancing back at the place where I had poured my soul into every dish.

I inhaled deeply; the familiar fragrances of the kitchen lingered in my nostrils, and I relished them one last time before stepping outside.

My strides were swift as I navigated the employee-only walkway, passing through the secluded garden pathway, vibrant with the late afternoon hues.

Reaching the parking lot, I unlocked my electric car, a

sleek vehicle that was one of my few indulgences. Slipping into the driver's seat with practiced ease, I placed my knife roll on the passenger seat.

"Cookie," I greeted the car's AI with a nod. "Drive me home."

"Welcome, Kael," Cookie responded in her smooth, electronic tone. "With moderate traffic, it will be a twenty-one minute and twenty-one-second drive to your destination home. Shall we proceed?"

"Go ahead," I murmured, reclining my seat and closing my eyes to the reality that awaited me.

The truth of my situation washed over me in waves of disbelief and concern for my future. Unemployed. The word echoed in my mind, a stark contrast to the years of dedicated service I had given.

I was now an unemployed private chef in a city where the cost of living was as high as the skyscrapers that pierced its skyline, too costly for someone without a steady income.

I lived frugally—my expenses few, my needs simpler than most—a habit born from my early years of struggling to make a name for myself in the culinary world. My savings were substantial enough to last me about six months if I were careful, but the thought of dwindling resources gnawed at me.

It was the thought of diving back into the job market, of finding another employer who would appreciate my culinary style and unique flair, that was daunting. I could take a position at a fine dining restaurant, certainly, but the idea of toiling under another's banner, climbing the ranks in a kitchen that wasn't truly mine, was unappealing.

Personal chef work was my calling, my art. It was the intimacy of creating meals for someone, learning their tastes, their desires, that drove me. Now, that connection was severed, leaving a hollow void where once there was purpose.

Another reminder that at the end of the day, I was an unmated feline, with no one to come home to. No one to love, to cherish, to spoil.

I'd put my head down, tail between my legs, focusing all my attention on my culinary skills to distract myself from the reality that, even after all these years, I hadn't found my fated mate.

My littermates had all found theirs and, through their love, had begun creating litters of their own.

I cringed, flicking my ears back, remembering the past summer's family reunion and how tired everyone appeared as they attempted to prevent their young from doing something they weren't supposed to be doing. I'd rather be the cool uncle that brought them delicious treats to take home so their parents could deal with their sugar high, hyper states.

Sighing, I pressed my head against the window, and gazed out at the fading sun shining off the cityscape.

The city streets blurred past under Cookie's guidance as the car's soft hum provided a soothing backdrop to my racing thoughts, which were loaded with worry about potential places to apply and the looming interviews.

As Cookie's soothing voice pierced the silence, an unexpected vibration across my wrist jarred me out of my reverie. "Incoming email from P-Harmony with the subject 'Match Found.' Would you like me to read it out loud?"

My heart skipped a beat, a surge of adrenaline coursing through me, ears twitching and tail flicking in alert interest. "Yes, read it," I said quickly, my voice betraying my sudden excitement. Eagerly, I grabbed my cell phone, my claws clicking against the screen as I opened my email app.

"Congratulations, Kael," Cookie's voice filled the car, reading the email that would change the course of my life as I followed along, unable to believe the news. "We have found your match. If you accept, now is the time to meet your fated mate, Grishka, at the Last Resort. Your life will forever change next Thursday."

As excitement coursed through me, I wagged my tail frantically, and a big grin formed across my face, so wide it felt like I would become forever frozen in my expression.

A match. My fated mate.

The job loss suddenly seemed trivial—a blessing in disguise.

Released from my previous responsibilities, with enough savings to see me through, I could fully immerse myself in the fated mate matching program. A new life awaited me, a life that included Grishka.

"Thank you, Cookie." My chest vibrated with a deep, resonant purr, a sound of contentment. It was unintentional, filling the space around me and blending with the faint rumbles of the car on the road.

Next Thursday couldn't come soon enough.

I would meet her, charm her, and serve her dishes that would delight her palate and win her heart.

The thought sent a thrill down my spine as it sent my imagination into overdrive.

The idea of cooking for my fated mate, sharing my culinary passions with her, was exhilarating. The possibilities were endless—would she prefer bold flavors, or something more subtle? Would she enjoy the delicate art of fine cuisine, or find joy in hearty, traditional dishes?

As Cookie continued to navigate the roads, my mind was no longer on the job I had lost but on the future I was about to gain.

Grishka—my fated mate—her name alone had a flavor, and I was eager to taste her…

And form a life intertwined with her by my side.

Chapter 3

GRISHKA

room 369

S tepping out of the limousine, the warm, humid air of the tropics greeted me like a soft caress. In comparison to the mountain woodlands I was used to, the local vegetation smelled exotic as it overwhelmed my senses.

I turned to the wolven male driver who had held the door for me, his amber eyes bright and welcoming. "Thank you for your service."

"I was only doing my job, miss." He nodded with a polite, professional smile, his eyes briefly meeting mine before he closed the door. "May the Moon Goddess smile down on you."

Turning my attention to the resort, I was immediately taken back.

It was nothing short of breathtaking.

"Last Resort" was emblazoned in gold lettering, framed with neon pink and green LED lights that added a touch of modernity to the tropical paradise. The entire place screamed of expense and luxury, a stark contrast to the rugged, earthy life I was used to in the mountains.

Tropical flora and plants were artfully arranged around the resort, their vibrant colors and exotic shapes adding to the sense of being in a secluded paradise. Palm trees swayed gently in the breeze, their fronds casting playful shadows on the ground. The air was filled with the scent of salt from the sea and the sweet fragrance of blooming flowers, creating an almost intoxicating aroma.

This definitely wasn't the mountains.

There were no deafening noises from the heavy machinery or workers going about their responsibilities. It was all... peaceful. And welcoming.

The architecture of the resort was a blend of elegance and wilderness, making me feel as though I was a queen, about to enter her summer home—or perhaps, palace, due to the size of the all-inclusive resort.

Every detail, from the polished stone beneath my feet to the intricate carvings on the columns, screamed expense and exclusivity. I felt out of place, like a seasoned warrior suddenly crowned a princess in one of my smutty fantasy romance books.

Kael could be my prince, in an arranged marriage driven by fate.

Rolling my luggage behind me, there was a lightness in my step, fueled by the excitement of meeting my fated mate. This was a moment I had dreamed of—that had always felt unattainable—yet it felt surreal, as if I'd stepped into a fantasy.

And this lavish lobby was designed to fulfill its customers' fantasies through their matchmaking service.

The Last Resort pulsed with life around me—with mostly other paranormal species, but a few humans were amongst the staff—and I felt the weight of their eyes on me, as if the workers and guests alike were fascinated with the freshly arrived female orc who dared to dream of finding her match through their program.

My heart pounded, not with fear, but with a mix of excitement and nerves that fluttered like wild birds in my chest.

A single thought circled in my mind—what if Kael doesn't like me?

The doubt was irrational—I knew the lore of fated mates, how they were destined to love each other eternally, for exactly who they were... regardless of our physical appearances and species.

It was a life altering phenomenon—where two souls discover each other—that all paranormal species yearned for.

But still, the uncertainty gnawed at me.

The concierge's eyes lit up as I approached the front desk, his smile as warm as the tropical sun outside. "Welcome to the Last Resort!" he greeted me, his hands gesturing grandly as if to embrace the entire lobby. "Where love stories aren't just made, they're destined."

"I assume you're not the one making the matches, though." I returned the smile as I leaned against the polished marble counter.

"That's right!" he exclaimed, his chest puffing with pride. "But oh, do I get to witness the magic of it all!"

I raised an eyebrow, intrigued. "Do tell."

"Oh, I will!" His smile broadened, and he leaned forward, eager to share. "You see, just last week, we had a feisty half-blood vampire check in. And guess who she was matched with?"

"Who?"

"A blue octopus shifter!" he exclaimed, his hands gesturing with theatrical flair. "Now, if that isn't a pairing straight out of a fantasy, I don't know what is."

"DID they create literal or figurative waves?" I laughed, the tension easing from my shoulders.

"Oh, he's an octopus shifter, not a kraken!" He flicked his hand dismissively and laughed heartily. "But they were the talk of the resort, their chemistry undeniable. The kind of love story that makes you believe in the magic of fate mates."

His enthusiasm was contagious, and for a moment, I felt a part of the fairy tale he described. "And you get to witness these matches all the time?"

"Every day," he affirmed, his eyes sparkling. "And each one is as unique as the creatures themselves."

"Well, I hope my story will be just as interesting." Curiosity piqued, I pressed on. "Do you know who—or what—I've been matched with?"

The shift in his demeanor was immediate, his excitement giving way to a practiced seriousness. "No one but the matchmakers know," he responded, his voice a low hum of confidentiality. "Even once we check you in, we aren't permitted to tell you. It would destroy the experience. First impressions only happen once."

I frowned slightly, unable to hide my disappointment. "You're no fun," I teased, trying to lighten the mood.

"With P-Harmony's track record, I'm certain you will be having fun soon enough."

His smile returned instantly, winking at me as he leaned forward. "He's waiting for you in room 369." He slid the room key across the desk. "Welcome to the Last Resort, where your love story begins."

With the room key now in my hand, the reality of the moment set in. The nerves were back, full force. "Thank you," I murmured, my voice barely above a whisper.

"Don't worry," he assured me, his tone confident and encouraging, his eyes sweeping over my attire. "You look amazing."

Glancing down at my clothing, I felt a twinge of self-consciousness. I wasn't used to dressing up—especially since I hardly had a reason to do so living in the mountains —but I had chosen my attire carefully, hoping to make a good first impression.

"You really think so?"

"Your fated mate will love your outfit."

"Thanks for the confidence boost," I said, feeling a warm flush spread across my cheeks, holding the key a little tighter. "It's strange to think I'm about to start a chapter like that myself."

"Your room is down the right hall, facing the waterfront," he instructed, his tone light once more. "Have fun!"

As I pulled my luggage through the hallway, my heart pounded with a mixture of excitement and apprehension. The resort was a tapestry of happy faces and luxurious decor, each smile from the staff and every passing couple amplifying the sense of romance in the air. They were wrapped up in each other, their contented murmurs filling the air a preview—perhaps, of what was to come for me. The elegance of the place was not lost on me, and I couldn't help but smile back, nodding in acknowledgment as I made my way.

Following the signs, I navigated the hallway, my heart thrumming with every step closer to room 369.

Outside, the view was breathtaking. The resort's high stone fencing was softened by the lush plant-life that clung to it. Ivy and flowering vines wove through the stones, creating a natural tapestry, their blooms a secret garden's whispered promises.

I wondered what lay beyond them…

The room number finally came into view, elegant script proclaiming the threshold to a new chapter in my life.

Room 369.

With a steadying breath, I slid the key over the scanner and heard the soft click of the door unlocking. Pushing it open, I was greeted by a scene that took my breath away.

The room was dark, illuminated only by the soft glow of

numerous little LED candles, creating an atmosphere of intimacy and magic. The backdoor stood ajar, the wind gently coaxing the sheer curtains into a delicate dance.

I stepped inside, leaving my luggage by the wall, my movements slow and deliberate, my senses heightened by the beauty of the setting.

Drawn to the outdoors, I quietly made my way to the door, stepping into a scene straight from a fairy tale. A path of exotic flower petals, flanked by more LED candles, led through the lush grass of the private yard. My eyes followed the trail to its end, where a blanket was spread out, a romantic picnic laid out under the setting sun.

A selection of fine cheeses, fruits, and a bottle of chilled wine were arranged on the blanket, their colors vibrant against the soft fabric. Crystal glasses shimmered in the fading light, waiting to be filled. The entire setup was framed by the serene beauty of a private pool, its still waters meeting the calm bay in the distance.

As the sun dipped lower, casting the sky in hues of orange and pink, the LED candles flickered like stars come to rest on the earth, their light reflecting in the pool and the tranquil waters of the bay. The air was filled with the scent of the sea and the subtle perfume of flowers from the tall stone walls that bordered the backyard.

I paused, letting the scene wash over me, the beauty of the setting sun casting a warm glow over the private oasis before me.

And then, I saw him.

Kael, my fated mate, a vision of primal grace.

He was bent over, arranging flowers around the plates of food with a concentration that spoke of his attention to detail.

The setting sun cast a golden light over his sleek, muscular body, accentuating the creamy orange and white stripes that adorned his skin and the sleek, powerful muscles that shifted with every movement. His tail swayed lazily, a hypnotic rhythm that drew my gaze to his nicely sculpted form.

Kael was not just a tiger catman; he was a breathtaking display of strength and sensuality, every inch the embodiment of feral allure, his presence commanding even in the gentle act of arranging flowers. The sight of him stirred something primal within me, a deep-seated recognition that this magnificent creature was mine, my match in every sense of the word.

My breath hitched in my throat, the air around me suddenly feeling thick.

His ears flicked back, a subtle sign he had sensed my presence. As he stood and turned around, I was struck by the creamy white fur that adorned his chest, leading up to his face. It framed his bright green eyes, which shone like emeralds as they met mine, and in that moment, the world seemed to stand still.

It was as if the world itself had shifted on its axis, everything snapping into a clarity I'd never known. Something deep inside me locked into place, a feeling of completeness, of belonging.

My soul had found its match.

"Mate..." His voice was deep, resonating in a way that sent a tingle up my spine, awakening every sense in my body.

In his eyes, I saw the reflection of my soul—everything I never knew I needed—the missing piece I hadn't known I was searching for until now.

His gaze held mine, unwavering, as he took a step closer. "Are you real?"

Chapter 4

KAEL

room 369

The world seemed to stand still as she stepped into the candlelight, her presence commanding the dusk like the moon goddess.

My breath hitched, my throat dry as an oven.

Her tall, muscular frame was a testament to strength and beauty, her emerald skin glimmering like precious stones under the warm hues of the setting sun.

Her long black hair, braided and tied high on her head, caught the light, revealing a violet sheen that added an ethereal quality to her striking appearance. But it was her eyes that truly captured me—piercing, black, and intense, they held a depth that seemed to see straight through to my very soul.

She was clad in a tight dark brown leather skirt and vest, both laced up with intricate leather laces that tantalized the imagination. The outfit hugged her curves, accentuating the valley of her breasts, a sight that sent a primal urge coursing through me.

Every sense I possessed homed in on her.

It was as if my soul had recognized its counterpart, and in that instant, she became my world—everything else faded into insignificance.

"By the moon, you're gorgeous," I found myself saying, the words slipping from my lips with reverence and awe.

A small, confident smile played on her lips. "You aren't so bad yourself," she retorted, her voice a melody that sang to the deepest parts of me. There was a twinkle in her eyes, a hint of the strong spirit that lay within.

Eager to bridge the space between us, I offered her my paw and cleared my throat, clicking my lips in a nervous gesture. "My name is Kael," I said, hoping she felt even a fraction of the connection I was experiencing.

She let out a giggle that sounded like the most delightful music pleasing to my ears, and her hand slipped into mine and squeezed tightly, her strength evident even in this gentle touch. "Grishka," she said, her voice rich with warmth. "It's nice to finally meet you, Kael."

Her touch sent a jolt through me, a spark that ignited my soul. I knew then, without a shadow of a doubt, that she was the one I was meant to spend eternity with.

"I'm glad to have finally met you, too," I told her, sincerity lining my voice. "Where have you been all my life?"

She laughed softly, a sweet smile lighting up her face that made my chest tighten. "I could ask you the same." There was a playful glint in her eyes as she posed the question on both our minds. "So, what do we do now?"

The purr that rumbled from deep within me was instinctual, a sound of contentment and desire. My tail swayed with barely contained excitement as thoughts of her, vivid and compelling, flooded my mind.

Images of her—holding her close, my body pressed against hers, marking her as mine in the most primal of ways—threatened to overwhelm my senses.

"Ultimately, that's up to you," I managed to say, trying to maintain a semblance of composure. "But I thought we could start by having dinner under the stars, getting to know each other."

It was important to me that she felt comfortable, that she knew this night was about us figuring out our future before getting lost in our connection, giving into each other passionately.

"That sounds perfect." She released my paw, and I had to suppress a frown at the loss of her touch, already missing the warmth of her hand, making me desire to feel it once again exploring my body.

As she sat down on the blanket, gracefully tucking her legs away, she smoothed her skirt in an attempt to appear presentable. The action, however, only served to draw my attention to her long, muscular legs, stirring a longing within me to feel them wrapped around me.

My tail twitched faster, betraying my thoughts.

I wanted to be the gentle-cat I had intended to be, to respect the pace she was comfortable with, even as every fiber of my being yearned to close the distance between us.

We were fated mates, yes, but that didn't give me license to rush her to fulfill my desires, while disregarding hers.

By the Moon, I realized I was falling for her—hard and fast.

The connection, the pull between us, it was undeniable, something beyond mere attraction. It was as if our souls had recognized each other, bound by a destiny written in the stars.

I knew what others had explained this would be, coming across your fated mate for the first time, but I didn't think it would feel like *this*.

I shifted to adjust my loincloth discreetly, trying to conceal the physical evidence of my arousal. Sitting across from her, I found my gaze lingering on her, admiring the way the dying light played over her skin, on every line of her beautiful form.

Grishka leaned forward, her movements deft as she selected an assortment of hors d'oeuvres from the plate. I watched, captivated, as she skewered two meatballs onto a toothpick and chose a few crackers spread with an assortment of toppings.

"What do you do for a living?" I asked, curiosity burning within me. "And where do you live?"

She took a moment before answering, sitting back up with her loaded plate.

"I live in the Emerald Mountains," she began, her voice laced with a sense of pride. "I work as a supervisor at our clan's lumber plantation and ensure we meet our quotas safely, lending a hand wherever it's needed." She paused, a hint of nostalgia in her tone. "My family were the first settlers in the area. Over time, as our family grew and others found their fated mates, a small town formed— Emerald Spring. Most of the townsfolk are part of our clan, connected to me in some way."

As she popped a meatball into her mouth, her expression transformed. Her eyes rolled back slightly, and a soft moan escaped her lips, one she muffled as she covered her mouth. The sound sent a thrill through me, awakening a desire to hear that moan again under different circumstances. She chewed for a moment before lowering her hand, reaching for the second meatball.

"These are good," she said, her voice carrying a hint of surprise.

Pride surged through me, a warm tide that swelled with her praise. "I made everything here, minus the drinks," I confessed with a grin, watching her reaction closely as I basked in the glow of her approval.

Her response was immediate and sincere. "You have talent. This is the best I've ever had."

The pride I felt was more than just a chef's satisfaction at pleasing a guest; it was the joy of pleasing my fated mate, filling me with a sense of accomplishment. To provide her with such joy through my cooking—it was a victory sweeter than any dish I could create.

"Thank you," I said, my gratitude genuine.

Her gaze turned inquisitive. "And what about you? What do you do for a living, and where do you live?"

"I was a private chef until recently," I began, the

memory of the kitchen I had commanded lingering in my mind. "The exact day I got my matched message, I was let go. The CEO I worked for, her new husband decided they didn't need my services anymore." As I confessed the recent turn in my life, my pride took a hit, and I found my ears tipping back, a clear sign of my distress. "Now, I'm unemployed..."

Grishka's reaction was immediate and comforting. She reached across the space between us, her strong hand enveloping my paw. "Then it's their loss," she said firmly, her conviction undeniable. "Because these are the best meatballs I've ever had." Her gaze was steady, encouraging. "You should consider working at the local restaurant, or maybe even opening your own."

But then she gasped, her eyes widening as she realized what her words implied. "I'm sorry," she rushed out, "I didn't mean to assume that you'd move to Emerald Mountains and start a life there... with me," she stammered, the blush on her emerald cheeks visible even in the moonlight.

But I couldn't let her fret over a future I already found myself longing for. I leaned in, driven by pure instinct, and silenced her worries with a kiss.

Her lips tasted of mint, crisp and inviting, as refreshing as a cool breeze on a hot day. She smelled divine; her scent was intoxicating, one that reminded me of morning dew on a field of wildflowers.

It was an aroma that made me want to rub myself all over her, marking her as my own, surrounding myself with her scent.

Grishka's response was immediate and fiery. Her fingers tangled in my hair, pulling me closer with an urgency that set my blood aflame. Our kiss deepened, becoming a dance of passion and longing.

Our tongues met, exploring each other with a fervor that mirrored the tumultuous emotions swirling within us, that sent sparks of desire coursing through me. The softness of her lips contrasted with the fierce grip she had on my hair, making me want to give into all her needs, her demands.

Every brush of her lips, every caress, ignited a fire that threatened to consume me. The taste of her, the feel of her, it was all-consuming, a storm of desire and need that I had never experienced before.

Her grip on my hair tightened, a delicious mix of pain and pleasure that only heightened the intensity of our kiss. I could feel her heart beating against mine, overwhelming my senses.

This wasn't just a kiss; it was a claiming, a mutual surrender to the bond that had been forged between our souls.

And as we finally broke apart, panting and flushed from our heated exchange, I knew that this was just the beginning, and there was no going back.

I was utterly hers—and I was willing to go to any length to be with her... to maintain the sense of completion she'd given me, knowing it would become stronger with time.

Chapter 5

GRISHKA

room 369

The intensity of my desire for Kael was overwhelming. His culinary creations had been nothing short of divine, but it was his presence, the soft silkiness of his fur, that I yearned to feel against my skin.

I wanted him with an urgency that was almost primal, yet I knew I had to temper my instincts. I wasn't some impulsive teenager, even if the bond between us was tugging at my self-restraint, urging me to give in to the hunger to touch and be touched.

Breathlessly, I pulled away, my apology tumbling out in a rush. "I'm sorry, I didn't mean to get so carried away."

Kael's purr was a low vibration that seemed to echo through me. His eyes, a dark shade of green, were filled with a heat that mirrored my own. "You can carry me away anytime you want," he said, his voice deep and reassuring.

"Is it okay that I may be stronger than you?" I asked,

wondering if my orcish strength would be a barrier between us.

"It's a turn-on. I'd love to be carried by you," he confessed. His response was immediate, his voice laced with a desire that sent a shiver down my spine. "Imagine me, your private chef, making you special lunch boxes with love notes for work, and you carrying me over your shoulder when you return, demanding me to service you."

I choked on a cracker, caught off guard by his forwardness. "Service me?" I echoed, a part of me thrilled at the idea of such a bold mate.

He nodded, a serious expression settling over his features. "Yeah, anything to keep you—my fated mate—happy."

Setting down the empty plate, I let out a sigh. This was all happening so fast… yet I couldn't fathom a reason to be cautious.

"For us to work, we need to be open and forward with each other," I stated, needing to lay the groundwork for honesty between us.

Kael moved closer, his paw enveloping mine, his touch warm and reassuring, sending a jolt of electricity through me. "I am being open," he assured me. "We're not young anymore—not that I'm going to ask your age just yet."

Without a second thought, I cut him off, embracing the honesty we both sought. "I'm thirty-five," I declared, meeting his gaze squarely.

He smiled softly. "I'm thirty-seven, and that's okay. Our ages don't matter to me. What matters is that we don't waste any more time—the time we lost not knowing each other."

As he cupped my cheek, I leaned into his touch, his warmth enveloping me. His green eyes held mine, seeming to see right through me. "I know this is just the beginning," he continued, his voice a gentle caress. "The completeness I feel with you, it's overwhelming, but I don't want to fight it. I want to fall feet first into this darkness with you, unafraid of how deep it goes. I know I can handle falling in love with you. We're fated mates for a reason."

His words were a balm to my soul, soothing the fears and uncertainties that had clouded my mind. "Do you feel the same?" he asked, his gaze searching mine for an answer.

His touch, his words, they resonated within me, echoing the depth of my own emotions. I did feel the same—overwhelmed, eager, and unafraid.

"Yes," I breathed, my voice laced with the weight of my admission. "I do feel the same. I don't want to waste another moment."

Kael's touch was tender as he combed my hair back, his fingers gentle against my scalp. He cupped my cheek again, his thumb brushing affectionately across my skin. "Tell me more about yourself and the Emerald Mountains."

I raised an eyebrow, a playful smirk tugging at my lips. "What is this, twenty questions until we fall asleep?"

His laughter was a warm sound in the cool evening air. "If that's what you want to do," he replied, his eyes twinkling with amusement.

"All right then," I said, deciding to play along. "What's your favorite color?"

"Green," he said without hesitation, a mischievous smile on his lips. "My new favorite color is green. And yours?"

I laughed, a genuine, carefree sound. "Maybe mine is orange," I teased back, watching his reaction closely. "Do you remember all three hundred questions from the program?"

He shrugged, a casual lift of his shoulders. "Only the important ones," he admitted. "Why does it matter? They matched us, and the instant, world-altering connection I feel with you proves they were right."

I took a deep breath, feeling suddenly vulnerable. "It matters to me," I confessed, "especially if you're considering moving to the Emerald Mountains, to start a life together."

His expression shifted to concern, his forehead furrowing slightly. "What's so important that you need to ask right now?"

I felt exposed, vulnerable, fearing that I might shatter the perfect moment we'd been sharing. But then he leaned in, pressing his forehead to mine in a gesture of intimacy and encouragement. "Ask me. Tell me."

Taking a deep breath, I found the courage to voice my thoughts. "I don't want to start anything under illusions. I need to know... do you want offspring? Children... cubs?"

He was quiet for a moment before muttering, "No, I'd prefer not to. But if my fated mate desired them, I'd be open to it." He met my gaze, searching. "What about you?"

"Some might call it selfish," I admitted, "but we've lost enough time. I don't want to share you with anyone. I want to build a life with just you—just us—without worrying about caring for someone else."

"Then that's what we'll do," he said firmly, a smile softening his features. "I have no great need to spread my seed, but I definitely want to... spread your legs, marking you as mine wherever we go."

His crude words sent a flush of heat to my cheeks, yet they sparked another, deeper heat within me, a mingling of arousal and relief.

As he picked up another meatball and fed it to me, I accepted it without hesitation, closing my eyes to savor the burst of flavor. A moan escaped my lips, unbidden, and I no longer cared about maintaining any facade of restraint in his presence.

Kael's purr was a deep vibration, a sound of satisfaction. "My goal is to make you moan, pleasing you with my talents," he murmured, his voice laced with desire.

My eyes opened, locking with his. "I might need a full resume of these talents," I said, half-challenge, half-invitation.

He winked at me, the promise in his eyes unmistakable. "Maybe after I've fed you."

Chapter 6

KAEL

room 369

T he conversation with Grishka was like a dance, back and forth we went, uncovering likes and dislikes, each revelation a step closer to understanding the heart of my fated mate. Handing her a glass of wine to savor, I tidied up our picnic, packing away the remnants of our meal. Wasting food was never my style, especially when I could envision delighting Grishka with a midnight snack.

Returning to her, following the LED candle-lit path, I found her gazing out at the vast expanse of water. She was bathed in moonlight, looking so magnificent that it seemed as if the moon goddess herself was presenting her to me. The primal part of me yearned to mark her as mine, to hear her moan my name in the throes of passion, surged within me.

"I've never seen so much water in my life," she confessed, a soft wonder tinging her voice.

Sitting beside her, I wrapped my arm around her,

comforted by her presence. "We could move to the beach if you want," I offered, half-serious.

She shook her head. "As pretty as it is, it's dangerous, unruly, unkind. I'd rather stay in the safety of my mountains than have danger in my backyard."

Her words piqued my curiosity. "What do you mean?"

"The large bodies of water are dangerous to my kind, particularly the muscular orcs who could easily succumb to its depths," she explained, with a harrowing look in her eyes. "Last summer, an orc teenager nearly drowned. He didn't heed the warnings about the deep water and tried to keep up with his wolven friends. If it hadn't been for them, he wouldn't have survived."

A frown creased my brow, saddened by her story. "I didn't know that."

"It's all right." Grishka shrugged. "Not everyone wants to talk about their species' weaknesses. We have enough orcs in our clan who are built sleeker than muscular, who serve as log drivers."

There was both pride and a hint of sadness in her voice as she spoke of her work and her people, yet there was an undercurrent of melancholy that didn't escape me.

"You really love your job, and the people there, don't you?" I asked, moved by her affection for her home.

"I do." She nodded, a soft smile on her lips. "Life is simpler there, but we don't go without. We've got electric charging stations, strong Wi-Fi, and other modern conveniences. The lumber plantation may be noisy, but we operate only on weekdays to ensure peace and rest for our workers. It's a dangerous job, but we do our best to keep everyone safe."

Her words painted a vivid picture of her life, one that I found increasingly appealing. "Do you truly believe there's a place for me there? As a chef?"

Grishka's eyes lit up. "Emerald Spring is growing. More people are seeking a quieter, simpler life. I know my clan would love your cooking. A small restaurant, even with limited hours, would be a great addition."

The thought of opening a restaurant was daunting, and I couldn't keep the laughter from my voice. "That would be a lot of work to do on my own."

She considered for a moment before offering an alternative. "Or you could be a one-man food truck, serving meals to the lumber plantation workers."

The idea sparked a flame of excitement within me. "That sounds perfect," I said, the possibilities unfurling in my mind like a rising dough, filling my mind with the wonders of a new beginning.

This could be a new opportunity for me to do what I love—and a chance to weave my life with Grishka's, to become a part of her world as much as she had become a part of mine.

Grishka's surprise was evident as she looked at me, her eyes wide. "You really like the idea?"

"Of course," I said, feeling a spark of enthusiasm for the future. "I've got enough saved to put a down payment on a food truck and equip it with everything I need. It'll take some time to get the licenses and perfect the recipes, but it's a start."

She nodded. "It'll be fine," she replied, her words soothing. "We have time, and I understand it'll take a while for you to settle in. You'd be uprooting your life to be with me. That's a big sacrifice."

I closed the distance between us, my nose brushing her neck, taking in her earthy, enticing scent that was already becoming my favorite fragrance. My tail wound around her back in a gentle embrace as I took her hand in mine. "There are no sacrifices when it comes to being with my fated mate," I whispered, my voice low and earnest, feeling her warmth against me.

Grishka inhaled sharply, her body leaning into mine. "I've been yearning for this," she confessed, her voice thick with emotion. "To be desired, all my life."

"It's too soon for love, but I'm already enjoying the fall..." I confessed, holding her gaze. "Being fated means the moon goddess has given us a connection. You're perfect for me, and I want to show you just how much."

She sighed; the sound was tantalizingly close to a moan. "How?" she breathed out, her eyes searching mine.

My heart raced with desire, a craving to show her all that I was capable of. "Now that we've had dinner, I'm ready for dessert," I said, with a playful yet suggestive tone. "I want to give you a taste... a sample of my resume."

Her eyes sparkled, a challenge and an invitation all in one. "Then show me," Grishka dared. "I want to see what skills you have."

As I rolled Grishka onto her back, she caught her breath

sharply, her strong hands cradling my head, guiding me as my lips found the tender skin of her neck. I kissed her there, feeling the pulse of her heartbeat against my mouth. The taste of her skin was intoxicating, a flavor of desire that I knew I'd never get enough of.

My lips traveled from her neck down to her chest, tracing the contours of her luscious body, marveling at the strength of her muscles flexing beneath my touch. Her skin was warm, a canvas of smooth emerald that begged to be adored.

Every caress of my lips was a silent vow of my affection and desire.

Reaching her legs, I continued my journey downward, worshiping every inch of her with my kisses. I unbuckled her sandals with quick, deft movements, tossing them aside without breaking the rhythm of my affections. My lips traced a path up along her other leg, savoring the sensation of her flesh warming under my mouth, until I reached the hem of her leather skirt.

Her moans filled the air, a chorus of need that echoed my own yearning. Her fingers found my tail, wrapping it around her forearm in a gesture of intimate connection. Her eyes locked onto mine, a plea written in their depths.

"I want you," she begged, and the raw honesty in her voice was my undoing. "I need you."

With reverence, I lifted her skirt, my fingers curling around the edge of her black panties, and carefully slid them down her legs, casting them aside to join her sandals.

She was helping now, caught up in the urgency of the

moment, untying her vest with eager hands as I unlaced her skirt, aiding her in shedding the last barriers between us.

Together, we removed the last vestiges of her clothing, leaving her gloriously naked before me, a vision of passion and strength. My loincloth remained, a final thread of restraint that I wasn't quite ready to discard.

Looking down at her, I was struck by a sense of reverence, struck by the sheer beauty of her. The moonlight cast her in an ethereal glow, her every curve and muscle a testament to her strength and femininity.

Her body was a temple, and I was the devoted worshipper.

"You are perfect," I whispered, the words falling from my lips like a prayer.

The intensity of desire in her eyes matched the hunger in my own. "I need to know how you taste," I murmured, my voice husky with want, "if you're as divine as your scent."

"Then have your dessert," she challenged; her response was a sultry invitation. "And perhaps, I can have mine too."

I eagerly buried my face between her strong thighs, my growl vibrating against her sensitive flesh. The scent of her was overwhelming, a heady perfume that fueled my desire to taste, to consume.

Her response was immediate, a sharp intake of breath followed by an exclamation of pleasure. "Oh Stars!"

When I enveloped her swollen nub with my mouth and lashed it with my tongue, her body arched up in a curve of ecstasy.

"Kael!" Her voice was a sweet torment, urging me on, driving me wild.

I lapped at her, my tongue delving deeper, savoring every drop of her essence. Each stroke was met with her cries of ecstasy, her hips bucking in rhythm with my tongue's strokes. Her hands found my head, guiding me, urging me on, lost in the waves of pleasure I invoked.

As I brought her to climax, her screams filled the night air, her essence flooding my mouth in waves of my dessert. I continued, relentless in my worship, until she was spent, her creamy essence a divine gift on my tongue.

Sitting back, I licked my lips, savoring the aftertaste of her pleasure, watching as her chest heaved with rapid breaths. Her dark eyes, heavy with satisfaction, held mine, and the air between us was charged with the scent of her need, now a storm of desire that matched the tempest within me.

Feeling my arousal pressing insistently against the fabric of my loincloth, I was ready to be consumed by the fire I had ignited in her.

My own desire spiked in response, my body reacting with an instinctual readiness. Her eyes fell to my loincloth, now clearly tented with my arousal.

She sat up, her gaze dropping to the evidence of my desire. "It's my turn."

Chapter 7

GRISHKA

room 369

My need for Kael consumed me, a fire ignited by his touch, his taste. He had awakened something primal within me, a yearning that demanded fulfillment.

My body responded with an intensity I couldn't contain, releasing pheromones into the air, a silent call to my mate, an invitation to claim and be claimed.

I watched him, noting his body's reaction to my need. His desire was tangible, a mirror of my own.

My lips parted as I took in the sight of his arousal, knowing it was for me, because of me. A moisture burst between my thighs, dripping down my legs at my body's sudden yearning to be filled—to have his cock deep inside me, milking his seed until he was dry.

Standing tall, I felt empowered, moving with purpose, my confidence as bare as my skin. Without hesitation, I scooped Kael up, tossing him effortlessly over my shoulder in a display of my orc strength.

He gasped in surprise, his claws embedding slightly into my back, a sweet sting into my flesh. His arousal pressed against my breast, a promise of what was to come.

"What are we doing?"

I was direct, my voice a growl of intent.

"I'm going to take my fill and have you until there's no more."

His body vibrated against mine, a purr of submission and desire that sent waves of heat through me. "I am ready to be claimed," he murmured, his voice muffled against the curve of my back.

The LED candles flickered as I carried him through the pathway, back into the sanctuary of our suite. I tossed him onto the bed, my bed, and watched as he lay there, looking up at me with wide, aroused eyes. His paws reached for me, desperate to maintain the connection, to feel the warmth of my skin against his.

I sat beside him, the bed dipping under my weight. Slowly, deliberately, I placed my hand on his leg. It wasn't a hold of restraint but a promise of what was to come.

His purrs grew louder, his body relaxing under my touch, the tension in his body melting away.

Kael's grip tightened on the blanket, his claws inadvertently slicing through the fabric as he maintained his intense gaze with mine. It was a look that spoke volumes, one of need, trust, and a hunger that matched my own.

Without hesitation, I reached for the ties of his loincloth. My fingers worked swiftly, untying them and yanking the cloth away, discarding it haphazardly onto the floor.

Gazing down at Kael, I was struck by the stark beauty of his naked form, something primal and majestic about him that was utterly captivating.

My gaze fixated on a part of him I had never seen before. His stav was unlike anything I had encountered; it was vastly different from an orc's.

The entire surface was lined with tiny, fine fleshy barbs, and while it wasn't particularly thick, its length was impressive.

My lips parted slightly, my breath hitching as I imagined the feel of him. Licking my lips, I found myself practically drooling, my imagination running wild with thoughts of how it would feel to have him inside me. My mind raced with images of us entwined, his stav ravishing me, fulfilling desires I hadn't even known I possessed.

As I took in the rest of his form, his allure seemed to magnify. I could detect the subtle scent of his need, a tantalizing aroma that cut through my own potent orc pheromones. He, too, was producing his own enticing aroma, beckoning me to claim him.

Though my scent was designed to be overpowering, his own desire called to me, a siren song of primal attraction. But nothing, not even the powerful pheromones of a wolven or catman in rut, could overpower an orc's.

His stav oozed with his uncontrollable lust, the pre-mating essence attempting to lure me in. The delicious scent radiating off him was impossible to ignore, a silent invitation that my body ached to accept.

I could no longer resist; reaching down, I wrapped my

hand around him. Kael hissed in pleasure, the sound sending a jolt straight to my core.

Feeling the rubbery barbs bristle against my fingers ignited an even deeper craving within me. I yearned to feel him inside me, a need so strong it was almost painful—to experience the full intensity of our connection.

"I know we've just met," I muttered, my voice husky with desire as I met his heated gaze. "But I don't think I can go to bed tonight without having you inside me. Without claiming you as mine."

"Claim me, take me," he urged, his voice thick with longing, his dark eyes pleading with me to fulfill our mutual need. "I was yours the moment I laid eyes on you."

His words, so raw and honest, echoed the primal need within me.

At that moment, any remaining barriers fell away.

I tightened my grip on his barbed phallus and began to pump, slow but deliberately, needing to make sure he was nice and hard for me. My fingers glistened in the slick precum oozing between them.

I was captivated by the fragrant scent wafting from his stav, and the increasing warmth spreading throughout my body.

I thrust my hand vigorously along Kael's twitching shaft, feeling every ripple of pleasure that coursed through him. His mewls increased in intensity as I pushed him ever closer to his climax, teasingly stroking him exquisitely until he was trembling with anticipation.

I wasn't ready for him to finish yet; I wanted to savor it.

Drink in the flavor of him, as much as feel its girth filling me.

"Please, please stop teasing me." Kael's plea was a raw, guttural sound that reverberated through the room, laced with desperation and desire.

His stav twitched in my hand, reacting to every stroke and touch as he shifted restlessly on the bed.

Smirking at his reaction, the power to elicit such a response from him filled me with a heady sense of control. "But I'm enjoying this too much," I teased, my voice a sultry murmur as I continued to stroke him.

His green eyes, dark with arousal, fixed on me, a silent entreaty that was almost my undoing. Yet, I held back, wanting this moment to stretch out, wanting to savor the anticipation building between us.

The air was thick with our combined scents, the primal aroma of desire that spoke of our deepening bond. I felt my own body responding, a yearning growing within me that mirrored the need I saw in his eyes.

With deliberate slowness, I leaned down, my breath hot against his fur. "I want you, Kael," I whispered, letting my lips graze his stav with the promise of what was to come. "And when I have you, it will be worth the wait."

I collapsed onto the fluffy rug, wedging myself between his furry legs and eagerly taking his hardness into my hands. I instinctively wrapped my lips around it, drawing out its flavor.

He emitted a low moan and purr of contentment, urging me to lavish him with more affectionate licks and sucks. His hips arched up to meet my mouth, his head flung back, his legs jerking.

Kael sat up and his paw found the back of my head, cradling it with a tenderness that contrasted with his wild nature. His claws, sharp but controlled, curled around the base of my ponytail, not to pull or possess, but to connect, to feel me there with him.

This simple act, so full of care and desire, sent a shiver down my spine.

The powerful grasp of his hand on my scalp conveyed his need for me.

His hips inched forward in a gentle rhythm, showing me that he was about to come for me.

My body responded to Kael's touch with a deep, primal yearning, a calling from the very core of my being. His touch unlocked something wild within me, stirring ancient instincts that coursed through my veins with ferocious intensity.

In an impulsive rush, I wrapped my arms around the backs of Kael's furry legs, drawing me closer to him. The sensation of Kael's fur brushing against my skin was both calming and thrilling. His legs, draped in a velvety coat of fur, felt sturdy and powerful beneath me.

Kael hummed a satisfied purr as I sucked the entirety of his stav into my mouth, feeling every prickly inch with pleasure.

Kael cupped two of his hands around the back of my head and pressed down, pushing more and more of himself into my open throat.

My moan echoed throughout the room as his hard flesh brushed against my tongue, tracing down my throat and allowing me to savor every inch of him. I enjoyed each prickly spine and rubbery nodule, using my tongue to give him the utmost pleasure.

His precum was reminiscent of vanilla flavored ice cream, and I wondered how delectably sweet his seed would taste as I sucked him dry.

He released a groan of pleasure as his climax surged. His hips thrashed in my grasp as thick streams of his creamy seed filled my mouth and cascaded down my throat.

A soft sound slipped past my lips as I swallowed his warm, rich essence. I gulped down what seemed like a massive amount of Kael's irresistible vanilla flavored cum, its powerful potency filling my belly.

Each droplet sent pulses of intense pleasure through my sensitive core.

The longing in me intensified, a visceral, aching need that pulsed through my veins. My body begged for Kael— to be filled by him and only him.

It was more than a physical craving; it was a yearning of my soul, a primal call that demanded to be answered. For him to ease the fire within me that had been building since the moment our gazes first met.

He dropped his hands from my head, releasing the gentle grip on my ponytail as he fell backward, his breathing deep and labored.

Pulling away, I caught my own breath as I watched him

for a moment, the sight of him laid out before me sending a thrill of power through my veins.

Fueled by instinct and desire, I climbed over him, straddling him, and seated myself above him, feeling complete in the position.

His reaction was immediate and primal. Kael reached up, instinctively cupping the weight of my heavy breasts, but I intercepted his hands, shaking my head with a sly grin.

"Don't move them until I say," I instructed, my voice firm with an undercurrent of desire as I placed his hands over his head.

Kael's frown was one of mock protest, but he nodded, submitting to my command. His heated gaze drank me in, a wordless confirmation of how much he still needed me, an almost physical caress that made my skin quiver with excitement.

The scent of our mutual need filled the air—intoxicating and overwhelming—enveloping us like a heavy blanket.

My hands roamed freely over his chest, fingers trailing through the silkiness of his fur and tracing the sleek muscles that lay beneath. Each discovery of his body was a revelation, each flex and twitch beneath my touch a sign of the passion simmering just below the surface.

His control was respectable as he let me explore him and feel his strong balled-up strength under my touch. I was stronger than him, but his species was more agile than mine. He could easily overcome me by altering our roles, but instead, he was entertained by my mating game.

With a grunt of satisfaction, I acknowledged the perfection of my mate beneath me.

Leaning down, I brushed his lips with mine in a soft, teasing peck, a promise of the intensity to come. The brief contact was a spark, a precursor to the flame that was about to be unleashed as I reveled in the sensation of Kael, my fated mate, ready and waiting beneath me.

My breath caught in my throat as I marveled at the feeling of his long, hard length between my inner thighs, pressing against my sensitive areas, and desire pooled in my core.

I ferociously dragged his glowing purple head against my aching lips, coating it with my slick wetness. His hot juices mixed with mine, and he let out an agonized hiss as I used him to coat me, preparing myself to take him in.

"Mate..." Kael's voice was strained, a hiss laced with unspoken pleas as his entire body tensed beneath me, yearning for release, heavy with need. "Please..."

The raw desire in his eyes was almost enough to make me reconsider, but I was determined to savor this moment,

"It's my turn to have fun." I moved deliberately, rocking against the firmness of his body, reveling in the sensation and the control I held. My eyes remained locked with his, a challenge and a promise all in one.

"We can do it your way another time," I continued, my movements deliberate and tantalizing. "We have a week before we return to the real world."

The reminder of our limited time together in this

secluded paradise only heightened my desire to make every moment count.

How many times could we do this when we returned to our normal life, indulging ourselves in honeymoon bliss?

Smiling, I leaned down, pushing his head toward my entrance and pressing it in. We both let out a deep moan. My body quivered as he penetrated further. Waves of pleasure rippled through me with each sensation of the ridges on his shaft against my inner walls. I moaned aloud, unable to contain the blissful feeling.

Slowly, I lowered myself halfway and then withdrew him almost out. The muscles in my pussy fluttered around his shaft. On the second pass, I engulfed him to the hilt, and letting the barbed shaft remain in me, I adjusted to the foreign stinging sensations.

"Oh...my..." Kael rasped, a sound torn from the depths of his being. His eyes slammed shut, lashes fluttering against his cheeks as his fingers twisted into the blankets beneath us, the fabric bunching in his desperate grip. "I need..."

His words trailed off into a breathless void, but I knew exactly what he yearned for. I leaned over him, my movements halting his frantic hands with a firm but gentle authority. "You're mine right now," I grunted. "Be a good kitty-cat and let me play with you."

He let out a low, rumbling purr of submission, his body tensing and then relaxing beneath me. Slowly, I began to move in steady, rhythmic motions, sinking down to take him in fully before gliding back up.

Each descent and ascent was a study in sensation, an exploration of the pleasure we could give to each other, a rhythm that we were both quickly becoming attuned to. The room around us seemed to fall away until there was nothing but the heat of our bodies and the synchrony of our desires.

Kael's restraint was palpable, his hands still obediently above his head, his body quivering with the effort to remain still under my command. The sight of him, so strong yet so willing to succumb to my desires, filled me with a heady mix of affection and power.

As I repeated the motion, sinking to his base and then rising up again, I focused on the different sensations that coursed through us both. I placed my palms on his chest, the soft fur a contrast to the tense, hard muscles underneath. With each of my movements, I felt him inside me, part of me, filling me in a way I had never known before.

My pace began to increase, the urgency between us building into a raging storm. I rode him with a growing fervor, each motion more insistent than the last, as we both chased the edge of release.

Our breathing became labored, synchronized gasps filling the room, mingling with the sounds of our union.

So full, so good. The drag of his barbs added a painful pleasure with each bounce.

"Fuck it all..." I hissed out in dazzling disbelief as I sank deeper onto the softness of the fur, feeling his stav pierce through me.

I threw my head back in pleasure and noticed Kael

watching me with his hungry gaze, his hands twitching. "Keep your hands where they are!"

The pace became a rhythm, a cadence that drove both of us wild. My thighs glistened, the evidence of our desire making them slick as I rode him, claiming him in the most primal way.

Kael's paws, which had once rested obediently above his head, now clung to my thighs, a small defiance that I welcomed. It was a comfort, a grounding as I controlled the pace, a sign of his growing need.

With each movement, my heavy breasts bounced unrestrained, demanding attention. Leaning forward, I pressed them to his face, my voice thick with desire. "Suck them."

"Gladly," he growled back, his voice muffled against my skin. His mouth covered my breasts with fervent licks and kisses, each pull at my nipples sending electric shocks straight to my core.

In response to his eagerness, I grabbed his hands. He offered no resistance, instead eagerly massaging them with a fervor that matched the intensity of our coupling. His touch was skilled, sending waves of pleasure coursing through me.

"Yes..."

As he worshiped me with his hands and mouth, I felt a powerful connection bind us, a tangible link that went beyond the physical. We were not just bodies joined in passion; we were souls intertwined, fated mates discovering the depths of our bond.

The room was filled with the sounds of our union—the

rhythmic creaking of the bed, our synchronized breaths, and the soft murmurs of pleasure. In this space, we were the only two beings in existence, lost in a world of sensation and desire.

With each thrust, each caress, I felt myself drawing closer to the edge, to the peak of ecstasy.

The inferno within me roared louder, an impending climax bubbling up from the depths of my being. I craved the searing heat, yearned to be consumed by the fire of our joined passion. I was ready to burn with desire, to have it incinerated in the most exquisite way by Kael, with Kael.

My gasps became unrestrained, primal sounds of raw passion as I rocked my hips with increasing aggression. Each movement was a deliberate search for friction, for that sweet, sharp sensation as his uniquely textured stav drove into me, ruthless in its pursuit of mutual pleasure.

Kael's reactions fueled my own arousal. He moaned beneath me, a sound of pure male satisfaction. His face contorted with ecstasy, the lines of his features etched with the intensity of the moment. His breath, once deep and controlled, now came in short bursts that mirrored my erratic panting.

His stav pressed deep into my inner depths, generating a wild pleasure that increased in intensity with each thrust. His barbs dug further and further into my soaked walls until the pain became almost unbearable as I sought out an orgasm.

My moans grew louder, more fervent, as I closed my

eyes, surrendering to the overwhelming feelings coursing through me.

He gasped, trembling under the force of my movements. His muscles twitched with each wave of pleasure that I drew from him, each gasp syncing with my own moans.

I slid my hands down to his chest. My fingers curled into his fur, grabbing instinctively. The softness under my fingers contrasted with the powerful muscles that rippled under my touch. I clutched at him, needing to feel grounded, needing something to hold onto as the pleasure threatened to carry me away.

Desire coursed through my veins as I feverishly thrust myself onto his stav, letting out desperate moans and shrieks.

In the crescendo of our movements, I felt the tether of control slipping. The fire within me coiled tighter, a serpent ready to strike.

A powerful scream of pleasure erupted from my lips as the hard, pointy stav plunged deep inside me for the last time. A hot stream of creamy cum burst into my core, filling it completely.

The sensation of the powerful seed swelling within me was overwhelming, unleashing a surge of pleasure coursing through me, electrifying every nerve.

I gasped for air as an intense orgasm racked my entire being.

A loud cry escaped my lips as I gasped, holding tightly onto him and pressing my face into his shoulder.

Before I could catch my breath, Kael's arms enveloped

me, drawing me into the warmth of his embrace. Carefully, he rolled us over, and I felt his stav as it deflated and slipped from me, leaving a palpable absence.

I nestled into his chest, a perfect fit against him. His fur was a soft contrast to my skin, a comforting presence that spoke of safety and affection.

He reached out for a blanket, draping it over us with tender care, his tail wrapping loosely around my leg in an intimate gesture.

The gentle kisses he planted along my neck were a soothing balm. Each kiss was a whisper of affection, a sign of the deepening bond between us.

A contented smile tugged at the corners of my mouth, a reflection of the deep-seated feeling of belonging that washed over me.

It was more than the afterglow of our passion; it was the knowledge that I was exactly where I was meant to be.

Chapter 8

KAEL

room 369

T he warmth enveloping me was unlike any I had experienced, softer and more comforting than the finest pillows ever crafted rested beneath my head. A deep, contented purr erupted from within me, the sound of a cat who had indeed gotten his cream, though 'content' seemed too mild a word to describe the elation coursing through me.

The scent of morning dew on mountain flowers filled my nostrils, a soothing aroma that seemed to seep into my very being. I nuzzled my face deeper into the pillow beneath my cheek, seeking the source of that delightful aroma.

Then, something—or rather, someone—grunted and wrapped their arm around my back, nestling their head atop mine and beginning to stroke it gently. My purrs intensified, a natural response to the affectionate touch, as I opened my eyes to find Grishka, my newly discovered fated mate, gazing down at me.

"Good morning," she said, her voice husky with sleep and tinted with amusement. She chuckled deeply, a sound that resonated in the quiet of the morning. "What a way to wake up."

I couldn't resist the opportunity to flirt, my mood light and playful. "I know better ways to wake you up," I told her, lifting my head from the comfort of her breast. A sly grin spread across my face as I traced a hand along her thigh, hinting at the pleasures we could revisit.

But she shook her head, rolling away from me with a playful swiftness, and swung her legs over the side of the bed. "I feel too sticky, dirty, and need a bath," she declared, just as her stomach gave a loud, obvious growl. She cupped it, looking down as if it had betrayed her. "I'm starving."

Stretching luxuriously in bed, my back arching as I took in the sight of her, I was struck by the ease and comfort with which she carried her nudity. It was a testament to the trust and intimacy we had already forged.

"You can climb back into bed, and I can serve you breakfast," I offered, the idea of catering to her needs appealing in every way.

Grishka threw her head back with a grunt of laughter, her hair cascading beautifully behind her. The sight filled me with an emotion I was only just beginning to understand—a deep, abiding affection mixed with a testament to the joy and ease that had quickly become the foundation of our budding relationship.

Grishka looked at me with a playful glint in her eye. "I'm afraid if I let you have it your way, you'd keep me satiated in bed all day, feeding me more than just your home-crafted food."

I raised an eyebrow, a smirk tugging at my lips. "And is there a problem with that?"

She chuckled, but there was a seriousness to her words. "I hardly ever leave the mountains. I want to explore the resort while we're here."

A frown creased my brow as the reality of our different lives settled in.

My career as a chef had allowed me to explore the world, to learn from different cultures and cuisines, while her responsibilities had kept her bound to one place.

Climbing out of bed, I felt the satisfying ache of muscles well-used, a reminder of our passionate night. I stretched, my body a canvas of lingering pleasure and slight soreness.

"If you want to spend our time outside our private sanctuary, then that's what we'll do," I said, my decision firm. "I want you to experience everything you desire."

Her eyes softened at my words, and she reached out, taking my paws in hers. "Thank you," she said, her gaze locking with mine. "We have our nights to explore each other..."

I shook my head gently, interrupting her. "We have the rest of our lives to spend together," I corrected her softly. "A little time out of bed won't harm our relationship. It'll strengthen it."

With that, I led her to the bathroom, ready to show her the luxury that awaited.

The bathroom boasted a large glass door shower, big

enough for two, with multiple showerheads that promised a variety of experiences. His and her sinks were set in a long, marble countertop, polished to a high sheen, reflecting the soft lighting of the room. Silver fixtures added a touch of elegance to everything they adorned.

The toilet was in a private closet, offering a sense of seclusion even in this shared space. Every detail, from the fluffy towels to the artfully arranged toiletries, spoke of luxury and comfort.

As I offered to assist Grishka, my intentions were pure. "I want to care for you," I said, the words laced with an earnest desire to be near her, to touch her. "I want to feel your skin under my paws."

Her nod and the smile that softly curved her lips were all the approval I needed. She agreed. "I would love your help."

I took her hand and led her to the full-size mirror that adorned our luxury bathroom, standing behind her as we both looked at our reflections. She stood tall, her height just surpassing mine if I discounted the pointed tips of my ears.

Grishka's reflection was a testament to strength and beauty.

Her emerald skin shimmered, a rich and vibrant canvas stretching over well-defined muscles.

Stray strands of her black hair escaped the messy high ponytail, framing her face in a way that only accentuated her wild beauty. Her eyes, a deep and endless black, reflected a strength and determination that matched the physical power of her form.

Her muscles rippled beneath her skin, each movement showcasing the layers of strength she possessed. It was an impressive sight, the very image of orcish strength, her body a testament to the rigorous life she led. To say she had muscles upon muscles was no exaggeration, and it filled me with an intense pride.

The memory of her carrying me, my body securely positioned on her shoulder as she effortlessly brought me into our suite, played through my mind. The feeling of being so easily borne by her was exhilarating, a wishful thought crossing my mind that she could carry me everywhere.

It was the knowledge that my fated mate was more than capable of taking care of herself that added a layer of respect and admiration to the already deep well of my affection for her.

Then she turned to me, her reflection mirroring the serious tone of her question. "Do you still want to move to Emerald Springs to live with me?"

The question hung in the air, a bridge between two vastly different lives now converging. The thought of leaving my past behind, of embracing a life among the mountains with Grishka, was both daunting and exhilarating. It was a decision that would shape our shared destiny, and as I gazed at her reflection, at the orc female who had swiftly become my world.

"Yes," I purred, combing a stray hair away from her ears. "I want to be with you, Grishka. Wherever you are, that's where I belong."

Chapter 9

GRISHKA

room 369

He leaned in and pressed his nose against the side of my neck. I watched him through the mirror as he closed his eyes and took in a deep breath. A satisfied purr erupted from him as his calming scent filled with oranges and sunshine wrapped around me like a warm blanket.

"Are you sure?"

His emerald eyes jerked open and found mine in the mirror's reflection. If it weren't for the clear confusion chiseled in his facial expression, I would've thought our position erotic, but the inquiry left unanswered from his kissable lips had stabbed a dagger laden with worry directly to my heart.

"What do you mean?"

"Are you sure you are willing to leave the city, being close to everything, to live in a small remote town in the mountains?"

He sent me a wide smile through the mirror and placed

his lips next to my ear. "The city doesn't want me, and it won't have you."

Leaning back, I pressed myself against him and enjoyed how we appeared standing beside each other in the mirror.

We radiated strength—power—and primal hunger.

I didn't miss how the air became heavier with our yearning, our pheromones swirling around us in this enclosed bathroom.

"Are you going to help me get clean?" I peered over my shoulder and rubbed my butt against his hardness. "Or are you too afraid of water to get wet?"

"Stand still," he purred, his eyes darkening as his citrus aroma engulfed me, setting my body on fire with need. "I don't want to ruin this moment, not when your body craves substance."

"My body craves many things…"

Without another word, he snaked his arms around my body. His hands pressed against me as one held my stomach and the other grabbed my breast. He placed light kisses against the juncture of my neck as his heavy breaths tickled against my skin.

I watched him through the mirror as he squeezed my breast, and I could feel the familiar warm tingle of arousal shooting up my spine. My mind was reeling as my body responded to the stimulation. I didn't know if it was his aroma wrapped tightly around me, flooding my senses with promises of pleasure, or the thundering purr radiating from him to me wherever we touched, but I couldn't move.

All I could do was stand there and watch one of his

paws hypnotically massage my breast and the other rub gentle circles below my belly button. I wouldn't have known such an odd place felt so good, as if his comforting gesture was preventing me from becoming too over-whelmed so fast.

"You are a jewel—the clearest emerald... a statue of the finest jade, Grishka," Kael purred. I hadn't missed the warm hardness against my ass, a clear sign of his arousal and what was soon to come. "I want nothing more than to place my mark on you so you would stop doubting our bond." Holding my gaze through the mirror, he trailed the back of two of his fingers along the side of my neck, making my body shiver with need. "Unless you have an objection, I want to claim you here, on the juncture of your neck, so you will be reminded of me whenever your gaze falls upon it, whenever something is pressed against it."

"Do it," I whined, wanting nothing more than his mark on my skin, forever being branded by him. "I want you."

"So impatient, aren't we?" He wrapped his arms around me and grabbed my breasts, shoving my bare behind against his hardened cock. Slowly, he rubbed my increas-ingly sensitive breasts as I reached behind me and gripped the sides of his legs not only for support but to make him feel what he was doing to me. "If this is how you are when aroused, I am going to be a goner when I'm in a full-fledged rut."

"I'll remember this when it comes that time," I chal-lenged as my voice came out more like an elongated moan.

"For I am sure you will be the one begging me after the first hour."

"That may be so," he chuckled as he licked my earlobe. "But I don't have any fears that you will be able to resist me and my talents."

"Well, I demand your stav in me, filling me wonderfully while you mark my neck," I whined, begging him to fulfill my wishes. "Why are you taking your time?"

"Because it will only be the first time," he explained, watching me in the mirror. "And I know that I won't be able to do this when my rut will demand quantity of orgasms over quality."

Kael slowly caressed, and lightly pinched my nipples, causing me to groan and thrash against him from his attention to my highly sensitive nubs. Then, gasping, I closed my eyes, unable to handle the pleasure radiating from my breasts and traveling down to my nether regions as his tail loosely trailed up and down my legs, teasing me.

I shivered when one of his paws left one of my breasts, and he dragged it down my chest over my ticklish belly and then cupped my pussy with his fingers. As his fingers grabbed me, I let out a loud moan as I pressed myself against his hard stav, teasing me from behind.

"You are so wet," Kael purred, pressing his middle finger between the center of my folds. "I can't wait to taste you again. I taste as divine as you smell."

Slowly, he started to grind against my ass cheeks, while his middle finger began to trace softly over my nether lips. It took all of my strength not to collapse onto the ground from how keyed up I was, on top of how weak my body felt. There was nothing more than what I wanted for him to place me on the edge of the large bathtub and fuck me until I passed out from orgasms.

If he was testing me, then I was willing to fail. And he could punish me.

"Let me show you how gentle I can be, so I won't feel as guilty when I rut you during the new moon," he explained, kissing along my neck. "I promise you. It won't always be this way, not unless you want it to be."

I nodded, too wrapped up in the overload of sensations that flooded through me. It was as if Kael had enveloped me within himself, and the only thing missing was his stav.

His middle finger pressed deeper and teased my entrance as the pressure from his other fingers parted my nether lips. It traced slowly in a circle as if he wanted to memorize it before he started to press in softly, only to retreat and start the maddening process all over again.

Moaning, I tried to move my hips back and forth as I attempted to force him to speed up and go deeper.

"You are doing so well, my perfect mate," Kael purred as he dragged his paw upward, spreading my slick in its wake, and his nimble fingers found my clit. "Just a little while longer and you will get what you want."

Chuckling, he nipped my earlobe as his fingers started to rub circles around my clit, sending shocks through my system from his skilled teasing. He worked with care, feeling my movements as I rocked against his hard stav, pressed against my ass cheeks. My slick was drenching my thighs as the coolness of the air blowing against its wetness combated the inferno radiating from his body.

His teasing fingers suddenly moved down to my nether entrance to my vagina. Kael released his grip on my breast and grabbed my leg, hooking it over his arm.

I gasped, but before I was able to ask what he was doing, he swiftly pushed his ring and middle finger into my entrance. The sudden movement took my breath away as I clawed at his legs in shock.

"You look so beautiful in my arms," he muttered as he thrust his skilled fingers in and out of my slick passage. "I can't wait to see you come undone before me. Over and over again."

His thumb found my abandoned clit. Every time he thrust his fingers in, his thumb would flick against it as he started to take me to new heights, building a delicious pressure.

My breathing became fast and shallow, and the rapid pounding of my heart drowned out his purring.

"That's it. Keep climbing," he soothed in time with his fingers. "I love the way you feel. All wet and how you squeeze my fingers. I can't wait to feel you wrapped around my needy stav, all hard and ready for you once again."

His erotic words, paired with the overload of sensations, ripped right through me. My eyes snapped open to the view of me shaking in his arms, screaming in pleasure, as his fingers continued to work my pussy and allow me to ride the waves.

"You are amazing," he whispered as he slowed down and removed his hand before lowering my raised leg onto the floor. He wrapped his hands around my waist to prevent me from becoming a pool on the floor. "I believe I've prepared you enough to take me once again. You're wet enough at least."

"I am ready," I announced, my voice sounding raspy to my own ears. "I want your knobby stav inside me as you claim me. I need your mark."

Picking me up, he nodded as a serious look crossed his face. "Tell me how you want to do this," he bit out as he gently placed me onto the bathroom counter.

"Take me as hard and as fast as you can," I muttered, beyond ready to feel him. "Delay any longer, and I will carry you to our bed and fuck you myself."

"Maybe I would prefer you to do that," he teased, gripping my legs as he yanked me to the edge of my new nest. "But I want you so very much that it was hard to sleep soundly last night just thinking about how you claimed me, mounting me on our bed."

"Then fuck me," I growled. "Give me a sample of how your rut will be."

Without a word, he stood as his long thick angry stav stared at me, fully aroused and leaking precum. It was as if it was begging me to milk it.

The display itself heightened my arousal as I witnessed how virile my catman was.

Right as I was about to touch it, Kael gripped my hand and used the momentum to flip me over onto my stomach.

Then, he snaked his arm around my waist and lifted me up onto my knees using the other hand.

"This is your last chance," he purred in my ear as his stav drooled on my inner thigh. "Tell me now to stop, and I will."

"I want this." Gripping the edge of the tub with my free hand, I raised my ass against his hard body, feeling its inferno of warmth. "I order you to mark me, claim me as yours."

"You aren't the one in power." Squeezing my hand tightly, he released it and jerked back. "I am, and I am going to make you mine."

I felt his stav trail up my leg until he placed it snuggly between my nether lips. Then, gripping my hips, he slowly pressed it in, spreading my walls ever so deliciously.

"I was right," he growled, see-sawing his stav back and forth, working my walls by stretching them out, rubbing them with his spines. "You are ready for me."

He lunged forward and pressed his hot hilt against the entrance of my pussy. I moaned. It was so hot and thick. And I was so desperate to have it in me, sealing us together. He jerked my hips back and grunted as he re-entered me.

I gave a grunt of my own as he pushed in a little more, rocking our bodies back and forth to widen myself to allow more of him in. I could feel myself become stretched open by his thick meaty knobs.

I felt so full and so hot. I loved how my pussy walls throbbed and squeezed his thickness, taking him in and preventing him from withdrawing.

Growling, he buried the rest of himself to the hilt.

Then, finally, he was entirely inside me, and as much as it stung to be stretched like this with his rubbery knobs, it also was exactly what I had been desperately wanting.

He paused his rocking, and I could tell by the heavy panting in my ear he was enjoying being able to feel my hot wet pussy shuddering around him. Now that I had taken him entirely, I wanted to climax all over him.

But, instead, I let out a small whimper and rocked my hips slightly, pushing back against him. He needed to fuck me, not bathe in my slick and take in my needy orc pheromones.

"I'm so happy to have finally found you," he growled and gripped my hips, his claws digging into my skin. "And now I am going to make you mine."

I shuddered as his hot breath tickled my ear and rolled my head to the side to permit him.

A scream ripped through my throat as his mouth bit down on the juncture of my neck in sync with a deep thrust. A shudder racked through both of us as he grunted and slammed into me hard.

Moans ripped through me as he continued to pound himself deep into me. His stav rocked against my entrance as if he were trying to seal us together more than what was possible.

He shuddered, releasing his mouth from my neck as an orgasm ripped through me. Then, wrapping his arms around my waist, he rolled us over until we lay side by side as his hot seed exploded from his shaft and filled me.

The coolness of the marble contrasted with the heat between us, creating a unique sensation as he continued to slowly pump within me.

Panting to a halt, he leaned over and licked my wound, cleaning the blood off the mark that sealed our fates together.

Then, combing my stray hair back, he peered down at me in awe.

"My mate," he purred. "My perfect mate. You honor me."

"How are we going to survive this trip?" I let out a slight chuckle. "We can't keep our hands off each other."

"Isn't that the point of this program?" He purred, as he slowly withdrew his stav from me, my body immediately missing the sensation of its fullness. "We answer the questions, give them a blood sample, and they find us our fated mate...

"I was told that once a match enters their suite, they are not permitted to leave until they are either fully mated or ready to depart the resort."

"They really want us to succeed, don't they?" I sat up carefully, taking in my orange striped catman's lethal beauty. "We pay them a fortune to do the research in order to find our match. It would be bad for them and their reputation if their guests failed, leaving them miserable and single."

"But we don't have to worry about that."

I watch Kael playing with the adjustments of the shower. Steam escaped the glass enclosure, heating the room, merging with his scent to create a unique combination.

An erotic thought about the steam cleansing me sent a rush of arousal through me. Then, growling, I placed a hand on his chest and pushed him into the enclosure.

His emerald eyes widened as I slammed my mouth on his and wrapped my hand around his stav. His hands found my hair and ass as they pressed me against him, sandwiching his growing need between us.

I yearned to have his stav inside me again, fucking me and pumping me full of his hot seed.

He knew how to please me well, and that was what I needed.

He flipped us around, pressing my back against the cool glass wall as he hooked a hand under my leg and wrapped it around him. Cupping my ass, he lifted me off the ground and sheathed himself in one fluid motion. My nails found his back as my legs clamped on around his waist for dear life as he pumped into me.

His grip on my ass tightened as he fucked me harder and faster, wrapping his tail around my leg. Then, baring his face into my neck, he sucked on my mark and sent a wave of electricity through me, instantly triggering an orgasm.

My eyes rolled in the back of my head as I hung on to him for dear life. His

pumping sped up as he chased his release while continuing mine.

Suddenly, his grunts filled my ears as his rhythm became unstable jerks, slowing down to a stop.

Pulling his mouth from my shoulder, I silently watched the water from the shower beam down on him as he licked my mark, not caring that he was getting his fur wet.

Satisfied with his work, he gave me a wide grin.

"Now that I've satiated your orc lust, let me take my time to make sure you are adequately bathed before your body makes any more demands."

Chapter 10

KAEL

room 369

We never made it outside our suite like Grishka wanted yesterday.

After spending another day exploring each other's bodies, the upcoming new moon had brought out a side of us I hadn't fully anticipated. Grishka's orc pheromones had unexpectedly triggered something equivalent to my mating heat, not just bringing it on early but bringing it into existence with fervor that left us both exhausted.

Now, as I sat across from her, my energy spent, I thought about the mess we'd left in our suite for the resort's housekeeping to attend, hoping they would let the fresh air clear the heavy scent of our day of mating.

Most importantly, I was eager to show Grishka around the resort.

I felt a swell of pride walking beside her, hand in paw, with my mark visible on her neck for all to see—a sign that she was mine and I was hers.

"What are you looking at?" Grishka's voice pulled me from my thoughts.

I purred, a sound of deep satisfaction, as I leaned across the tiki bar's table and cupped her face gently. My thumb caressed her cheek, and I savored the warmth of her skin against my pad. She leaned into my touch, her black eyes holding mine, seeking my response.

"I'm looking at you," I confessed, my voice low and filled with admiration. "And how good my mark looks on the base of your neck."

Her cheeks flushed a darker shade of green—a reaction I hadn't seen on an orc before—and it was endearing. "I'm happy to wear it," she admitted, and the pride in her voice matched the pride in my heart. "Maybe I should get a fancy collar for you."

"I would wear it with great pride." As I wrapped my tail around her leg, I let out a deep purr from deep within my chest. "As long as it doesn't have one of those bells on it. Then how am I supposed to sneak up on you to surprise you at work?" Dropping my palm to my mark, I traced it with a claw, observing her reaction as she closed her eyes and let out a faint sigh. "Are you fine with the fact that your skin will be scarred?"

She raised an eyebrow, a smirk playing on her lips. "I have scars all over my body."

A surge of curiosity washed over me. "When we return to our suite, I will have to map out your body," I promised her with a mischievous glint in my eyes. "To discover each and every mark and hear the stories of how you got them."

"I would be foolish if I believed your suggestion would remain just story time over a drink," she quipped, a twinkle of mischief in her eyes. Grishka's words were a playful challenge, suggesting our conversation could evolve into something far more intense than idle storytelling.

In response, I raised my tail higher on her leg, letting it tickle the hemline of her skirt. "I can't help it; I'm endlessly curious about you," I admitted, letting a playful note enter my voice. "It's part of my feline nature."

She shot me a look, one that was filled with a teasing warning. "You're playing with a flame that might engulf you if you're not careful," she teased.

With a grin, I leaned in closer, my voice dropping to a sultry whisper. "If it's by your hand that I am to be burned, then I welcome the flames. I would gladly kneel and worship at your altar."

The dark green of her cheeks deepened, a sign that my words had their intended effect. She glanced away toward the waterfront, a subtle shift of her legs betraying her restlessness. "You're making it hard to resist the urge to throw you over my shoulder and carry you back to our suite," she confessed, her voice dropping to a husky murmur that sent shivers down my spine. "So that you could use your tongue to clean the essence flowing between my legs."

I sat back, a satisfied purr vibrating deep in my chest at her admission. Knowing that she was as affected by our mate bond as I was filled me with a profound sense of connection, that our desires were perfectly aligned.

She wanted me as fiercely as I wanted her, and that knowledge was intoxicating.

Our intimate moment was interrupted by the approach of a brown wolven male waiter. "I'm Jacob, and I'll be your server today," he introduced himself with a friendly smile. "Are you ready to place an order? Or do you need more time?"

I had been so absorbed in Grishka that I had forgotten about the menus. My attention had been entirely on her, on the bliss she had already given me.

The Moon Goddess had indeed blessed me with the perfect mate.

She turned her attention to Jacob. "What's the special today?"

Jacob, with the affable ease of a seasoned server, leaned closer. "Today we have a new themed drink," he announced with a broad, welcoming smile. "It's called Sweet Shifter Passion."

Intrigued by the name, Grishka probed further. "And what's in that?"

Jacob's smile widened as he listed the components with enthusiasm. "It's got sparkling wine, dragonberry flavored rum, passionfruit juice, and grenadine."

The mention of each ingredient seemed to tantalize Grishka, her tongue darting out to moisten her lips—a gesture that didn't go unnoticed by me, stirring a warmth in my chest.

"That sounds delicious," she declared with the certainty

of someone who knew exactly what she wanted. "We'll have two, please."

I raised an eyebrow in surprise. "Two?"

She winked at me playfully, a mischievous glint in her eyes sending a familiar warmth through me. "If it's as good as it sounds, I won't be inclined to share," she teased. "Best if you have your own."

Jacob nodded, his professionalism unfazed by our banter. "Don't worry about it. It's included in the resort's all-inclusive mate program." He glanced at Grishka's neck, at the mark that I had bestowed upon her. "Congratulations on the successful completion of your mating bond," he said with a genuine smile.

Caught off guard, I snatched up the menu, the paper crackling under my sudden grip. I scanned the images and descriptions, my mind a whirlwind of choices. "Could we have a bit more time?" I asked, my voice tinged with sheepishness.

"Of course, take your time," Jacob replied before departing to prepare our drinks.

Turning back to Grishka, I felt a surge of pride, but then frowned, realizing my mistake. "I'm sorry," I began, feeling a flush of embarrassment for my lapse. "I was so caught up in you that I forgot to consider if you were ready to order."

Her laughter was a soothing balm, dismissing my concerns with a wave of her hand. "It's okay. I wasn't ready either," she confessed. "I've been thinking about the collar I want to have made for you."

At her words, my hand instinctively went to my neck,

where the phantom weight of her claim seemed to rest. The thrill of her words raced through me, igniting a fervent pride. The idea of wearing her collar, a symbol of our bond, appealed to every fiber of my being. It was not just a collar but a declaration, a testament to our union—a sign to the world that I was hers and she was mine.

"I want that," I admitted, my voice low and earnest. "I'd wear it proudly. To show everyone that I'm mated to you, Grishka. That I belong to you."

Her gaze softened, and she reached across the table, her hand finding mine. "And I'll wear your mark with equal pride."

Jacob's timely return drew our attention, carrying two drinks that looked like they had been crafted with as much care as a fine piece of art. They were pink and red, layered beautifully over ice, each garnished with strawberry slices and a heart-shaped cookie.

Grishka's reaction was pure delight. "Wow," she exclaimed, her eyes sparkling with excitement as Jacob handed her one of the drinks first, then passed the other to me.

I lifted my glass, the cool surface slick against my fingers, and met Grishka's gaze. "To our future."

Chapter 11

GRISHKA

room 369

As I stepped into the villa, I was immediately struck by the opulence that surrounded me. Every detail seemed to whisper luxury, and I couldn't help but marvel at the thought that had gone into making the place welcoming for monsters in all forms. The open floor plan was a breath of fresh air, and the double-wide doors stood ready to welcome guests of any size or shape with a grand, inviting gesture.

The furniture around me was no less impressive. Stools had been chosen over chairs—a considerate nod to the specific needs of someone like Krakens or any avian species equipped with a tail and wings. It was these small touches that warmed my heart, knowing that someone had thought of creatures unlike myself.

Even though Kael only had a tail, I was glad that he wouldn't have problems sitting down. I understood how uncomfortable it was to be forced to sit in a chair with armrests that dug into your sides.

But it was the bed that truly captured my attention and held it. Enormous didn't quite do it justice; it was colossal, a sprawling expanse of comfort that seemed to promise endless dreams. It was the sort of bed that wouldn't just fit a fairy-tale princess but could easily accommodate her and her seven monster companions.

And yet, whenever we cuddled and fell asleep, Kael always found my chest to lie on.

I was astounded by the silky softness of the cyan comforter as I combed my hand over it. I had never felt anything so exotic, having always opted for generic and low-cost versions of household items.

I justified this to myself as a necessary sacrifice to save money for emergencies and the occasional extravagant things like this fated mate program.

Why buy expensive things when I was never home to use them?

After unpacking the rest of my luggage and arranging the suite to my liking, I laughed at myself for how long it had taken me to do this.

I've been here for three days, this was the first time I was able to take a breather by myself, without Kael attached to my hip. We hadn't been able to take our eyes and hands off of each other—amongst other things.

Which wasn't a bad thing, but I kept wondering when the honeymoon period of our new relationship would end —and whether it ever would.

It wasn't that I didn't want to be around him; it was just that I needed a break—we both did—especially after constructing a life without someone, and now... we had each other.

Picking up the note on the desk, I read the contents. Kael had decided to spend some private time sunbathing on our suite's private beach, inviting me to join him.

It seemed the perfect moment to explore the beach before the midnight dinner cruise.

I slipped into my black bikini and threw on a matching sundress and shawl, which billowed out behind me as I tied it around my waist. With my flip-flops on and a towel in hand, I headed out, eager to spend the rest of the day with Kael.

The warmth of the setting sun kissed my skin as I stepped outside, the coolness of the wind blowing through the leaves offering a delightful contrast.

As I walked along the beach, the rhythmic lull of the waves seemed to wash over me, and I took in the diverse assembly of monsters along the shore.

Some frolicked in the water, their laughter echoing across the beach, while others reclined on the sand, basking in the dying afternoon light.

A group of orcs was engrossed in a spirited volleyball match, girls versus boys, their competitive banter filling the beach. I stopped to watch them for a moment, their game attracting a crowd of entertained onlookers.

In the water nearby, a flock of birdmen swam, their wings skimming the surface with a graceful ease. Gargoyles and wolven had joined them, their playful splashing contributing to the vibrant atmosphere.

Beside our suite's gazebo, my tiger catman lay sunbathing on a beach bed curiously designed just for cats. A line of empty lounge chairs stretched beside him, their umbrellas closed, awaiting more guests to shield from the sun.

In an attempt to be discreet, I walked toward one of the empty chairs and placed my towel beside my sunbathing catman. His orange and white fur stood out starkly against the vivid hues of his beach bed, and as I settled myself, he opened one eye to give me a sly smirk.

Kael's laughter was a comforting sound against the symphony of the beach, his tail swaying contentedly behind him. "I heard you the moment you opened our suite's doors," he confessed with a grin, his eyes sparkling with amusement. "And your scent reached me as soon as you stepped onto this sandy shore."

I returned his smile, though I playfully rolled my eyes. "I wasn't built for stealth, like you, but for strength," I said, flexing an arm in half jest, half pride.

He sat up, the movement fluid and graceful, a stark contrast to my more robust manner. Grasping my hands firmly yet gently, he looked into my eyes, his own reflecting a deep sincerity. "None of that matters to me," he said earnestly. "We both have our strengths and weaknesses. What matters is that we have each other, and that we work things out together."

His words stirred something deep within me, a fluttering sensation that spread like warm honey through my chest. I felt cherished, loved in a way I had never known before.

It was a feeling of being loved, truly and deeply, without reservation or condition. And it ignited in me a fierce desire to love him back with equal intensity.

Looking into his eyes, I saw not just my fated mate—but my life partner, my equal. His acceptance of my orc strength and his acknowledgment of our differences made my heart swell.

There hadn't been a moment when I felt he wished the Moon Goddess hadn't chosen me as his match—that I wasn't a catwoman like him to share his experiences and challenges.

As soon as we locked eyes, he welcomed me for who I was—green skin and all—and wanted to go headfirst into our relationship.

And I couldn't lie: I had felt the same way, and I still did.

That's why I was willing to leap into bed with him to test our chemistry and accept his mark on my neck the next morning.

We were in our thirties and had wasted nearly twenty years of our life searching and yearning for our fated mate —for each other—and neither of us wanted to waste any more time waiting any longer.

And he made falling for him so easy...

With his hands in mine, the fluttering in my heart trans-formed into a powerful surge of love, pouring over me like the gentle lapping of waves behind me.

I couldn't wait to start a new life with him once we left the Last Resort.

"Since we have time to kill before tonight, do you want to take a stroll along the shore?" he inquired, his eyes warm. "I recall you saying that you rarely leave the Emerald Mountains and would like to tour the resort while we are here. We only have a few days left since we've already accepted our bond, so we might as well make the most of it."

I gazed at him, touched by his thoughtfulness. "I would love that."

The thought of walking beside the ocean with him, feeling the sand beneath my feet and the sea breeze against my skin, appealed to a part of me that craved new experiences.

He stood up, offering me his paw with a smile that reached his eyes, his tail swaying gently behind him. His enthusiasm was infectious, and I found myself eagerly taking his paw.

We set off down the shore, side by side.

The beach was a beautiful expanse of white sand, the waves lapping gently at the shore. The sound of the ocean was a constant, soothing backdrop, a soundtrack to the thoughts about Kael and our future swirling through my mind. The setting sun was warm but not overbearing—painting the sky with shades of orange and purple—a gentle presence that seemed to bless our quiet excursion.

As we walked, I felt a sense of peace.

Kael spoke little as he walked beside me, allowing the

tranquility of the beach to envelop us, but his paw held mine, with our fingers intertwined.

I knew that this day would be etched in my memory forever.

As we strolled along the beach, hand in hand, I found myself captivated by the beauty of the setting sun. Sparse clouds dotted the pastel sky, casting a spectrum of stunning colors onto the pristine white sand beneath our feet.

Kael, walking beside me, held a net bag he'd found hanging up in our gazebo in his other hand, ready to collect any treasures we might find during our walk. His touch was warm and comforting, and his tail occasionally brushed against my legs.

Breaking the peaceful silence, Kael's soft voice asked, "How was your shower?"

"Refreshed," I responded, glancing up at him while the breeze played with his blonde hair. "But I can't help worrying about the midnight dinner cruise."

"If it's making you uneasy, we don't have to go. We could enjoy a romantic picnic right here on the beach, and watch the fireworks from a safe, comfortable spot on the sand." He studied my face, then scanned the rest of my body, as if checking for any sign of discomfort or pain. "Is something wrong? Should we visit the resort's clinic?"

Confessing my apprehension, I glanced at the horizon. "I do feel uneasy. I mean, I can't swim. My body isn't buoyant; I sink. And I don't want my limitations to prevent us from experiencing something potentially once in a lifetime."

Kael sighed softly, squeezing my hand a little tighter. "I

wouldn't want you to do anything that makes you uncomfortable," he said quietly. "Your enjoyment is paramount, and I don't want to push you into something when you have a real fear that could endanger your life."

Suddenly, Kael's attention snapped to something in the distance. He released my hand and darted forward, his tail swaying with urgency. Driven by curiosity, I chased after him.

He knelt and scooped something from the sand, lifting it toward the diminishing light of the sun. It was a piece of sea glass, the color of sea foam and incredibly smooth, its edges worn down by years at sea.

"Take a look at this, Grishka," he exclaimed, his eyes alight with excitement as he placed the sea glass in my palm. "It's in perfect condition."

The glass felt cool and heavier than I expected. I turned it over in my hand, watching the sun's rays filter through it, bathing my skin in a warm, verdant light. I lifted it to my eye, the world appearing a green-tinted wonder through its transparency.

But Kael wasn't done yet.

He stepped past me and picked up another piece of glass from the sand, this one a deep sapphire blue, its smoothness rivaling the first piece. He added it to our growing collection, a testament to the sea's hidden treasures.

A little way off, I spotted a pink marble shell, partially buried in the white sand. I picked it up and examined it, a smile spreading across my face. Its surface was iridescent, reflecting the twilight's soft glow, and the pink hue shone vibrantly in the fading light.

"Kael, look at this!" I exclaimed, lifting the shell for him to see. He hurried over, his eyes shining playfully and his tail bouncing behind him.

"That's stunning, Grishka," he remarked, taking the shell gently from my grasp to inspect it. Carefully, he placed it into our net bag, which was now teeming with a spectrum of sea glass and a variety of unique shells.

We continued our search along the shore, uncovering more and more treasures that a recent storm must've brought in. Each discovery sent a thrill of excitement between us, our shared joy in these simple finds was tangible, making me appreciate this fated mate program for connecting us even more. I realized I had never felt this relaxed and genuinely happy with anyone before in my life.

Could this be what being fated mates was all about?

As we made our way back to our private beachfront with my sandals in my hand, our treasure bag full of shells and pretty rocks, I found myself savoring the feeling of the cool water lapping at my feet on the warm sand.

Curiosity bubbled up inside me as I watched Kael move with such grace beside the water. "Is it true that your species hates water as much as house cats?" I asked, half-expecting him to leap away from the next wave that rolled in.

His hearty laughter filled the air. "Most of us do, yes," he admitted, shaking his head with a smile still playing on his lips. "It's the drying off that we disdain, and how long it takes our fur to do so. Unlike the wolven, who seem to revel in getting dirty and don't mind the mess, many of us prefer to always be on perfect display, especially when we're unmated. It's all about attracting our fated mate any way possible."

The image of Kael trying to remain perfectly groomed brought a chuckle from my throat. I couldn't help but recall the steamy sessions we had shared in the shower, the way he had eagerly embraced the water when it was just the two of us.

"You didn't seem to mind getting wet in the shower," I reminded him, the memory of how he couldn't keep his paws off me—his paws roaming over my skin as water cascaded around us—vivid in my mind.

He gave a thoughtful nod, his gaze meeting mine. "I don't mind the water," he confessed. "But I don't enjoy the fuss of grooming afterward, trying to brush out the hard-to-reach spots to prevent knots from developing."

A smile curved my lips, and as I took a step closer to him, I offered a solution. "Well, now you have me," I said, a playful lilt in my voice. "I can brush all those hard-to-reach spots for you."

The look in his eyes shifted, a spark igniting in their depths, and his lips curved into a sly smirk. "I would very much enjoy that," he said, the promise in his eyes sending a warm shiver down my spine.

I gazed at the gentle waves caressing the shore, feeling their rhythmic call. "Would you mind if I wade into the waves for a bit?"

He stretched out, a contented look in his eyes as he settled into one of the beach chairs, the sun casting a golden hue over his striped fur. "Go ahead," he encouraged with a lazy wave of his hand. "But don't take too long. We need to catch the boat before it leaves."

"Thank you," I said, feeling a surge of affection for him.

With the sun setting and casting its last golden rays around us, I couldn't resist the pull any longer; I smashed my lips against Kael's.

His response was immediate and fierce; his hands gripped my back and the back of my head, pulling me closer as his tail wrapped around my waist, securing me against him. I felt his power and his passion, and it ignited a similar fire within me.

In a playful tease, I nipped the bottom of his lip, earning a deep growl that vibrated into our kiss, sending a thrill straight through me.

As our lips moved together in a fervent caress, I slipped my tongue past his lips, meeting his in a passionate dance, neither fighting for dominance.

Every emotion, every ounce of affection and love I felt for him, I poured into that kiss—the joy of finding my fated mate, the wonder of our connection, overwhelming me.

Eventually, we had to pull away, both of us panting from the intensity of the kiss.

My first instinct was to carry him back to our suite, to continue what we'd started, but I knew that would mean missing the midnight dinner cruise we had been looking forward to. I didn't want to sacrifice that experience for either of us, especially when I didn't know when we would be able to have a vacation like this once we returned to real life.

Hoping the cool water would tame the fiery need growing within me, I took a step back, but Kael's senses were too sharp. He inhaled deeply, his eyes darkening with desire. "I can smell your arousal," he murmured, the intensity of his gaze holding me captive. "Your mating pheromones are rolling off you."

With a laugh that held a hint of desperation, I placed a hand on his chest and pushed him gently. "We need to be good."

"I am good," he retorted, but the smirk on his lips suggested otherwise.

"Maybe too good," I replied with a laugh, backing away further. In a swift motion, I removed my black sundress and tossed it to him.

He caught it with a predatory growl, burying his face into the fabric to inhale my scent. "I can't get enough of you," he admitted, his voice rough. "Your scent is like a drug, my very own brand of catnip, making me want to press my body against yours."

"You can," I assured him, "after our cruise."

His head snapped up, his gaze locking on to mine. "That's a promise."

Laughing, I turned and ran into the water, hoping to cool the heat that his touch, his scent, his very presence had ignited within me. It was a playful escape, a temporary respite from the overwhelming desire that Kael stirred in me.

The gentle lapping of the waves and the warmth of the sand under my feet beckoned soothingly. As I waded in further, I relished the comforting push and pull of the water against my legs, coaxing me to venture deeper.

With each step that took me further into the water, a surge of joy bubbled within me. Swimming... it had been such a missed pleasure.

It had been ages since I last swam, not since before my body had begun to change with puberty and gained all my muscles. Growing up, swimming in rivers and lakes with friends was a treasured activity, a piece of freedom we all relished.

Now, surrendering to the sea's welcoming arms, I felt a part of myself reawakening, a piece I had forgotten. The water enveloped me like a silk blanket as I ventured deeper into the dark waters, gazing upward at the vast expanse of the young night sky. The noises of the resort faded into a distant murmur, overpowered by the soothing whispers of the waves.

As the water enveloped me, I had a feeling that tonight, under the stars on our cruise, we would experience something that would change our lives forever.

Chapter 12

KAEL

room 369

A s the sky deepened into twilight and the stars began to glimmer above, I noticed the change in Grishka. Her breaths came heavily, a sign of her unease. Taking a dinner cruise at night was a sacrifice for her, especially given her discomfort with swimming. I couldn't stand the thought of her not enjoying herself, especially since she seldom left the safety of her mountains.

But I was determined to make sure that she would enjoy this experience.

I made a silent vow then, a promise to myself and to her.

I would change this.

We would venture out, maybe take mini weekend vacations once a month. She deserved to see the world, especially now that we had each other.

Stepping up behind her, I wrapped my arms around her waist and pressed my front against the strong curve of her back.

By the Moon Goddess, I loved this female. She was everything I could have ever hoped for, fitting seamlessly into my life.

Her hands came to rest atop mine, pressing them closer to her as she leaned back into my embrace. Her warmth seeped into me, and her heart's steady rhythm was a comforting lullaby against my palms. I nestled my face closer, breathing in the scent of her that I had come to adore.

"You're brave for being here, my perfect mate," I whispered into her ear, my voice soft yet filled with admiration. "I am so proud of you tonight, and I promise to show you just how much once we return to our suite."

Holding her, a pang of regret washed over me, knowing our wonderful day was drawing to a close. Yet, there was also a burgeoning excitement for what the future held. I had plans for us, starting with a visit to the resort's hair stylist. I wanted to spoil her, to show her how it felt to pamper herself, to make her feel as cherished as she truly was.

Beneath the expanding blanket of stars, I marveled at their splendor, a beauty I had only ever known through city lights and in pictures. "The stars are amazing tonight."

She chuckled, a sound that was music to my ears. "You'll get used to it in the mountains. We see auroras and shooting stars all the time," she said, and I could hear the smile in her voice.

I squeezed her gently, the idea blossoming in my heart. "Can we make it a tradition to watch the stars every night before bed? Just us, our own little ritual?"

Her response was a gentle tightening of her grip on my hands. "I would love that."

With the stars above and the promise of countless nights spent under their watchful gaze, just like this stretching out before us, I felt a profound sense of completeness.

While I had a lot to plan, with getting a new food truck purchased, permits accepted, ingredients gathered, and recipes tested, I couldn't wait to start a new chapter in our lives, together.

As our boat abruptly veered back toward the resort, a surge of alarm shot through me. Dark clouds were massing on the horizon, ominously rolling in to obstruct our way.

How could we have overlooked this? Storms on the open sea could arise suddenly and wreak havoc on the unprepared.

"What's happening?" Grishka inquired, her voice tinged with the onset of panic she detected in me.

"A storm, and it's coming in fast," I said quickly. "We need to find shelter immediately, and hope we make it back to shore in time."

A vise of fear clenched my spine as I held Grishka's hand in my own, my eyes scouring for any hint of land. But the encroaching clouds shrouded everything. The stars that had been twinkling just moments ago were now obscured.

The wind began to howl, the waves growing more insistent, and I ushered her inside.

I was aware that tempests on the open sea could be ruthless. Alone, perhaps I would have been less concerned, but with my mate at my side, the stakes were too high.

The possibility of her being torn from my grasp by the relentless wind, lost to the sea's depths, was unbearable, especially after I had reassured her that this romantic dinner cruise would be safe.

I felt like I had failed my fated mate, by not being proactive and looking up the weather before we boarded.

As I tried to reassure Grishka, a growing unease gnawed at my chest, a premonition of something amiss. Then, without warning, the boat began to pitch and heave violently beneath us. Panic surged through me as the serene dinner cruise transformed into a nightmare.

The small ship, once a haven of romance and tranquility, rocked violently on the waves. An unexpected and terrifying storm had brewed outside. Huge waves crashed against the vessel, moving it up and down with such force that it felt like we were in the grasp of some monstrous kraken.

The gentle rocking of the boat had turned into violent, unpredictable jerking motions.

Couples gasped and clung to each other, their expressions mirroring the fear that had taken hold of my heart. Crew members moved swiftly, trying to reassure everyone, their voices barely audible over the roar of the storm and the creaking of the ship.

I held Grishka's gaze, my paws gently cupping her face as I tried to pour every ounce of reassurance into my words. "I love you," I told her firmly, trying to sound more confident than I felt. "Everything will be okay. We will be okay."

The words were barely out of my mouth when the boat

began to pitch and heave beneath us with a violence that seemed to come from the very wrath of the sea itself. The small dinner cruise ship was no match for the towering waves that assaulted it from all sides, rocking it as if it were a mere toy in a bathtub.

Around us, other couples gasped, their faces a mixture of shock and fear.

The waves moved the ship up and down, a sickening motion that left us weightless one moment and crushed the next. The boat rocked violently, each tilt a terrifying reminder of how small we were against the might of the ocean.

"I love you too," Grishka replied, her voice steady even as fear flickered in her eyes.

Guilt gnawed at me, and I wished then that I had chosen a different path for our evening. "Forgive me," I said, regret lacing my voice. "I should've made you a homemade dinner and had us repeat our first night together on the beach."

She shook her head, her voice firm despite the fear. "You have nothing to be forgiven for," she assured me.

But then, the boat lurched to the side more violently than before, tilting at an angle that sent a surge of terror through me. Grishka's instincts were immediate; she gasped and latched onto a support pole with one arm, pulling me close with her other, securing us both with her formidable strength. I clung to her tightly, my own arm wrapping around her waist, determined not to be separated from her.

As the ship tilted further, going almost vertical, the sound of breaking glass filled the air, followed by the rushing of water. I held on to her tightly, my heart racing with the fear of being separated from her.

In the chaos of the capsizing boat, with the water rising rapidly around us, I knew we had to act quickly. "We have to get out of here. We need to find something—anything—floating to cling onto," I told Grishka, my voice firm despite the fear that gripped me.

Her eyes, wide with fear, met mine as she gripped my paw with a strength that spoke of her terror. "Please, don't let go of me," she begged, her plea almost lost in the roar of the storm.

"I won't let go," I promised, and I meant every word. "Not now, not ever."

With a nod of understanding, she let go of the support pole. Using her incredible orc strength, she led us up the vertical stairwell, fighting against the current as the water rose higher and higher. When we finally broke the surface, gasping for breath as the waves crashed over us, I clung to her, relying on the buoyancy of our life jackets to keep her afloat.

As I scanned the chaotic water surface, I saw other terrified faces, their cries for help almost drowned out by the roaring storm. They were tossed by the merciless waves, disappearing and reappearing, their positions changing constantly under the sporadic light of lightning strikes.

My fur was soaked, heavy with water, making it difficult to move my limbs. The darkness of the storm and the sea seemed to drown me in fear. But I couldn't succumb to it. I had to be strong for Grishka; her life depended on it, and her risk was greater than mine.

Suddenly, a wooden table floated into view. With each wave that passed, I struggled to reach out, my attempts hampered by the weight of my water-logged fur. Finally, after several agonizing tries, my fingers closed around it. I pulled it closer with all the strength I had left.

"Get on the table," I told Grishka, my voice firm with the command.

She didn't argue and listened.

With difficulty, she managed to climb onto the makeshift raft, her powerful muscles working against the pull of the water. Once she had secured herself, without hesitation, she reached for me and yanked me on top as well, her arm wrapping around my neck in a vise-like grip, securing my leg with her own.

As we clung to the table in the raging sea, Grishka looked at me, her eyes fierce even in the dim light. "I didn't wait my whole life to meet you just to be separated by some storm," she declared, her voice fierce against the howling wind. "If we go down, we go down together."

I nodded, unable to speak past the lump in my throat.

We were fated mates, not just destined to be together in the calm, but to fight through the storms of life, side by side, unwavering. The storm raged around us, but we had each other, and that was all that mattered.

I knew that together we would survive.

No storm, no matter how fierce, could tear us apart.

Chapter 13

GRISHKA

room 369

As the storm raged on, I clutched the table that was our lifeline, with a determination born of desperation. I could feel the strain in my arms, but I was acutely aware that not only my life but Kael's too depended on it.

The tempest raged around us, a relentless fury that seemed to stretch endlessly into the night. The cries of others caught in the storm became distant as the night wore on, their voices swallowed by the fury of the sea.

Kael was pressed against me, his fur soaked through, drenched to the bone. He shivered uncontrollably under my arm, pressing against me for warmth. I tightened my hold on him, trying to give him as much warmth as I could muster.

Under any other circumstance, the sight of him seeking comfort in my strength would have filled me with a sense of pride and affection. But out here, adrift at sea, the gravity of our situation weighed heavily on me.

The storm showed no signs of abating, and with each passing moment, my energy waned.

I could feel the energy draining from my body, the relentless struggle against the storm taking its toll. The need to stay awake battled against the overwhelming exhaustion that crept over me. My eyelids grew heavy, and my head began to nod, lulled by the rhythmic motion of the waves.

In the darkness, with only the sounds of the ocean and the storm for company, it became increasingly difficult to keep my eyes open. The adrenaline that had surged through me was ebbing away, leaving behind a profound tiredness. Every time my head dropped, I jolted awake, fighting to maintain consciousness. But each time, it became harder to resist the pull of sleep and my grip on the table.

I battled the darkness that crept into the edges of my vision, the temptation to just close my eyes for a moment and rest. But I knew I couldn't give in. For Kael, for us, I had to stay awake.

With a silent prayer to the Moon Goddess for strength and deliverance, I held on, determined to see us through the night, and for a miracle to guide us back to safety.

I AWOKE ATOP A TABLE, drenched and surrounded by sand.

As the memories of the previous night rushed back, I quickly scanned the area for my mate. The thought that fate could be so cruel as to take him from me just as we had found each other was unbearable.

My heart lurched as I spotted Kael, lying motionless in the sand a short distance away. "Kael!" I shouted, desperation seeping into my voice. "Wake up!"

The chill wind tore at me, while dark-gray clouds roiled above, obscuring the sun. Lightning sliced through the sky, and thunder crashed violently, as monstrous waves assaulted the island's edges.

With each wave, the water swirled around us, threatening to drag us out with the receding tide. My gaze was fixed on Kael's still figure.

Leaving him was not an option; he would surely drown.

Panic surged within me. I bent down, grasping his forearm, pulling with all the strength I could muster, but he was immovable. His drenched fur added weight, and I cursed my own lack of strength, vowing to become stronger to protect him in the future.

I gritted my teeth in frustration when he barely moved.

The scenarios that ran through my head were bleak—I couldn't move him, couldn't leave him, and couldn't conjure any other solution. The water level was rising perilously fast. I lifted his head onto my lap to keep his face above the rising tide.

I was chilled to the bone as another wave washed around us. In desperation, I clutched my sundress against my chest, hoping the sodden fabric might offer some illusion of warmth.

Glancing down at the soaked dress, a spark of an idea

flickered through my mind. The sundress could be useful. A faint smile touched my lips as the plan took shape.

We were going to make it through this.

The rain hammered down in relentless torrents, transforming the sand into a sludge of mud. I stripped off my sundress and knelt beside Kael. Rolling the dress lengthwise, I laid it along his body, shoving as much as possible underneath him. I hurried to his opposite side and pulled, managing to slide the fabric under him. Then, I tied the sleeves securely around his shoulders.

Positioning myself by his head, I took hold of the sundress's hood and started to pull. He was still a great weight, but my makeshift stretcher held. The fabric slid across the mud-slicked sand as I dragged him, inch by painstaking inch. My muscles screamed in protest as I trudged up the slope away from the beach, but I was determined. We weren't going to perish here, not on this day.

With my head bowed against the onslaught of rain, I forced my legs to keep moving. Each step was a battle, yet we were inching forward, and that was all that counted. Once we were a safe distance from the encroaching tide, I lifted my hand to shield my eyes from the downpour, searching the surroundings for any form of shelter.

My whole life, my parents drilled survival skills into me and my siblings. Initially, we resented these lessons, but they insisted on their necessity, should we ever find ourselves lost in the mountains. Over time, we grew to cherish those excursions with our family. Looking back, I can see the wisdom in their teachings.

Shelter, water, food: these were the essentials my father had emphasized as paramount. With Kael unwell, finding shelter was my immediate priority.

"One thing at a time." My father's words echoed in my mind as I made my way up the beach. Spotting a rocky overhang on a cliffside, it didn't seem too distant, though appearances in such conditions could be misleading.

"Difficult, but not impossible," I muttered to myself, turning to haul Kael toward the shelter.

My muscles protested with a fiery ache as I dragged him, but I was resolute. Kael was depending on me; I couldn't, I wouldn't leave him behind. It didn't matter to me that Kael was a catman—he was my destined partner, the one I loved. That was all that mattered.

It felt like an eternity before I finally reached the rocky overhang, my mind foggy with fatigue. The terrain around was mountainous, blanketed in dense, green foliage. On any other day, this place would have seemed enchanting—a perfect retreat for a romantic getaway.

The overhang itself formed a horseshoe curve overhead, and a waterfall cascaded from the mountain above into a pool below. If the water was as fresh as it appeared, we had found our water source. Now, food was the next concern.

The land around the pool, tucked under the overhang, was elevated enough that I wasn't worried about flooding. The water seemed to drain into a river that flowed away from our refuge, vanishing into the jungle's lush greenery.

With some protection from the storm, I took a moment to really look at where we were. The vividly colored plants gave the impression of a tropical island paradise, rich with exotic flora.

Yet, unfamiliarity bred caution. Concerned about the possibility of large predators or venomous creatures lurking on the island, I dragged Kael behind a boulder, seeking concealment from any prying eyes that might be watching.

Panic threatened to overwhelm me as I looked at Kael's motionless body, but I forced it away. I needed to stay clear-headed.

Oh, how I wished for the fae's healing earth magic at that moment. I couldn't fathom what was ailing him. As I ran my hands over his body, searching for injuries, I found nothing. It made no sense—he had been fine, albeit soaked, atop the table in the storm, yet now he lay unresponsive.

His breathing was soft, even, not strained—surely that was a positive sign. Yet, the weight of the unknowns chipped away at my composure.

Isolated, with no way to call for help, and ignorant of any nearby settlements, I felt utterly helpless. Even if I could scream for aid, I wouldn't know how to guide a rescue party here, clueless as I was about our location.

Gently, I cradled Kael's face, turning it toward mine, my thumb tenderly stroking his cheek. "Wake up, Kael. Please, open your eyes for me. Tell me what you need, my love." The words 'my love' slipped out naturally—a truth I had tried to deny but couldn't. It might be too soon for most, yet it was undeniable. I loved this catman, and I wanted nothing else but for him to wake up so I could tell him once again, but without our lives in danger.

A ghastly possibility crept into my mind—that he might never wake up, might never look at me again, might die and leave me here alone, without the fated mate I had longed for all my life.

I swallowed hard against the growing lump in my throat, my eyes drifting to the jungle at the edge of our makeshift haven. I knew enough about the wild to survive, but the prospect of being alone, of losing Kael, was unbearable.

Ignoring the pangs of hunger, I resolved to stay by his side as darkness approached. Food would have to wait; we had water, and that was enough for the moment. Kael was my priority—everything else was secondary.

I took a deep breath, shivering as the realization set in that my sundress was completely soaked, leaving me in just my bikini. Catching a cold was the last thing I needed, so I stripped off my wet clothes without a second thought. Everything had to dry. I spread my sundress and bikini over a nearby rock, and I didn't hesitate to take Kael's loin-cloth and lay it out as well.

Kael was shivering, prompting me to check his fore-head, which felt unnaturally warm. I had no baseline for a catman's normal temperature; my previous touches had been of a different nature, my mind on entirely different matters. With no other options, I curled up next to him, pressing myself against his chest, hoping my body heat might bring him some comfort.

His closeness brought me a measure of warmth as well. A brisk breeze swept through our shelter, and I instinctively buried my face in the fur of Kael's chest. He let out a faint moan, and I gently stroked his cheek. "Kael, I found us shelter. We're safe for now, my love. Just rest, and let yourself heal, okay? I'm here to take care of you."

Even in his unconscious state, my voice seemed to reach him, as he soon settled and his breathing steadied once more. The constant rhythm of his chest rising and falling and the feel of his heartbeat mingling with mine was comforting. He was alive, and that was all that mattered.

I SHUT MY EYES, attempting to drift off, but the tumult of the storm outside made rest elusive. My mind wandered back to my parents, replaying the memories of nights spent camping in the mountains with my siblings. Though my mother and father framed those trips as survival lessons, it was clear they reveled in those mini-vacations as much as we did.

But now, the stakes were real, not just a playful escape. Those camping trips never harbored any genuine peril, which was partly why they were so enjoyable. I found myself questioning the usefulness of those survival skills in this unfamiliar tropical environment.

A deep sigh of frustration escaped me. Orcs were far from primitive; we had technology like everyone else, which, admittedly, made us complacent about traditional survival techniques—'glamping' as those social media influencers called it. I regretted not taking the time to reconnect with nature and maintain my survival skills.

My mind had been preoccupied with planning upgrades for the lumber plantation, my studies to become an arborist, and the latest methods in cultivation.

I knew I could spend the whole night agonizing over what I should've done, but it would be more productive to get some rest and start searching for food at dawn. Despite my reluctance, I acknowledged that there must be fish in these waters. They were a safer bet than the purple berries I had seen on some bushes earlier.

I couldn't—wouldn't—entertain the thought that Kael might not wake. He had to.

When he woke up, he would need both food and water, and I was determined to have them ready for him.

The thought of predators lurking nearby was a nagging worry, yet my exhaustion was so overwhelming that I struggled to keep my eyelids from falling shut. Finally giving in to my weariness, I closed my eyes, sending a silent plea to any entity that might be out there, hoping fervently that we would be left undisturbed. With that wish in my heart, I surrendered to the engulfing darkness of sleep.

When my eyes fluttered open, I couldn't tell how much time had slipped by.

Kael was still beside me, unmoving. The tempest had lessened, the worst of it seemed to have passed. The sky was a blanket of thick gray, the sunlight dimmed, but visibility was no longer an issue.

Our bodies had entwined during our restless sleep, and I felt something firm against my abdomen. With a flush of realization, I identified it as Kael's 'stav'—the term furred paranormals used for their manhood.

I tried to shift away discreetly, but his arms constricted around me, and he murmured my name with a sigh.

"Kael?" I whispered, hoping for a clearer sign of consciousness.

His eyelids remained shut, and he muttered a possessive "mine." A growl vibrated from his chest as he nestled into my hair, his tail curling around my leg.

It was a relief to feel him move, yet I wished he would

fully awaken. As comforting as his embrace was, we had pressing needs to attend to. I waited for his grip to loosen before I gently extricated myself from his arms.

This was not the moment to indulge in the closeness with my catman, not with the mystery of his condition hanging over us, and our survival uncertain without food or water.

My bikini had dried, but our other clothes were still damp. Nudity wasn't a concern for our kinds, yet practicality dictated caution—especially with the potential hazards of running around unprotected on the island.

After dressing in my bikini and the slightly wet sundress, I knelt by Kael. Cradling his cheek, I turned his face toward me. "I'll return as quickly as I can," I assured him. "I'm going to find you something to eat."

His expression creased faintly, suggesting he heard me but perhaps didn't comprehend. I smiled, kissing his forehead lightly before I set out to verify the presence of fish in the waters.

Stepping out from under the shelter, I surveyed the aftermath of the storm. Fallen trees, scattered branches, and debris were everywhere. Pushing aside the sight of the destruction, I centered myself on the task ahead.

My father's words rang in my head: survival in the wild was possible for anyone who maintained their wits.

With that thought anchoring me, I began my search.

Ahead in the sand, something stirred. I halted, heart pounding, as I realized it wasn't just one thing but several. With careful steps, I moved closer, my tension easing into a sigh of relief at the sight of fish flapping in the shallow water.

They were like no fish I'd seen back in the mountains—larger and more brilliantly colored. The storm's waves must have swept them ashore, leaving them stranded on the beach.

Realizing I needed something to carry them with, I quickly stripped off my sundress to use as a makeshift bag. It wasn't long before I had collected a dozen of the stranded creatures, bundled them in the fabric, and returned to our makeshift refuge.

The next challenge was to start a fire. Even if Kael had been awake, I doubted he'd be of much help.

The branches scattered around were soaked through, and while the small dagger attached to my thigh harness could generate heat, I lacked tinder that would ignite and hold a flame.

Then an idea struck me...

I collected several broken limbs, setting them aside to dry. I could use a lock of my own hair as tinder, hoping to catch a spark from the sunlight at just the right angle. Alternatively, I could attempt to start a fire through sheer friction, relying on my orcish strength—though I was loath to expend the energy I'd barely managed to regain, not knowing what lay ahead for us.

I laid the fish out on some rocks, pondering the possibility of having to consume them raw. The mere thought made my stomach turn, but the urgency of survival was clear.

I may not have liked sushi, but I knew it wouldn't be an issue with Kael, and that was what mattered. There was no room for me to be picky.

We would have to adapt, to use what we had. That was the only way to make it through.

I tore a long strip from my sundress and carried it to the pool. After dipping it into the water, I wrung it out several times, making sure it was clean. The water had a fresh scent, and when I tentatively tasted a drop, there was no hint of saltiness or bitterness. With no other means to verify its safety, I had to trust it was potable.

With the wet strip in hand, I went back to Kael, squeezing it gently over his lips, hoping he would drink. Initially, there was no reaction, but then he opened his mouth, capturing a few precious drops.

Feeling hopeful, I cradled his head in my lap and continued to carefully administer the water, wanting to avoid any risk of choking. His eyelids fluttered, and I couldn't help but smile at him. "Kael, I'm here. You're safe. I'm taking care of you, but you need to wake up, my mate. Please."

His hand reached up, his grip weak but somehow still reassuring.

"Do you want more water?" I asked softly.

He nodded faintly, and I fetched another wet strip.

Once he had drunk his fill, he slipped back into sleep. It was disheartening to see him unable to stay awake, but the fact that he had regained consciousness at all was a good sign—he was getting better.

"All right," I spoke to him, even though he was sleeping. "I have a dagger, but I'm going to make us a spear. Two weapons are better than one."

He didn't stir, but that was fine. He had managed to drink and that was enough for now.

I had to remain vigilant. The island had been quiet, save for the sea's constant murmur, but that didn't guarantee we were alone. I didn't know what creatures might call this place home, and I had to be ready to protect us.

I couldn't just wait idly for P-Harmony—or anyone else —to send help. Not with Kael's condition uncertain and our future up in the air.

Spotting a suitable branch, I began to sharpen one end against a rock. It took some effort, but eventually, I fashioned a makeshift spear. Examining my handiwork, I allowed myself a moment of satisfaction. Now, not only did I have a means to fish, but also an additional weapon for protection, just in case the dagger proved insufficient.

I settled next to Kael, leaning against a boulder with my dagger grasped in one hand and the spear in the other. "I'll keep watch," I assured him, though he was unconscious. "You just concentrate on recovering."

He let out a faint moan, and a surge of hope washed over me. Perhaps he would awaken again before long.

My eyes snapped open to a scene I didn't recognize. My head was throbbing as I turned to see Grishka, slumped against a boulder beside me, asleep. In her slumber, she still clutched a dagger in one hand and a spear in the other.

I wondered how long I had been unconscious. Had she been watching over me the entire time?

I sat up, feeling dizzy for a moment before the world stopped spinning. I looked again at Grishka, noting she was only in her bikini, and saw that her sundress and my loin-cloth were spread out on rocks to dry.

Next to our clothes, I saw several dead fish on the rocks. Had she collected those for us? Watching her peaceful expression, I realized she truly had a survivor's spirit.

"Grishka?" I called out gently, hoping not to alarm her.

Her eyes flew open, and the instant she saw me awake, she lunged forward, her arms encircling my neck. She planted a flurry of kisses across my face, her relief palpable.

I couldn't help but purr, overwhelmed by her response, as I wrapped my tail around her, drawing her closer.

"Thank the Moon Goddess you're awake," she whispered into my ear, her embrace tightening.

"How long have I been out?" I asked, my voice rough.

She looked up at the sky, now shrouded in darkness. "I'm not sure. The storm's over, but the sun... I haven't seen it since our walk on the beach." Her hand came up to my cheek, her frown etched with worry. "I don't understand what happened. We were having such a good time on the cruise, and then the storm just swept it all away."

The sharpness of my headache and the queasiness in my stomach hinted at mint poisoning. I knew a bright red tongue was a telltale sign.

"Is my tongue red?" I inquired, opening my mouth wide for Grishka to see.

She looked at me incredulously but checked my tongue all the same. "Yes, it's red. Why?"

"I think I might have ingested some mint by accident," I explained, connecting the dots between my symptoms and the potential cause.

"Mint?" She looked surprised, her eyebrows climbing high.

I dug through the foggy recollections. "I must have eaten it with those desserts I wolfed down," I said, recalling the incident.

A wave of irritation washed over me as I remembered the server's assurance that the dessert was mint-free.

Her expression mirrored my frustration as she pieced it

together. "How could they be so careless? With so many people with allergies, some of them severe... Do you remember what the server looked like?"

I nodded somberly.

"Right now, that's not our main concern. We need to focus on survival until help arrives," she said, her voice firm.

I clenched my jaw, filled with a mix of emotions.

"If not for you, my mate, I don't want to think about what might have happened..." I trailed off.

Grishka's cheeks and the bridge of her nose flushed a dark green with embarrassment or perhaps modesty at my words. She started to deflect. "But, Kael, I was just—"

I reached out and took her hand, feeling a new roughness against my own skin. I turned her palm upwards and caught my breath at the sight of blisters forming on her flesh. My eyes darted to the sharpened end of the spear.

She withdrew her hand, rubbing the blisters lightly. "It's nothing, just a few blisters," she insisted, downplaying her discomfort.

Shame washed over me at the thought of not being able to protect her. The memory of how I'd collapsed on the beach during the storm came rushing back. "How did we end up here?" I looked up at the rocky overhang that sheltered us, noticing the trickle of water nearby. "Did you... carry me?"

She shrugged slightly, a noncommittal gesture. "Sort of."

My jaw dropped. "But how?"

As she explained how she used her sundress to drag me,

I was dumbstruck. The distance she must have pulled me from the beach was unclear, but it was an impressive act of resourcefulness and strength after surviving the storm and everything.

"Do you recognize this island?" she queried. "Where are we in relation to the resort?"

A twinge of frustration bit at me, and I shook my head. "I'm sorry. The mint—my senses were dulled, and I—"

"Shhh," she hushed me gently, placing a finger to my lips, her gaze earnest. "No apologies needed." Her touch was tender on my face, her blue eyes searching mine. "I'm just relieved you're awake." She motioned toward the fish. "I collected those. Can you eat?"

Again, I shook my head. "My stomach is still unsettled. But some water would help."

I attempted to stand and approach the waterfall, but my balance failed me. Grishka's arm came swiftly around me, lending support.

Though I leaned on her briefly, I was aware she couldn't bear my full weight. I murmured my thanks and allowed her to guide me to the pool beneath the ledge. Without hesitation, I scooped up the water, savoring its purity.

Turning back to her, I asked, "What about you? Hungry? Thirsty?"

"Both," she confessed, her smile faint. "But I wasn't sure about the purple berries there." She indicated a nearby bush.

My eyes snapped to it. "They're toxic."

Gratitude filled me. "Good to know," I murmured,

silently thanking the Moon Goddess for blessing me with such a discerning mate. Had Grishka not exercised caution, she might have eaten those berries in her ignorance and succumbed before I had even stirred from my stupor.

She glanced at the fish. "My parents taught me a variety of survival techniques. I'm pretty sure I can start a fire."

I was curious. "How?"

As she supported me back to where I had been resting, I noticed for the first time that she had arranged a small collection of branches and twigs beneath the overhang.

With a grin, she said, "Watch and learn."

My concern heightened as she pulled several strands of her own hair, a slight grimace crossing her face. I shook my head firmly. "Please, use my hair instead. I can't bear to see you in pain."

She brushed off my worries with her characteristic thoughtfulness. "You're sweet, Kael. But I'm fine. You need to focus on recovering."

I couldn't help but feel a pang of helplessness. It was supposed to be me looking after her, not the other way around.

"Stand back," she instructed gently, drawing me out of my self-reproach.

I observed as she used her dagger, angling it with the sun's rays to focus on the hair and the pile of wood. To my amazement, the hair caught fire, igniting the twigs beneath.

She looked back at me, her triumph evident. "Ta-da!"

I echoed her, smiling. "Ta-da!"

Her laughter rang out, the sound more delightful to my

ears than any music. Her beauty and ingenuity left me in awe.

"Where did you learn that?" I asked, my admiration clear.

"My dad showed me how to make fire," she replied with a nonchalant shrug. "He was big on survival training."

"Your father sounds like a wise orc," I commented.

Her eyes dropped to her hands. "He is," she confirmed softly. "So is my mom. They're both retired now, helping my siblings with their horde—teaching them how to survive and contribute to our clan's lumber plantation."

Her smile was radiant, and I felt an immense pride in having her as my mate. I silently hoped that we would be found soon, so I could accompany her back to the Emerald Mountains and meet her remarkable family and clan.

As she speared two of the fish on a twig, she settled in to cook them over the fire. "You can eat the first two while I prepare the others."

Her simple, practical kindness was yet another reminder of how fortunate I was to have her by my side.

She was a true survivor, my destined partner.

"You are as intelligent as you are beautiful, Grishka," I said with a bright smile.

But her face fell, and I realized my words had somehow landed poorly. "I'm sorry, I—"

She cut me off with a soft shake of her head. "No, Kael. It's me who should be apologizing."

Confusion furrowed my brow. "What do you mean?"

Her eyes dropped. "I—I have feelings for you, Kael.

But..." Her words trailed off as her eyes flicked to my chest. "I'm ashamed I didn't tell you I loved you before... before we almost drowned. You deserved to hear those words in a moment not driven by disaster."

My hand found her cheek, and I leaned in, pressing my forehead gently to hers. Gazing into her deep black eyes, I spoke my truth. "Grishka, you are the one I want. No one else. You have captured my heart, and now that we're mated, only the Moon Goddess herself could part us."

Our eyes locked, and then she kissed me, a simple touch that halted all thought.

Her lips were warm, softer than I'd ever imagined, and her tongue gently requested entry. I obliged, and as our tongues met, a sense of rightness washed over me.

I relished the taste of her, the feel of her tongue exploring mine. I wanted to savor this, to draw her in closer. My hand cradled the back of her neck, the other arm wrapping around her waist, my tail curling around her.

Her heart raced against mine as my fingers wove through her silken black hair. "You're perfect," I breathed out. "Tell me you're mine, for I am surely yours, my perfect mate."

She looked away, a whisper of vulnerability in her voice. "I was always yours, even from the start. But I was so scared of losing you..."

I lifted her chin with two fingers, ensuring her eyes met mine. "Listen to me," I said firmly. "I want you, Grishka. I love you and nothing can alter that. I vow it upon the Moon Goddess."

"I love you too. So much it hurts." Tears glistened in her eyes as she absorbed my words. "All that's happened... it's made me realize I can't take anything for granted. We searched for nearly two decades to find each other, only to nearly lose it all to a storm. I don't want to waste another moment."

"Neither do I," I vowed, drawing her close again. "I want nothing more than to grow old with you, until my stripes fade to white."

Chapter 16

GRISHKA

room 369

He cradled my face in his hands, his gaze intensely scanning my expression. The soft glide of his thumb across my cheek ignited a burning path that made me shiver. Gradually, he leaned closer, his lips barely brushing mine, a teasingly light caress before he withdrew slightly, looking into my eyes for any sign of hesitation.

I couldn't resist reaching up to trace the contour of his cheek in return, awed by the striking features that seemed to cut right to my soul. "May I kiss you again?" he whispered, so softly it was almost lost in the breeze.

"Yes," I whispered back, and his lips met mine again, this time with a softness that spoke of tenderness and longing.

A sigh escaped me as his tongue met mine, a gentle exploration that prompted me to tighten my hold on his shoulder, guiding him to turn onto his side. He responded with a low groan, our bodies aligning in a harmony of movement. The firm press of his desire was evident even through the fabric of my bikini, igniting a deep yearning within me.

Like the forest reaches for the light of the sun, I yearned for him—my catman—with an intensity that surprised me.

His hand slipped beneath the edge of my bikini, a rush of anticipation flooding my veins as his fingers trailed along my thigh before resting on the small of my back. Kael's movements against me sent waves of pleasure coursing through my body, and I couldn't help but moan softly, the sound absorbed by his kiss.

His claws, careful yet assertive, grazed my skin as he drew me even closer, the sensation sending my heart into a frenzied dance. The whirlwind of need inside me grew, a maelstrom of desire that I had never known before, all-consuming and impossible to ignore.

He held me close, his embrace firm and his tail entwined around my leg. "I love you... As long as I live, I will protect you, Grishka."

My heart surged with emotion. His declarations of love, though not new, never failed to stir something deep within me.

"Say it again," I urged, needing the affirmation.

His hold tightened. "I love you more than anything," he confessed, his gaze falling briefly. "And I know it's been a short time, and I didn't expect—"

"I love you too," I interjected swiftly, not wanting him to doubt.

His eyes locked onto mine, filled with a profound affection. "Say it again," he murmured, the rumble in his voice like a soft purr. "I need to hear it again... to savor this moment, no matter how we arrived here."

"I love you, Kael," I affirmed, my hand caressing his cheek.

His smile was quick and full of joy before his lips met mine in a kiss that engulfed all my senses.

Suddenly, he broke away and gathered me in his arms, our bodies rolling until we lay atop my sundress laid out like a makeshift blanket. He positioned himself above me, capturing my lips again with an urgency that sent my heart racing.

A moan vibrated in my throat as he pushed my bikini top aside, exposing me to his touch. His hand cradled me, his thumb teasing a sensitive peak, eliciting a gasp from my lips.

He moved from my mouth to my breast, his tongue tracing circles that sparked waves of delight.

The barrier of fabric between us became too much, and I wanted nothing more than his bare stav between my slick folds. With a flick of my hands, I untied my bikini bottoms, baring myself completely to his gaze.

My fingers wandered through the thick fur that adorned his muscular frame, marveling at the contrast of strength beneath such silken strands.

A low groan emanated from deep within his throat as he surrendered to the sensation, his eyes closing, his purrs growing louder.

But then his eyes flew open, the green darkening to an

intense raven-black as his gaze roved over me. The sight of his fangs, revealed as he licked them, sent a jolt of desire through me, affirming the influence I held over him.

"You are perfect," he whispered, his voice a velvet rumble. "My beautiful mate. And you are all mine."

"If I am yours," I replied, my voice a mere breath, "then you are mine just the same."

A growl of arousal vibrated from him at my words, and he brought his lips down on mine with a passion that ignited my senses.

My fingers found his length, eliciting another groan. "Careful," he rasped, "my stav is sensitive. If you continue, I won't be able to restrain myself."

"And would that be such a bad thing?" I teased, my heart racing as his lips blazed a path down my neck. My other hand found the back of his head, scratching gently in the way I knew he loved.

His response was a deeper growl, and he swiftly kissed his way down my body, his hand gliding up my inner thigh. "Open for me," he murmured against my skin.

With a quickened pulse, I complied. His hungry gaze never left mine as he lowered his face to my most intimate area. I gasped, a mix of shock and pleasure overwhelming me as his tongue swept through my wetness. He focused intently on my most sensitive spot, sending waves of pleasure through me.

My heels pressed into his shoulders, my body arching under his expert touch. "Kael," I managed to say, a plea laced within the single breath of his name.

His fingers found their way inside me, skillfully reaching depths that heightened my pleasure, while his tongue danced along my folds, an exquisite contrast of sensation. It was overwhelming, yet I craved more.

"Just let go," he coaxed gently. "I've got you."

The low growl that vibrated from his throat resonated within me, sending shockwaves of desire through my entire being. I was teetering on the brink, and with his urging, I surrendered to the sensation. My release crashed over me in an all-consuming wave, and I called out his name as I was swept into a rapture of ecstasy.

I couldn't bear the distance between us any longer. With an insistent pull at his shoulders, I brought his mouth back to mine, our lips meeting fiercely. "I want you," I confessed breathlessly, my hands finding his stav, desiring to share the intensity of pleasure I had just experienced.

"Grishka," he warned in a deep growl, a sound that held both a promise and a plea.

"Please!"

Kael's eyes, deep and black as a starless night, locked onto mine, a silent claim in their depths. As he entered me, a sharp twinge of discomfort momentarily pierced through, but it was swiftly engulfed by a rush of pleasure that cascaded through my body as his unique anatomy rubbed against me in a way that felt purely divine.

A warmth spread from my core as he filled me, his movements deliberate and measured. With each undulation of his hips, he drew deeper, until he was completely enveloped within me.

"Are you okay?" he asked, his voice a low whisper as he paused, giving me time to acclimate.

"Just give me a second," I managed to say, feeling my body start to yield to his presence. A slight shift from me drew a groan from him, and he delved deeper, the base of his length pressing insistently at my entrance.

Our eyes remained entwined as I started to move, and he met each of my motions, creating a symphony of friction that resonated within me, sending waves of bliss coursing through every nerve.

He caught my hair in his hand, drawing my mouth back to his, our tongues meeting in an intimate dance as he filled me completely. A sharp intake of breath escaped me as I felt him swell, locking us together, the sensation intensifying the storm of desire brewing inside.

Then his thumb found the most sensitive part of me, and I couldn't hold back the cry that erupted from my lips. My body tensed; the world narrowed to the point of unbearable tension and then released as I clamped around him, shouting his name as a wildfire seemed to ignite my veins.

With a pulse that matched the beating of my heart, he claimed me as his own, a heat unfurling deep within as he released into me.

His climax sparked another in me, overwhelming in its intensity, a tidal wave following the first.

His tail tightened around my leg, each movement he made was relentless, his expression one of pure ecstasy.

I wrapped my arms around him, holding him as close as

possible, feeling the strength of his body, the power of his affection.

As he looked down at me, I reached up to caress his face, feeling the raw power and tender care emanating from him.

He was magnificent, a perfect balance of fierceness and beauty, and he was all mine, just as I belonged to him.

His arms enveloped me with a protectiveness that was almost tangible, his tongue tracing the mark he had made on my neck as his thrusts grew longer, deeper, more potent.

"You're perfect," he whispered against my ear, each word punctuated by his deep movements. "Absolutely perfect, Grishka."

As waves of sensation cascaded over me, I clung to him, my arms and legs entwined with his form, while the crescendo of my impending release gathered momentum within me. The intense pleasure wound itself tightly around my core, every small muscle within me pulsating and tightening around his penetrating presence.

A sharp gasp escaped me as his fangs pierced my skin, marking me unequivocally as his—once again.

Any twinge of pain was swiftly eclipsed by the profound sense of completion as my body clenched around his stav, a rush of warmth enveloping me as he spilled his essence into me once more.

With a tenderness that contrasted his primal act, he soothed the mark with his tongue, his actions sealing the bond as much as the bite itself. When he finally leaned back, he brought his forehead to rest softly against mine, a silent communion in the aftermath of our passion. "You are mine," he murmured, his breath a caress as he bestowed a gentle kiss upon my lips.

I caressed his face, feeling the truth of our connection in the depth of my being. "And you are mine," I affirmed softly, the words a solemn vow. "Always."

room 369

The sound of helicopters tore through the roar of the ocean and the howling wind. I jolted awake, my senses suddenly alert. Grishka, already on her feet, was scanning the sky, searching for the source of our hope.

"We must get to the shore," she commanded.

In a swift motion, she grabbed a limb she had prepared earlier with vines and leaves, fashioning it into a makeshift torch. She lowered it to the fire, and within moments, the flame caught. Handing the torch to me, she scooped up her sundress and dashed toward the shore, her movements swift as a warrior's.

Thank the Moon Goddess for giving me a fated mate with survival skills.

She didn't bother to dress; time was of the essence. Every second we delayed could mean the difference between being rescued or remaining stranded. Bare as she was, Grishka ran down the shore, waving her sundress in the air and yelling loudly, trying to catch the attention of the helicopter in the distance.

Joining her with the torch, I hoped our combined efforts would be enough to attract the pilot or anyone else on board. We waved and shouted, our voices carrying over the waves, desperate to be seen, to be saved.

Suddenly, the helicopter jerked and then surged forward toward us.

A wide grin spread across my face, relief and joy flooding through me.

This was it; salvation was at hand.

I ran to Grishka, unable to contain the elation bubbling within me. As I reached her, I wrapped an arm around her and pulled her into a passionate kiss, pouring all my relief and love into the embrace.

"We're going to be saved," I breathed out, our lips parting, the promise of safety finally within grasp.

Grishka slipped on her sundress and, in a burst of joyous strength, hoisted me onto her shoulders. A surprised grunt escaped me as she spun us around, her laughter mingling with the wind.

"Kael, we are going to be saved," she proclaimed, her voice brimming with relief and happiness.

Waving my torch at the approaching helicopter, I felt a surge of gratitude.

With Grishka by my side, my perfect mate, we had survived the unthinkable. She had been my strength, my beacon in the storm. Without her, I would have been lost, but together, we had weathered the storm and were now on the brink of rescue.

As the helicopter drew nearer, I knew that this was just the beginning of our story, a tale of survival, of love, and of two souls fated to be together against all odds.

And it all started with both of us taking a chance at the last shot at love.

AUTHOR'S NOTE

If you've received this note, Amazon has delivered the
wrong file to your kindle. Please re-download the eBook. If
your Kindle doesn't automatically update, you may have to
manually do it from the settings.

I'm sorry for the inconvenience.

ABOUT THE AUTHOR

USA Today Bestselling author, Jade Waltz lives in Illinois with her husband, two sons, and her three crazy cats.

She writes character driven romances within detailed universes, where happily-ever-afters happen for those who dare love the abnormal and the unknown. Their love may not be easy—but it is well worth it in the end.

Jade enjoys knitting, playing video games, watching Esports, green tea and writing all the stories that live in her imagination.

Website: www.jadewaltz.com
Newsletter link: https://jadewaltz.com/#newsletter
Email: authorjadewaltz@gmail.com

ROOM
88

SEDONA ASHE
WRITING AS
DARCI R. ACULA

Room 88

Sedona Ashe writing as Darci R. Acula

Cover artwork by Gombar Sanja

https://bookcoverforyou.com/

Interior artwork by Cauldron Press

www.cauldronpress.ca

A huge thank you to-

Allison Woerner for Alpha Reading.

Maxine Meyer for Copy Editing.

Imogen Evans for Proofreading & Editing.

Why is 88 better than 69?
Because you get eight twice!

Get it? Ate twice?
Okay, fine... I'll stop now so you can get on with reading the
book.
Love y'all!
Sedona

A quick author's note regarding the word octopus...

*I grew up believing the plural form of octopus was octopi.
However, while the term octopi is commonly taught as proper, it
is incorrect. There is a long reason for this, but it boils down to
the word octopi having a Latin plural ending, while the word
octopus is based on a Greek word. Technically, this means that the
correct term should be octopodes... which I think sounds freaking
cool, but alas, it's not accepted as the correct term either (and
people might give you weird looks if you use it).
Since English has adopted (a.k.a. kidnapped) the original Greek
word októpus, and made it octopus, the correct term is considered
to be octopuses based on the English pluralization rules.
Also, in case you were wondering, cacti and cactuses are both
acceptable terms for a group of prickly acupuncture plants.
Yes, my whole life has been a lie.*

**I am American, so the above is based on American English
standard.*

Chapter 1

BERYL

My driver opened the door of the sleek black rental car. Mack held out his hand to steady me as I stepped out. I loved being self-reliant, but I was thankful for his chivalry because of my clingy, sequined gown's habit of wrapping around my ankles.

The absolute last thing I wanted to do was face-plant on the concrete sidewalk outside Luxe Hotel. It would definitely make for a memorable entrance, but not the impression I preferred to leave.

"Enjoy your evening, and try to do something you wouldn't normally do," Mack teased.

"Like have fun?" I asked, brow raised.

Mack was a tall man, but with my heels on, we were at eye level.

His gray eyes crinkled with laughter, making his aged face appear several decades younger. "Yes. You really should try that sometime, Miss Beryl."

Rolling my eyes, I patted his arm and made my way toward the imposing glass doors of the grand ballroom.

A tuxedo-dressed host greeted me.

"Good evening. May I have your name?"

"Beryl Latos," I answered with a smile.

The host quickly searched the guest list. "Ah, yes! There you are. And will you have a plus one or a husband joining us this evening?"

"No, just me." My smile tightened.

Why did it seem like the entire world was focused on my relationship status?

The host's brows rose in surprise, a reaction he quickly hid. "Apologies, miss."

See? That reaction just made it worse. Because now I wasn't sure if he was apologizing for the fact that I was single, or if he was apologizing for being forward in assuming I had a husband... or even wanted one. Which, for the record, I didn't.

I'd done the calculations, and I didn't have time for a relationship. It was a fact of life and one I wasn't sad about.

I was living the life I'd always wanted. A life filled with challenging work and expensive vacations—when I managed to sneak away, which wasn't often enough. I really needed to make traveling a priority.

How long had it been since my last vacation?

There had been my trip to Bali, but I'd been there to meet with a client. I'd ended up spending much of that trip locked away in an office, so I suppose it didn't count.

Ah, yes! Three months ago, I visited Tokyo. That was

exciting... at least until there had been an issue back at my office in the US, which had required me to spend the next four days ordering room service while I worked remotely to get our systems back in order.

I ran through a mental list of the countries I'd traveled to over the past decade and realized with a start that I hadn't taken a true vacation.

I was a twenty-nine-year-old woman who'd never had a vacation filled with nothing but relaxation and fun. Pulling my phone out of my clutch, I typed a quick memo to add 'taking vacations' to my to-do list.

"Follow me, miss." The host led me through gold-trimmed doors and through an elegantly decorated dining area.

He stopped by an open doorway that led to a private dining room. "You'll find your party in there."

Tilting my head in thanks, I made my way inside the room. A chandelier the size of a car hung over the middle of the floor, casting warm light around the room. Linen-covered tables were scattered around the deep-red carpeted room. A few guests had taken a seat, but most stood in small groups.

My stomach grumbled, and a wave of dizziness washed over me, reminding me I'd skipped lunch to prepare for a meeting. I was starving! If I wanted to remain upright on my silver stiletto heels, I'd need to grab a snack.

Making my way to the buffet table against the wall, I picked up a small plate and placed several hors d'oeuvres on it.

"I can't believe your husband let a woman as gorgeous as you out of his sight," a masculine voice said from behind me.

Turning, I found myself face-to-face with Tony Harris, the CEO of one of my company's smaller holdings. His ruddy red cheeks matched his hair—which he'd combed over to hide a growing bald spot. Tony chuckled over his joke, patting the white dress shirt straining over his stomach.

"Mr. Harris, how good to see you!" I lied through my teeth, purposely ignoring the 'husband' comment. "I look forward to hearing how our new policies are being implemented. Be sure to find me before the evening is over."

Not giving him a chance to respond, I moved toward the largest group of people who stood by the floor-to-ceiling windows that looked out at the sparkling lights of the city.

As I made my way into the circle, several people greeted me with warm smiles.

Douglas Archer stepped forward, raising his champagne glass. "I'm so glad you joined us, Beryl. Our stocks have already doubled in value since Chiroptera acquired us. The stockholders are thrilled, and it is thanks to your skill!"

"I'm so pleased for you, Douglas. I've seen nothing but positive reports over the past six months." I politely tapped the rim of my champagne flute against his, and the other glasses lifted in my direction.

Smiling, I listened to the various CEOs share their own stories of company growth. I made appropriate sounds of delight and surprise while they spoke, even though I was well aware of each company's growth and current value.

My company, Chiroptera, was a large investment firm. I acquired companies that were doing well but had the potential to do far better if given access to funds for expansion and an experienced managerial team to guide them.

Sometimes, Chiroptera arranged mergers, matching companies that complemented each other's offerings or products. The combined companies would create a boost in profits and make the stock appear far more attractive to potential investors.

My team and I created detailed growth plans for each acquisition to increase their profits. When the companies had blossomed and multiplied their value, Chiroptera would begin searching for another investment firm interested in acquiring assets. This allowed the companies I owned to continue growing under the guidance of another investor.

While I had an amazing team of skilled experts, I personally followed up on a daily basis with each of my assets, checking reports for growth, stock worth, and analyzing overall company statics.

Other parts of my life might be sorely neglected, but I was dang good at my job.

"I'm trying to convince him to take some time off to visit our vacation home in Costa Rica, but I can hardly drag him away." Mrs. Archer, a tall brunette with a breathtaking smile, laughed and squeezed her husband's arm. "He promised we'd take a long vacation after the deal closed, but I think he's working twice as hard now."

Douglas patted her arm. "It's hard to pull myself away when the growth plan Beryl laid out is showing such incredible results!"

I agreed with Douglas; why take a break when things were going so well? But that didn't seem like the most appropriate response.

Summoning a laugh, I gave his wife a pained smile. "I think you're right. Douglas needs to take you on a vacation as a thank you for everything you've put up with."

Mrs. Archer beamed up at her husband. "Did you hear that, Dougie? She agrees we both deserve a break!"

"And what about you?" Lennie, the grandfatherly CEO of a small natural supplement company we'd acquired, shot me a playful frown. "Last time we chatted, you were heading to Japan for a getaway. Did you enjoy it?"

"Yes! It was lovely—"

I was cut off by Roger Tyne. "I know that's a lie because you spent your time there working on a merger for my company."

The gathered group laughed, and I shook my head at the good-natured ribbing.

"How does your partner deal with your long work hours?" the blonde bombshell at Mr. Tyne's side asked, her eyes filled with sincere curiosity rather than judgment.

"That is something I don't have to worry about since I don't have a partner to notice my work habits. Goodness knows I don't have time to care for a pet, let alone a partner." I kept my tone light, trying not to give away my twinge of frustration at yet another reminder of my marital status.

They didn't mean to offend with their curiosity, but the constant reminders and questions were becoming old.

"You'd better make time for love, Miss Beryl. There will be a day when you'll find yourself wishing there was more in your life than just work." Lennie's kindly blue eyes met mine. "And for Pete's sake, take an actual vacation. You've more than earned it."

"I'll keep that in mind, Lennie." Lifting my glass, I sipped at the bubbly champagne.

To my relief, the conversation drifted to other topics for the next hour. When my feet began to ache, I found a table in the corner to sit down for a few minutes. Pulling my phone from my clutch, I flipped through emails, wanting to make sure I hadn't missed anything of importance.

"Beryl?"

I glanced up at the dark-haired man, who grinned down at me.

"Do you mind if I sit? I had a couple of questions I wanted to ask before we close in three weeks."

"Of course. Sit, please." I motioned to the chair across from me.

The deal with Timothy's company, Tenser Enterprises, would put both of our companies in a really lucrative position. I'd spend the next few years helping Tim's company grow and become more profitable. And when I sold the company to another firm in five to ten years, it would likely create a return on investment in the high millions, possibly even billions.

It was the highest stake acquisition I'd tackled in my career, and it had become my main focus.

Timothy spent the next few minutes going over several questions but then stopped abruptly and leaned back in his chair.

"Was that all?" I asked, confused by his sudden silence.

"No, but I just can't think about business when I'm sitting in front of a woman as stunning as you. Brains and beauty, it's an intoxicating combination."

With practiced effort, I kept from clenching my jaw in frustration. His comment was sweet enough, but this type of thing had happened far too often.

Why did the single men feel the need to interrupt important business conversations to shoot their shot? I'd never dream of letting my hormones disrupt business.

He was a very attractive man; his dark hair was carefully brushed away from his chiseled face. His eyes shone with a keen intelligence that could be alluring or intimidating. The man was a once-in-a-lifetime type of catch, but I wasn't interested in fishing or catching…

"Thank you. Do you have any other questions? We can also schedule a meeting at my office to go over any other concerns prior to signing the contracts." I tried to redirect the conversation.

"Yes, I have one more question." He leaned forward, his dark eyes drilling into mine. "What would it take to get a date with you?"

Keeping my mask in place, I gave him a fake smile. "I'm flattered, but I don't date people I'm closing deals with."

I'd expected Timothy to be disappointed, but his eyes lit up. "You didn't say no. So what I'm hearing is that I have a chance after the contracts are signed at the end of the month."

Not giving me a chance to respond, he stood. "I look forward to signing those papers. For more reasons than one." Giving me a wink that would have made any other girl's ovaries explode, he walked away.

I swallowed a groan of frustration. Deciding I couldn't handle any further socialization, I quickly made my way out of the hotel.

Sending a text to my driver, I waited just inside the hotel doors until I saw my sleek black car pull to the curb. Not giving Mack time to get out and open my door, I yanked the handle and slipped inside.

Mack's eyes met mine in the mirror. "Everything okay, Miss Beryl?"

I blinked hard, surprised to find tears springing to my eyes at his fatherly concern.

"Yeah. No. I don't know." I rested my forehead against the cool glass window. "I'm... I'm just tired."

"Then let's get you home, miss." Mack pulled away from the hotel and drove me home in blessed silence.

Chapter 2

BERYL

room 88

Arriving home thirty minutes later, I moved through my condo, not bothering to turn on any lights as I made my way into the bedroom. With my abilities, it wasn't like I needed lights to see, anyway.

Entering my bedroom, I kicked off my shoes and went to stand in front of the windows at the panoramic view of the ocean. For several minutes, I stared at the crashing waves, hugging myself to ease some of my pent-up anxiety from the evening.

With a sigh, I turned to my desk and flipped on a tiny desk light. A stack of mail sat waiting to be dealt with. Deciding I was too agitated to sleep, I settled into my chair and picked them up.

As I sorted through the letters, one caught my eye.

P-Harmony Agency.

Slicing through the envelope with a deadly sharp nail, I unfolded the single sheet of paper. It was an invitation to be matched with a mate.

Hysterical laughter bubbled from my throat. No matter what I wanted, the entire universe seemed to be hung up on my personal life. I laughed until my sides ached and tears streaked down my cheeks.

But as my giggles faded away, I reread the invitation. The gears in my mind turned, and my mood sobered. Maybe I should do it.

Did I want to be matched by an agency? No, not particularly.

But I was exhausted by the constant needling into my personal life and the distraction my marital status seemed to cause in my work life.

Perhaps it wouldn't be the worst thing to be matched.

Resting my chin on my hand, I stared unseeing out at the ocean. What would it be like to come home to a house where the lights were on? What would it be like to come home from a long day of work, crawl into a warm bed, and have a strong set of arms wrap around me?

I could sign checks for millions of dollars without so much as a heart flutter, but the thought of falling in love terrified me. But maybe I didn't need to fall in love for this to work... maybe I could just fall in *like*.

Flipping open my laptop, I typed in the URL written on the invitation. It led to a password-protected page. My fingers trembled as I entered the password written in the invitation.

P-Harmony's mate matching agreement loaded. Now, I was back in my element, and my nerves eased as I combed carefully through every word of the contract. Everything was straightforward, and I liked that they took care of everything.

Reaching the end of the document, I found the line where I needed to sign. I worried my lip between my teeth, my fingers hovering over the keyboard.

The logical choice would be to make a decision like this when I wasn't tired, stressed, and frustrated. But tonight was the last dinner party I wanted to attend as a single woman.

The agency promised most matches took place within two weeks, which meant I'd be mated before the big closing happened. There were typically several parties I had to attend after the large acquisitions, so getting this taken care of sooner rather than later worked for me.

Frankly, I didn't have the time or the interest in navigating the dating world, which made this the best option.

Not giving myself time to second guess my decision, I quickly typed in my information and signed the agreement.

Wedding bells chimed on the website, and digital confetti rained down on the laptop's screen.

It was one more thing I could check off my to-do list.

For better or for worse, my days as a single woman are numbered.

FUMBLING WITH MY ROOM KEY, I pushed open the door and pulled my rolling suitcase in behind me. My eyes scanned the room, taking in the stunning decor.

It was as though the resort had specifically designed this room with social media travel influencers in mind. Heck, I'd traveled to countless incredible hotels for various business meetings, but this one definitely ranked in the top five.

The floor was made of smooth stones in various shades of sandy brown, charcoal, red, and black. An artist must have spent hours arranging the stones to create the mosaic that curled around the sprawling room.

Heavy glass and polished oak doors opened out onto the patio and a large infinity pool with the ocean behind it; this setup gave the illusion that the pool poured directly into the ocean. The patio's courtyard had tall walls and large, perfectly manicured shrubbery to give it privacy from the neighboring rooms.

Reminded that there were other couples being matched at the hotel, my gaze focused back on the open floor room. I really hoped the resort had added soundproofing insulation inside the walls.

I had no interest in listening to a newly mated couple bang all night long. Because that is what most newly-mateds did, wasn't it?

After signing the contract, I spent the week that followed studying everything on P-Harmony's website. I still hadn't figured out what the P stood for, though.

Paranormal Harmony?

Penis Harmony?

I snickered. Yes, it was probably the latter, and I wouldn't hear otherwise.

The password-protected website featured countless testimonials where the happily matched couples extolled the agency's incredible skill at pairing mates. They spoke of things like love at first sight, instantly falling head over heels, and most had alluded to a first night filled with a wild passion like nothing they'd ever experienced.

I'd rolled my eyes so many times while reading the reviews I'd grown dizzy.

There was no denying that those were the types of things you'd want to hear if you were starved for love and desperate for a mate.

But for those of us who viewed this as a business arrangement, it sounded horrible. The last thing I wanted was to be pounded all night so I could wake up exhausted and with a pounding headache.

I was here to close on a mutually beneficial partnership agreement. And yes, I understood that my partner and I would have biological urges that would need to be met now and then.

But I didn't see why that would need to take up an extended length of time. I wasn't high maintenance, so I figured we could easily consummate the bond within thirty minutes.

That would leave plenty of time to get a good night's sleep so I could get an early start the next morning on my emails and text messages. In fact, I could probably even squeeze in a Zoom call with my assistant if she needed me.

My partner should be happy with that, right? Didn't most guys just want to get their rocks off, anyway? I was saving him the trouble of wooing me or trying to impress me with extended foreplay.

Besides, I was more interested in speaking with my contractually matched regarding what arrangements I'd need to make for his arrival in Boston with me. One of my stipulations in the agreement was that I would not relocate, so my matched would need to move in with me—or at least move to my city, and we could purchase a home we both liked.

P-Harmony had taken care of the rest of our arrangements and dealt with the contracts between both parties. It was something I very much appreciated since it would've been annoying to show up at the resort only to have both our time wasted.

I knew what I wanted and expected from my partner, as well as what concessions I was willing to make to ensure the partnership worked out.

What I wanted was a man to stand to travel with me for business meetings and attend all the elbow-rubbing parties at my side. I could side-step awkward conversations and unwanted male attention by flashing a wedding ring—a ring I was more than willing to purchase myself.

Having a husband at my side, I could redirect conversations with the businessmen who seemed more interested in their ability to get me in bed than in my ability to close a deal that would make both of us a crap ton of money.

I was willing to provide for my partner's needs and

wants. Hades knew I had more than enough money for that. Aside from public engagements, my mate would be free to do whatever he wished with his time.

There were a couple of other things that were important to me as well. I wanted a man who was intelligent enough to carry on conversations and not embarrass me at parties, meetings, and around colleagues.

My mate also needed to be faithful. I didn't want to deal with the annoyance of a scandal, nor did I wish to be distracted in the office by my employees whispering behind my back over who my husband was sleeping with.

A sharp twinge shot through my chest, and I massaged it with my hand. Fine, I wasn't being 100 percent honest with myself.

I'd never been a romantic, and it didn't seem likely that would change in the future. However, a small part of me longed to have someone who was mine. Not as a pet or a toy. I didn't want purchased affection.

Deep down, I wanted someone to look at me like I was the only woman who mattered. It was probably an unrealistic dream at this point in my life.

But surely there was someone out there who wanted to pursue scholarly interests or philanthropic work, and also had enough control to keep his penis in his pants until our scheduled sex. I knew I wasn't the most cuddly person, so that was likely the most I could hope to have in a partner.

Miraculously, the agency had found a mate willing to agree to my terms less than a week after I'd agreed to be matched. We'd signed agreements, and they'd made the reservations for us here at the paranormal-friendly resort. Then they gave us the date we needed to arrive.

Today.

My stomach quivered. I was about to meet my match, my mate, my husband.

But this was just one more business arrangement, so there was absolutely nothing to be nervous about… right?

Chapter 3

BERYL

room 88

S itting in the cushioned chair on the patio, I took another sip of my liquid courage. Aponté, the skilled mixologist in the resort's expansive bar, told me it was called a Passion Shifter, and I knew at first sip it was my new favorite drink.

I tapped my phone screen to check the time. The sun was low on the horizon, and the chatty concierge had told me my mate would arrive shortly before sunset.

Lowering my sunglasses, I studied the sky and decided I had less than two hours before he arrived. That gave me just enough time to go over the growth plan for Timothy's company, which we planned to implement after the acquisition was final.

I brought the swing to a stop and reluctantly stepped out of the sunshine and into the darkened room. Sitting my drink and sunglasses on the desk, I rifled through my briefcase.

The first folder I pulled out held the documents I

wanted to go over with my soon-to-be-mate. Setting them to the side, I grabbed the second folder.

I flopped onto the California king bed and began going through the acquisition paperwork, looking for anything our team of attorneys may have missed. I'd been reading for about twenty minutes when my eyes grew heavy.

Blowing a fallen strand of light-brown hair from my face, I pinched the bridge of my nose. Traveling must have taken more out of me than I'd thought…

Something cool brushed against my cheek, and my eyes flew open. My pupils shifted, allowing me to see better in the dimly lit room.

A man sat on the edge of the bed, watching me without saying a word.

His pale blonde hair brushed against his shoulders, falling around his face and dripping water on the bed.

I barely kept from hissing in surprise, a reaction I blamed on still being partially asleep. No one had ever snuck up on me, even in my sleep. So how had he gotten so close without my instincts waking me?

"Sorry. I didn't mean to frighten you." The man's voice was soothing, and my body responded instantly, my taut muscles relaxing and my breathing evening out.

What the heck? For all I knew, this man was a serial killer, yet all my instincts had calmed at the sound of his voice. At least if he was here to murder me, I'd be chill about it.

The guy gave me an abashed grin. "I thought about waiting for you to awaken naturally, but figured I would come across as a creeper sitting in the corner watching you. So I decided it was best to wake you. Unfortunately, clearing my throat, coughing, and even speaking didn't rouse you. You must have been sleeping well."

"It's fine." My throat was tight. Not from fear but from something I couldn't quite put my finger on.

I was betting at least part of it was due to the fact that this man could have played a Greek god in a blockbuster film, and the team wouldn't have needed to use any special effects on him.

His tan skin shimmered and glowed as though reflecting the waning light coming through the open doors.

The chiseled angles of his jaw and cheekbones, combined with his Romanesque nose, gave him a sculpture-like beauty. He was so perfect that I bet he pulled people to him like a spider drawing its prey into a web.

And did I mention he was butt-freaking-naked?

I shouldn't keep staring, but I couldn't seem to find the strength to look away.

Pull yourself together. I gave myself a little shake.

Hades! I'd grown up around vampires, a species known for their exotic beauty, so I should have immunity to it. So why was he affecting me so much?

The fine lines around his eyes and the slightly sharper angles of his face told me he was no longer in his twenties. Yet, his looks and easy-going vibe reminded me of the thousands of sandy-haired surfers who flocked to beaches around the world.

This man was aging like a fine wine. He was the type of

guy who could wear a suit and look like distinguished royalty rather than like a washed-up hippie.

Which might create a problem for me.

I'd never be able to take this man to a business meeting because there wasn't an eye in the room, male or female, who'd be able to look away from his beauty... I still hadn't managed to drag my gaze from him.

The whole point of accepting the arranged partnership was so I could get people's focus off my personal life and keep their attention on business matters.... and there was no way that would happen if I showed up with the real-life version of a certain ridiculously handsome squid in a TV episode of a popular kid's show.

His brow furrowed. "Does my appearance displease you?"

I slowly shook my head. "You're gorgeous. It's just... Well, if I find you this distracting, I can't imagine what would happen if I took you to a business meeting. How often do people drool on you?"

The man chuckled. "Darling, if you're worried about me stealing your thunder, you needn't worry. I'm an expert at blending in, the king of wall-anemones."

"You mean wallflowers?" I asked.

"Oh, yes. Wallflowers. It is an ability my kind excels at." His words were smooth, rising and falling like the waves of the sea. "Besides, I can't imagine I'd be noticed in a room with a woman as beautiful as you."

An unfamiliar sensation bubbled in my chest. Was it heartburn? Hiccups?

No, it was pleasure.

He thought I was beautiful.

I'd spent my life frustrated with men flirting with me, yet I was delighted with his compliment. Catching my bottom lip between my teeth, I chewed on it, trying to work through my odd reaction to him.

Lifting my gaze back to his face, I watched his eyes slide to my mouth, and for a moment, a blue color seemed to flash beneath his skin. It happened so fast I thought I might have imagined it.

"What are you?" I asked, suddenly curious.

His royal blue eyes met mine. "An octopus shifter. And you?"

"Vampire." I studied his reaction, looking for any sign of disgust.

P-Harmony made each applicant fill out long questionnaires to aid in creating a perfect match. So, although we didn't choose what species we were to be matched with, they wouldn't have matched us together if he had a problem with vampires.

"I've never met a vampire before." There was no judgment in his tone, only open interest.

"Would you like me to give you a quick rundown?" I pushed myself into a sitting position, bracing my back against the headboard.

"Please." He shifted positions until he was sitting cross-legged at the foot of the bed, facing me.

"Vampires have intermingled with humans over the last few centuries. We can produce offspring with humans, and the vampire traits are passed on to the children, but in a slightly weakened form. With each progressive generation, the vampire features will continue to grow weaker."

He leaned forward, resting his elbow on his knee and propping his chin on his palm. "And you? What are you?"

"I'm a halfling," I answered without embarrassment. "My father is a vampire, and my mother was a human. I inherited several of my father's traits. For instance, I'm able to shift to a vampiric form. I inherited his fangs, although mine are slightly shorter than his, but thankfully, I have my mother's digestive system."

Sneaking a glance at him, I once again searched for disgust but found nothing but curiosity in his eyes.

I took a breath and continued. "Other than the occasional glass of blood, I'm able to keep my vampiric hunger under control by regularly consuming rare meat. So if you're concerned that I'm a danger to you or that you'll wake up to find me latched onto you like a bloodsucking leech, you needn't worry. I've never taken blood directly from a living being."

As soon as the words tumbled from my mouth, I wished I could take them back.

I'd just admitted to still possessing the vampire equivalent of a V-card. Most vampires did away with both types of virginity during their high school years. This was an extremely personal detail about myself I hadn't intended to reveal to anyone... ever.

His brows rose. "Is that common among vampires?"

I paused, trying to decide whether I should be honest and embarrass myself, or if I could brush it off with a lie.

The latter didn't seem a great way to start a relationship with the person who'd signed a contract to be my mate.

Taking a breath, I blew out a long sigh and dropped my eyes to the brilliant white bedspread.

"While vampires no longer feed upon unwilling humans whom they've stalked and turned to prey, it's an extremely..." I searched for the right word. "It's an intensely sensual experience to drink from another living being—or so I've been told. Apparently, nothing compares to the taste of fresh blood straight from a vein."

My cheeks burned. "The experience is like eating at a 5-star restaurant while having mind-blowing sex at the same time. It's a highly erotic experience that almost always ends with sex."

"And yet you haven't—"

"No." I cut him off, hoping we could move on to other conversations.

He wasn't ready to let it go. "Why not?" A gold ring formed around his deep blue irises.

"I haven't had time for it," I stated matter-of-factly.

It wasn't a lie, but it was only half the truth.

I'd been busy, and there'd been no one who'd aroused me enough to stir my vampiric urge to feed. And there'd been a part of me that only wanted to experience it with the person I wanted to spend my life with.

I certainly wasn't a virgin, and when my biological needs grew distracting, I had no qualms about letting my hair down and blowing off some steam with a romp in the bedroom, but I'd never given all of myself to my sexual partners.

And now that I'd signed the mating agreement with the golden god in front of me, I might never experience that. Because I'd never sink my fangs into him without his consent.

Some people had a kink for being bitten, but there were far more who'd be squeamish at the idea of having a vampire's fangs sink into their necks.

Chapter 4

CERULEAN

room 88

I watched as her eyes sparkled and her sexy, full lips moved as she spoke.

She was heartbreakingly beautiful.

Appearance had never mattered to me, and I'd arrived on land with no expectations... so finding a living goddess sleeping in our room had been a shock.

Other than her name, I'd purposely chosen to not find out about my new mate until we met in person. The downside to being matched through a business transaction was that it was far from being romantic.

By waiting, I'd hoped to have my mate tell me about herself rather than reading those facts on a legal document. For that reason, I asked the agency to provide me with only the essential information.

Things like her requirements for our relationship. One of the most important had been her insistence that I move to her area, as her job was the highest priority for her.

She'd even offered a generous allowance if her mate was

willing to agree to her terms. I'd been fine with moving, and the allowance was unnecessary, but I figured I'd tell her that later.

My biggest surprise had been that for such a savvy businesswoman, she'd failed to request a prenup to protect her assets. Maybe there was a romantic part of her buried deep down that believed in lifelong love.

"What are you staring at? Is there something on my face?" Her fingers brushed across her cheekbone before trying to pat down the stray locks that had come loose from her tight, no-nonsense bun.

"Here, let me." Leaning forward, I undid the coil, allowing her long, dark-blonde hair to cascade wildly around her face.

The gentle waves of her hair added a soft vulnerability to her face. My heart thudded painfully. I'd never seen a woman as stunning as the one sitting in front of me.

I'd come to shore to find a person who was willing to be mine and with the determination to make her fall in love with me. There was nothing I wanted more than to be the type of man she could fall in love with.

My only type when it came to a mate was that she had a kind heart.

Whether she was thin or curvy, tall or short, red-headed or blonde—none of that mattered to me. Not even her species mattered to me. I knew my heart would have found my mate beautiful no matter who the agency had matched me with... but Beryl had a type of beauty that I didn't believe existed outside of paintings.

She was the type of woman who could pick from any man on earth by wiggling a finger. So why was she willing to be matched by P-Harmony? How could I make a woman like her fall in love with me when she'd likely been wooed by men from the moment she'd turned eighteen?

Beryl flipped on the bedside lamp, reminding me of the hour.

"I don't know why I'm so anxious over all this." She reached for a folder on the bed. "It's a simple partnership agreement which requires an understanding of what both parties bring to the table, how the assets will be distributed, and a working plan to make the partnership a success."

Beryl spread a document in front of me on the bed. I quickly scanned it, recognizing it as the marital contract we'd already agreed on.

"I know you already signed, but I want to make sure there are no issues you haven't voiced before this goes any further." She spun a gold-tipped fountain pen between her fingers, her piercing green eyes studying my face.

"Beryl, I have zero issues with the agreement. I'm looking forward to seeing your home and having you show me your city," I reassured her.

Beryl grabbed a notepad and scribbled a note. "Yes, of course! I'll have my assistant hire a guide to show you around."

While I'd refused to accept the full brief on my future mate from the agency, they'd felt it necessary to ensure I understood ahead of time that my mate was a highly driven, quick-witted, business-oriented woman.

After meeting her, I could read between the lines of P-Harmony's emails and understand what they'd been trying to warn me about.

Rather than wanting to talk to me, Beryl was flipping through business documents. She definitely wasn't looking for romance. Which was the opposite of my reason for signing with P-Harmony, and there was no denying the twinge of disappointment that pierced my heart at the realization.

I refused to regret my decision. This simply meant I had the opportunity to show my mate how wonderful losing your heart could be.

Who knew? Maybe I'd be her first love.

My chest filled with hope and desperate longing at that thought. Yes, I would spend my life trying to sweep my gorgeous mate off her feet.

It was going to be a challenge, but I was ready. I could already tell she'd be worth it.

"Or perhaps you could show me around yourself?" I kept my tone light and teasing, not wanting her to feel pressured.

"Um, maybe?" Beryl chewed her lip. "I'll have to check my work schedule once we return to the city, but I should be able to pencil some time in."

I had to admit, the last comment stung a little. She viewed me as a burden rather than her companion.

Patience, Cerulean. She doesn't understand how pleasurable spending time with a lover and a friend can be, I reminded myself, taking a calming breath.

Beryl pulled out a checklist, her manicured fingertip sliding down the page and her pouty lips moving as she silently read over the items before checking several things off.

"Okay, the last thing I wanted to bring up is a prenup." She turned to me. "Since you've willingly agreed to all the terms I laid out, I didn't think a prenup was necessary. And I accept that if we divorce, you will get 50 percent of my companies, stocks, properties, and other assets."

I shifted positions until my back was against the headboard, and I was sitting beside her. Every fiber of my being and beast longed to scoot closer until our thighs touched, but I didn't want to risk crowding Beryl or making her uncomfortable.

"I'm fine with no prenup. Beryl, you'll be my mate. What I have is yours. Besides, there won't be a divorce."

The vampire bombshell next to me shrugged. "Maybe it's that way in the sea, but on land, people divorce with the same regularity as buying a new car. Even among paranormals, divorce has grown more common."

"But how? Mate bonds are for life!" I tried to keep the horror I felt at the idea of separating from leaking into my tone.

She met my eyes, giving me a sad smile. "Well, sure. The mate bond can't be broken, but the legal partnership can. While neither person can ever create a mate bond with a new partner, it doesn't stop them from remarrying and creating a life with a new partner."

For the first time since I'd accepted P-Harmony's invitation to be matched, I experienced a pang of regret. Not over being paired with Beryl, but over my decision to leave the ocean and live predominantly on land.

How could paranormals defile the sanctity of the mate bond by creating a life with those they weren't bonded to?

Beryl chewed her lip, her eyes tracking every microexpression that crossed my face.

Reaching out, I gently pried her abused lip from between her teeth. "Darling, I will never dishonor our bond. My body and beast will not allow me to find another woman desirable after our mating."

Her eyebrows rose. "You mean you can't have sex with anyone else after we complete the bond?"

"Nope." I grinned at her. "You will be the only woman I will crave."

An adorable blush tinged her cheeks. "I've heard there are a few species where arousal can only be achieved with one's bonded mate. If you can only be with me, are you really sure you want to be tied to me for the rest of your life? We don't even know each other."

Delight shot through me at the sudden emotion shimmering in her eyes. Beryl wasn't asking because of the contract. She was asking for more personal reasons.

"I think it's important that you know I didn't agree to be matched through P-Harmony because I was looking for love—"

"Are you against falling in love?" I asked softly.

She looked surprised. "N-no. I don't think so."

"That's good enough for me." Taking a risk, I reached

out and interlaced our fingers together, giving a tiny squeeze. "It means I have a chance to sweep you off your feet."

"But why would you want to bother?" Beryl looked genuinely confused. "We'll be sharing a bedroom, and I won't deny your sexual desires. If you'd like, we can even set up a schedule to ensure your biological needs are met. All your expenses will be covered, and my assets will be shared with you. I don't understand why you'd want to put in the effort to sweep me off my feet?"

This time, it wasn't disappointment but pity that ricocheted through my chest. Beryl couldn't understand the value of love... which meant she'd likely never experienced it.

"You'll see. Besides, you're more than worth the effort." I winked and swallowed the lump in my throat while trying to keep my tone light.

"Fine." She shrugged. "You're free to do as you please with your days. If that's how you want to spend them... it's your choice."

Picking up the papers from the bed, she rifled through them. "While I don't require a prenup, I wanted to make sure you didn't have one you wished for me to sign? I don't mind signing it so you can have reassurance that I'm not after your assets."

The tone of her voice gave me the distinct impression Beryl believed I was broke and spent my days lounging on a beach.

I rested my head back against the wall. "Nope. I told

you, there is only one mate for my species. What I have is yours."

Beryl didn't look at me, but the corner of her mouth twitched up for the briefest of seconds in a hint of a smile. "Okay, Romeo."

"Cerulean," I corrected.

"What?" She lifted her eyes to meet mine.

"My name, it's Cerulean."

Beryl's eyes widened in horror. "I can't believe I hadn't asked you that already. How rude! This whole thing has me rattled and feeling off-kilter. Plus, there's a big acquisition I close on at the end of the month, so I am trying to resist the urge to check my business emails, but it's making me terribly anxious."

"Have you eaten dinner?" I brushed my thumb against the back of her hand.

Beryl gave a breathy laugh. "No, I was waiting for you and fell asleep."

"Then how about this? I'll go find us some dinner, and you check your emails while I'm gone. When I get back, we can eat, and maybe you'll be a little less stressed."

I'd come to land hoping this evening would go far differently, but the last thing I wanted was for my mate to be worried.

Beryl spun her pen between her fingers, something I was finding she did when anxious. "Are you sure? I don't want to be rude..."

"I'm positive. Are there any foods I should avoid? Or food that is your favorite? And how do we feel about garlic?" I added the last with a smirk, knowing it was a ridiculous rumor that vampires and garlic didn't mix.

Beryl rolled her eyes. "Seriously, Cer?"

My breath caught. She'd already given me a nickname. I tried to ignore how pathetic it was that something so simple could give me so much joy.

"Sorry, I couldn't help it." With a last tender squeeze, I released her hand and pushed to my feet.

"I'd kill for a rare steak or even a nice carpaccio. But I'm not picky. Oysters are the only thing I'm not a fan of." She shivered.

"Got it." I strode toward the door.

"Uh... aren't you going to dress first?" Turning, I found Beryl's cheeks turning an adorable shade of pink.

"You don't think this looks good?" I couldn't resist teasing her.

"The problem is you look too good!" Bright red bloomed in her cheeks. "I mean... you don't want women mobbing you in the halls."

Beryl thought I looked good, and she didn't like the thought of other women seeing me. It was all I could do not to fist pump the air. With a grin, I allowed my magic to rush across my skin, leaving the illusion of clothing in its wake.

Her eyes widened in surprise. "If you could magically make clothes appear, then why were you naked this whole time?"

This time, it was my turn to shrug. "I don't spend a lot of time on land, and I forget clothes are the norm. Besides, it was fun watching you trying to take peeks at my body when you thought I wouldn't notice."

Her jaw dropped, and she tried to stammer a denial even as I laughed and made my way out into the hall.

Mission 'woo my mate' was off to a wonderful start!

Chapter 5

BERYL

room 88

I spent the next thirty minutes checking emails and texts and trying not to think about the gorgeous man I'd be sharing a room—and my life—with. My assistant was doing a wonderful job of holding down the fort, so there wasn't anything that needed my immediate attention.

Slipping both my phone and laptop into my bag, I sat drumming my fingers on the polished desk and listening to the sounds of the ocean drifting through the open balcony doors.

It had been thoughtful of Cerulean to go get us dinner to give me time to work. I doubted the rest of the couples in the resort were allowing their partner to work. Yet, he'd given me the space, which had worked wonders to calm my nerves.

I wanted to return his thoughtfulness, and I racked my brain for a handful of minutes before landing on something.

Hopping to my feet, I hurried to my suitcase and pulled

out my bathing suit. He might have preferred me naked, but I needed a bit more alcohol before I was going to be ready to strip in front of a stranger... even if, on paper, the stranger was my husband and soon-to-be bonded mate.

Once dressed, or rather dressed down, I made my way out to the infinity pool and slowly sank into the warm water.

When Cerulean returned, I watched him search the room before his eyes landed on where I floated in the pool.

"I've brought food. Would you like to come out and eat?"

I smiled. "I thought maybe we could eat in the pool?"

His eyes glowed, and, for the second time since we'd met, his skin took on an iridescent quality. Colors rippled across his skin faster than my mind could process.

Unsure what the flash of color meant, I asked, "Is that okay with you?"

"Yes. I'd like that very much." His voice was husky, deeper than it had been earlier.

I said nothing as Cerulean made his way onto the stone patio and down the steps leading into the pool. He held the tray, keeping it above the water as he settled beside me.

Placing the tray on the stones surrounding the pool, he rearranged the plates, setting a lovely beef carpaccio drizzled with olive oil and capers in front of me.

"Mmm," I moaned, mouth watering. "It looks delicious."

Cerulean gave me a soft smile, the lights from the room dancing in his eyes.

Finding it difficult to eat while floating, I stood but frowned when I realized I would need to bend down for each bite. Maybe I could squat in the waist-high water and hold my plate?

"Would it bother you if I shifted forms? I could help you be more comfortable while we eat," Cerulean offered, his brow creased and his voice hesitant for the first time.

Surely he wasn't worried that his paranormal body would repulse me?

"Of course, I don't mind."

Cerulean's shift rippled over his form, gills appearing on either side of his neck and royal blue rings flashing across his skin before disappearing. Beneath the clear pool water, his legs disappeared, replaced by six thick tentacles.

"Don't panic. I'm going to slide a tentacle beneath you," Cerulean warned.

A moment later, one of his powerful tentacles moved beneath my butt and curled around my waist, creating a stable seat for me. With him holding me suspended in the water, I was at the perfect level to eat.

A pair of tentacles held the floating tray between us, keeping it anchored so it didn't drift away.

"Comfortable?" He still seemed worried I was going to freak out.

"Yes, very." There was a part of me that wanted to ask to see his tentacles out of the water, but despite my curiosity, I didn't want to overstep a boundary.

For some species, shifting from their human form to

their natural form was considered a private thing—something you only did around those you trusted.

Wanting to make him more comfortable, I closed my eyes and unclipped the leash I kept on my vampiric form.

I was a halfling, so it wasn't as dramatic of a shift as when my father shifted. Even so, Cerulean sucked in a harsh breath at my change.

Opening my eyes, I found the night had grown far brighter. My vampiric abilities allowed me to see well in the dark in both my forms, but when I shifted to my vampiric form, my eye structure changed completely.

This gave me the light-reflecting qualities of the feline eye and the ability to see my surroundings in infrared if I focused. As a vampire, I was a creature of the dark, which meant I found comfort in the dark in probably the same way he found it in water.

I couldn't drag my gaze from Cerulean's face. Having looked at myself in the mirror many times, I knew what he was seeing, but now I wanted to see his reaction.

My usually lightly tanned skin had grown pale, the surface taking on a translucent quality that reflected the moon's soft light and caused my skin to glow. Some people found this glow beautiful in an otherworldly way, but others found it eerily ghostlike.

Other things besides my eyes and skin had also changed with my shift. Changes like the slight lengthening of my canine teeth into sharp fangs, the tightening of muscles throughout my body to give me the strength of a powerful athlete, and finally, the gentle plumping of my lips and breasts.

My shift served two purposes. The first was to enhance the features that men tended to notice first. This allowed female vampires to lure them in willingly, which often allowed for feeding without a fight. However, the strengthening and toning of my body ensured that should the need arise, I could take down and subdue prey that was larger than me.

In modern times, vampires no longer needed to lure their meals to them as we didn't hunt other living beings, which had rendered our vampiric form pretty much useless... other than as a tool to arouse potential sex partners.

His eyes drifted lower, and I tried not to be self-conscious at the way my breasts were straining against the itty-bitty string bikini top that was now too small.

"Wow. I don't know what to say." Cerulean's voice was a scratchy rumble that did unexpected things to my insides. "I'd heard vampires were painfully beautiful in their shifted forms, but I thought that was a rumor."

His eyes focused back on my face, and he swallowed hard. "Beryl, you were already the most stunning woman I'd ever laid eyes on. But you've somehow found a way to top even your own beauty."

Warm pleasure blossomed through my chest.

He wasn't freaked out by my fangs.

"You're the first non-vampire to see this form," I admitted, then wanted to kick myself.

Why on earth had I told him that? What was it about Cerulean that had me pouring out secrets I'd planned to take to my grave?

It wasn't like I had a large group of friends I got together with for wild girls' weekends where we could all let it hang out.

As for sexual partners, I'd always told myself I hadn't bothered to show them my natural form because I already had them in bed, so why bother to seduce them?

Deep down, silly as it was, I'd wanted to save this form for my mate. It embarrassed me to acknowledge that maybe there was a romantic bone somewhere in my body.

Cerulean took a ragged breath. "You've never shown a partner your natural self?"

Shaking my head, I nibbled at my lip.

"That means more to me than you could know." Cer reached out, brushing a finger across my cheek.

His touch left a trail of tingles in its wake, and my stomach quivered. What was wrong with me? Hades knew I'd been aroused before, but it had always been a quick thing for me—a business transaction to scratch an itch so I could return my focus to work.

Foreplay and tender caresses were completely unfamiliar. I'd always thought they were an unnecessary waste of time, but now I wanted to scoot closer. My body ached with the longing to feel his touch everywhere.

Cerulean cleared his throat and dropped his eyes from my face. "Maybe we should eat."

Blowing out a breath, I pulled myself together before I threw myself at him. "Yeah, that's probably a good idea."

How was this man affecting me this much when it had been less than three hours since I'd met him?

I tried to tell myself it was a good thing I was attracted to him since we were soon-to-be mates. It would have sucked—and not the good kind of suck—if he'd been a turnoff.

We ate in companionable silence, his gaze rarely leaving the dark sea that lay in front of us.

Finishing the last of my meal, I sipped the mixed drink he'd brought for me. "Do you live far from here?"

The tentacle wrapped loosely around me twitched, and his eyes jerked to meet mine. "Sorry, I was lost in my thoughts. Yes. I live close to the Australian coast, so it is a long way from here."

It was my turn to be surprised. "Surely you didn't swim all the way here?"

"A witch owed me a favor and used a little magic to teleport me to the Bermuda Triangle portal. After that, I hitched a ride with a whale friend up the coast. It has been years since I've traveled, so it was an enjoyable experience."

The alcohol was sending cozy warmth through my veins, and I found myself relaxing further into his tentacle.

"Do you work?" I asked, trying to focus on business and not the way I enjoyed the flex of his muscles as he adjusted his grip around me.

"Yes, in my family's business with my sister and brother. Things run smoothly between us and my father."

"A family business? That must be so nice." I popped the strawberry garnish from my drink into my mouth. "My father tried to execute a hostile takeover of my company a couple of years ago, so in my life, business and family don't mix."

Cerulean's grip tightened around me. "That is terrible, darling."

I shrugged. "It's fine. We laughed about it over New Year's dinner last year."

My mate looked horrified. "You still talk to him?"

"Of course I do. Stuff like this is common in vampire families. If you see a weakness that you can exploit to your advantage, you are duty-bound to take it. Blood or not. It is the vampire way." My bark of laughter lacked any genuine amusement.

Cerulean was silent for so long that I assumed he was thinking about other things. "Have you done that to one of your family members?"

I wiggled the straw in my drink, knowing that if I looked up, he'd see the emotion in my eyes. "No. Although I've seen plenty of opportunities where I could have easily taken business away from my father and brother. Instead of seizing those opportunities, I let them pass. According to the vampire code, that is a testament to my weakness."

Cerulean set the tray on the stone at the edge of the pool and turned toward me. Now that they no longer needed to hold the tray, his tentacles moved around me like eager puppies wanting to play.

The tentacle around my waist shifted, pulling me closer

to Cerulean until he could capture my face between his palms.

"Beryl, you aren't weak, and you're one heck of a businesswoman. You saw the opportunities because you are smart, but you let them pass because you are kind. That isn't a weakness... regardless of what other vampires might say."

My heart began thudding hard in my chest at his praise. Or was I reacting to the nearness of his lips and the way his playful tentacles were brushing against my bare thighs?

"Thank you." Blinking hard, I tried to clear the fog of lust that was causing my eyelids to grow heavy.

Cerulean's arms wrapped around me, pulling me into a tight hug. There was nothing sexual about the hug. It was just immensely comforting. I wanted to stay there forever, relaxing in his arms, being rocked by the water surrounding us, listening to the methodical crash of the ocean's waves in the distance.

room 88

Chapter 6

BERYL

room 88

"Come on, let's get you into bed. Your body isn't made to sleep in water." Cerulean's lips brushed against my forehead, sending another wave of unfamiliar tingles skittering across my skin.

I made a move to pull away, but his arms tightened around me.

"I've got you." He moved through the water with effortless ease.

Cerulean must have shifted before we reached the steps because, when he stepped from the pool, he had two legs instead of six tentacles.

He carried me into the room and lowered me gently onto the bed.

"I'm going to dry you, so don't start panicking," he rumbled.

I watched in stunned silence as his hand trailed across my skin, and the droplets of water moved toward his hand like metal beads to a magnet. When his hand brushed featherlight up my thighs and near my breasts, I fought back the urge to squirm. He didn't linger in those areas, but it was still an erotic experience.

Within minutes, I was completely dry, and Cerulean held the gathered water in a swirling globe on his palm. With a grin, he tossed it through the open doorway, where it splashed into the pool.

"If you can dry water, why were you still dripping wet when you woke me up?" I asked, running a hand through my dry hair.

My hair was so thick it took close to twenty minutes to dry it with a blow-dryer, yet he'd done dried it in under a minute.

Cerulean chuckled. "Water doesn't bother me, so I often forget to dry myself. But I know land-dwellers are uncomfortable being wet unless they are bathing or spending time at a pool or beach."

His head tilted as he studied my skimpy bikini. "That doesn't look very comfortable. Did you bring something comfortable to sleep in?"

"Um, yes. I brought something special to wear to bed." My cheeks burned, and I wondered if he could see them in the darkened interior of the room.

He cocked his head to the side, an unreadable expression on his face. "But is it comfortable?"

I burst out laughing. "Cerulean, none of the sexy things women wear to bed are made with comfort in mind."

He shook his head. "Then I don't understand the point."

"Women wear pretty things to make their man want them more and to ensure their man finds them attractive."

Cerulean stalked toward where I sat on the edge of the bed. Leaning down, he caged me in with his powerful arms.

"I already believe you are the most attractive woman I've ever seen. I don't think you could do anything to make me want you more." He gently nuzzled my neck, his warm breath blowing across my skin.

My stomach clenched, and desire flared to life inside me.

"I suggest we sleep as the sea-dwellers do." Cerulean stood and made his way to the opposite side of the bed.

Pulling back the duvet and the sheet, he slid beneath them.

"Oh? And how is that?" I raised a brow.

Surely, he didn't mean what I thought he...

"Naked." The bright white of his teeth glowed in the dark.

I caught my breath.

He wanted me to undress.

Right now.

Everyone on earth knew what happened when two adults who were attracted to each other got naked in bed together.

Was I ready for that to happen?

Somehow, when I'd thought of it as a business agreement, the thought of sex to seal the mate bond hadn't seemed like a big deal. I knew how to make it pleasurable for a man, and if I was lucky, my partner would make it nice for me, too.

Sex was just sex.

No emotions, no strings.

But somehow, this was different.

This time, it mattered—or at least, I wanted it to matter.

For the first time in my life, it wouldn't be 'just sex.'

Still struggling with my inner turmoil, I slowly undid the ties of my bikini top. Then I untied the strings on either side of my hips that held up my bottoms. Taking a deep breath, I dropped them to the floor.

Not giving me time to overthink things any further, Cer's arm hooked around my waist and pulled me beneath the covers.

I yelped in surprise, earning me a deep laugh from the shifter.

He didn't stop pulling until my back was pressed tight against his chest. I was considered a tall woman, but Cerulean was far bigger and easily tucked my body into the safety of his arms.

He rubbed his face against my hair before placing a soft kiss on the top of my head. "Goodnight, Beryl."

Goodnight?

Shut the fraggle-rockin-front-door!

What did he mean by *goodnight*? Why wasn't he pushing to mate?

I'd seen the rigid evidence of his arousal when he'd sat me on the bed. But now he was going to—what was this called? I tried to remember the word, but I hadn't had time to read or watch television for several years and couldn't recall.

"What is this called, Cer? What you're—*we're*—doing?"

"Do you mean snuggling? Well, more accurately, we're spooning."

"Spooning?" That was a word I hadn't heard.

"I'm the big spoon, and you're the little spoon." He chuckled, his warm breath stirring my hair and causing it to tickle my cheek.

I snorted, tucking the offending hair behind my ear. "I think you just made that up! What would it mean, and why are we spoons?"

Cerulean was quiet for a long minute. "It means we fit together."

Oh. It did make sense in an oddly sweet kind of way.

"Now stop over-analyzing everything and go to sleep." His playful growl sent a fresh group of butterflies taking flight in my stomach.

I didn't do sleepovers with sexual partners, which made this the first night I'd ever slept in a man's arms.

And not just any man, but the most gorgeous man I'd ever laid eyes on.

A man who, on paper, was technically my husband.

It turns out I've never slept better.

I AWOKE to the sound of gently lapping waves, exotic birds calling happily to each other, and Cerulean's steady breathing.

We'd shifted positions during the night, and blinking open my eyes, I found I was facing him. He'd tossed his leg over mine, and his arm was resting across my lower back.

The sheet had slipped and now pooled around our waists, which meant my bare breasts were on display. I gently tugged the sheet up to cover myself, relieved Cerulean was asleep and hadn't noticed.

Don't be silly, Beryl. He saw pretty much everything last night, so why are you getting bashful now? My inner voice was always grouchy before coffee.

Staring at his face, I was once again struck by how stunningly gorgeous he was. Seriously, it should've been a crime for a man to look that beautiful. I bet if we slapped his face and body on romance book covers, women would be demanding the paperback version instead of an e-book just so they could stare at him all day.

And Cerulean was mine…

Well, at least on paper.

I'd made it sound like I'd adopted a puppy instead of a whole smexy-arse man. Laughter bubbled in my chest, and not wanting to wake him, I struggled to stifle it.

Cerulean's blonde eyelashes fanned against his tanned skin, and his lips were slightly parted. He was as sweet as he was stunning, which was a lethal, heart-stopping combination. I'd come into this match from a business stance, but I could feel my internal walls trembling.

What would he taste like? What would it feel like to have his lips brush against mine?

Since I hadn't shifted forms before falling asleep, my vampiric saliva had kept any morning breath at bay. I was staring temptation in the face, and unable to resist, I leaned forward and caught his bottom lip between mine.

His taste exploded in my mouth, like the little juice-filled candies that coated your tongue with intense flavor. I moaned in delight and sucked his lip, being careful not to cut him with my fangs.

Over the years, I'd experienced some mind-blowing kisses, but never one this addictive... and Cerulean wasn't even kissing me back.

My body moved on its own, scooting close and hooking my leg over his hip. So lost was I in his taste that I didn't even notice when his hand moved to grip my butt. It was when his mouth captured my lips in a burning kiss that I realized he'd awakened.

"Good morning to you too, beautiful," he laughed against my mouth.

Reluctantly pulling away and feeling more than a little embarrassed at my lack of control, I watched him from beneath my lashes. "Hi."

Cerulean yanked me close again. "Hey, you don't have to stop just because I'm awake."

With my mouth still tingling from our kisses, I couldn't resist his offer. Sliding a hand to the back of his neck, I pressed my lips to his again.

"Why do you taste so good?" I murmured between kisses.

"My venom breaks down when exposed to air and becomes sweet."

He has venom? Well, isn't that just freaking great? That meant I was probably going to die.

Oh well, since it was already too late for me, there was no reason I should stop kissing him now. Why not die happy, right?

Intensifying our impromptu morning make-out, I slipped my tongue into his mouth to dance with his. From there, our kiss went from steamy to rated XXX in about two seconds flat.

It was Cer who pulled away first, gasping for air. "Hades, woman! Are you insane? I told you I have venom, and instead of being horrified, you nearly kissed the soul from my body."

Like a self-satisfied feline, I licked my lips and savored every last bit of his taste. "If I'm going to die, then I'm going to do it enjoying myself."

"Wow. If you thought you were dying, I'd have expected you to run to your phone and give your assistant last-minute instructions on how to run your business." Cerulean drew in another ragged breath and ran his fingers through his messy, sun-bleached hair.

His comment gave me pause. I'd been awake for a while now and hadn't thought of work... not once. Instead of reaching for my phone, I'd reached for Cerulean.

How the heck had this man affected me so quickly?

A sharp arrow of worry pierced through my dreamy, lust-filled haze. I couldn't risk losing focus on my work, especially not when I had the acquisition of a century lined up, a deal that could fund an early retirement if I wanted to take it.

I'd never planned to retire, but lying in Cerulean's arms, listening to the sounds of the tropics through the open patio door, had me questioning how I wanted to spend the rest of my life.

Get it together, Beryl. I gave myself a mental shake.

Flings were okay, but falling in love came with a huge time commitment... time I didn't have to give.Rolling away from him, I pressed my fingertips to my eyes. "You're right. I really should check in with work."

I moved to roll out of bed, only to remember I was naked beneath the sheet. And although Cerulean had seen me naked the night before, it had been dark and felt different in the daylight.

"If you don't mind, while you check in with work, I'm going to take a swim. It's strange being on land for so many hours." Cerulean lifted the sheet from his waist and stood, making no effort to hide himself.

I swallowed hard, steadying my voice. "If it's uncomfortable for you on land, how will you be able to live in the city with me?"

He shrugged his broad shoulders. "It's not painful, merely unusual."

It made sense. Most shifters got an uncomfortable itch that could only be scratched by releasing their natural form.

I spent so much time in my human form it had become easy to go long stretches of time without feeling the need to shift. My father, on the other hand, could only go about twelve hours in his human form before he grew antsy and needed to shift to his natural form.

Vampires and most other shifters could train themselves to go longer between shifting forms, but it would take some time for Cerulean to get used to staying in his human form the majority of the time.

"I live near the ocean, so you could visit the sea every day. But there are only a few months out of the year that it's warm enough to swim in."

Cerulean chuckled. "While I prefer warm water, I'm able to regulate my temperature. Swimming in the Atlantic in December wouldn't be an issue for me."

I shivered. "Well, don't expect me to come swimming with you. I'll watch from shore while wrapped in a blanket."

Cerulean's eyes softened, reminding me of a puppy. It was so dramatic I couldn't help but wonder what he was thinking.

"I'd like that," he whispered.

Unable to hold his gaze, my eyes trailed down the chiseled lines of his body. He wasn't overly bulky, like the guys who spent half their waking hours in a gym. His tall frame had the beautifully sculpted muscles you'd expect from a dancer... or a guy who spent twenty-four hours a day swimming.

There was no denying I was incredibly attracted to him. *The man is exactly my type.*

Despite my best efforts to keep my eyes from drifting lower than his chest, I failed miserably. And just like

Dorothy on the yellow-brick road, I eagerly followed the thin line of golden hair. But unlike Dorothy, who'd needed to tap her slippers, there was something far different at the end of my path that I wanted to tap... and I wanted to do it more than three times.

Forget a magician; the man should have been a carpenter with the magnificent wooden tool he was working with.

Afraid he would notice that I'd begun drooling, I slid my tongue along my bottom lip and the corner of my mouth.

I hissed as the stale, coppery taste of my blood hit my taste buds. I touched my finger to my bottom lip. When I pulled it away, it was smeared with my blood.

"Seriously?" I stared at the blood, absolutely incredulous. "I haven't bitten myself since I was a toddler!"

Cerulean moved faster than should have been possible. One minute, he'd been standing near the patio doorway, and the next, he was crouched over me, his eyes a solid, inky black.

I would have screamed, but I found myself spellbound as he wrapped his lips around my finger, and his tongue began lapping at my bloody fingertip.

A deep, guttural groan came from his chest, as though he were tasting a delicacy, which was strange, since vampires weren't exactly known for possessing tasty blood since it was aged rather than freshly made. To be honest, vampire blood tasted downright disgusting.

Reluctantly, Cerulean released my finger. "I've tasted

nothing like that." His voice had gone so rough and gravelly I could barely understand his words.

The inky abyss of his eyes called to me, stirring the desire that had burned under my skin since meeting him.

"Oh, really?" My vampiric nature was intrigued and excited to play. Pouting slightly to better display my tiny injury, I purred in a husky tone I didn't recognize, "It seems I've cut my lip. Maybe you could kiss it and make it better?"

Cerulean responded with a vicious snarl.

I'd expected a gentle, sucking type of kiss. I definitely hadn't expected my teasing challenge to release his inner Kraken.

But *dang!* I was totally there for it.

His right hand sank into my hair, hauling my mouth to his as his body crushed me into the pillowy mattress.

I arched toward him, and his left arm quickly wrapped around my waist. His kiss was demanding, and I eagerly gave him what he wanted.

His arm curved around my neck…

Hold your seahorses!

My foggy mind struggled to understand how Cer could have more than two arms, but that confusion cleared as the tentacle around my neck tightened, the tip flicking against my skin.

It wasn't tight enough to cut off my breathing, but it was enough to hold me in place and remind me I wasn't the one in control.

Cerulean had shifted forms, and this time, his tentacles

weren't as curious and gentle as they had been in the pool; they were dominating and determined as they twisted around my body.

Two tentacles coiled around my ankles and stroked against the sensitive flesh of my inner thighs. Cerulean swallowed my moan when a fifth slithered around my breasts.

His tentacles coiled around me like a serpent around its prey while his mouth devoured mine, his tongue lapping at the blood. I was pinned beneath him, and even if I'd used my vampiric strength, I doubted I could have fought him off.

Even while lost to his beast, Cerulean was keeping his full weight off me, and his tentacles were restrictive but not painful. He didn't want to hurt me, and that sent a strange, gooey warmth trickling through me.

Cerulean's chest vibrated each time he got a drop of my blood, causing my desire to rise.

I was used to being in charge... everywhere. And being in control during sex had become a quick way to release my pent-up stress.

So why was Cer's aggressive dominance causing my body to send wave after wave of wet heat rushing between my thighs?

This differed from the wham-bam-thank-you-ma'am sex I'd grown accustomed to, and I was becoming intensely curious about what it would feel like to experience sex that was filled with a wild passion.

The cut on my inner lip was already healing thanks to

my vampiric abilities... but I wasn't ready for our fiery kiss to be over.

Letting go of all reason, I swiped my tongue along my fang. The sharp tip sliced into my skin with such ease I didn't feel the pain.

Fresh blood pooled in my mouth, and Cerulean instantly took the bait. And once again, he responded with a primal hunger that caused a powerful ache to build low in my stomach.

His tongue delved into my mouth, stroking against mine. The tentacle around my waist curled around my upper thigh, the tip inching ever closer to my soaked core.

When another tentacle brushed against my aching breasts, I whimpered, eliciting a rumbling growl from the man devouring me.

As though he wanted to make me whimper again, the tentacle rolled against my skin until the underside stroked my skin—were those his suction cups?

I got my answer when one of those cups latched onto the hardened peak of my nipple and pulled gently. It was as though his mouth was in more than one place at a time, and my body nearly short-circuited.

"Cerulean!" I arched, breaking our kiss to pant his name.

He responded with a frustrated growl, his mouth traveling up the column of my neck to claim my mouth again.

I struggled in his hold, not because I wanted to be freed, but because I longed for more. His mouth, his scent, his body pressed against mine, his tentacle teasing and sucking my breasts… it was too much and not enough all at the same time.

The tentacle around my waist slid low across my stomach until the tip brushed against my slit. The simple touch was too much for my brain to process, and my body stiffened.

For the first time since he'd licked my finger clean, Cerulean spoke, his voice raw. "Do you want me to stop?"

He was motionless, not a single wandering tentacle twitching as he waited for my response.

"No," I whispered against his lips. "Please don't stop."

The tentacles holding me flexed slightly, and I got the distinct impression they were pleased I hadn't pushed him away.

The tentacle between my legs rolled until the edges of the cups rubbed against my soaked entrance.

My body came off the bed as though I'd been electro-cuted, the delicious friction too much to handle.

An alien clicking came from Cer's chest, and his lips found my ear. "If you liked that, you're really going to love this."

As he spoke, one of the suction cups pressed between my lower lips. My body quivered with terror and excitement.

Surely, he's not going to….

The cup attached itself to my clit and immediately began a steady sucking rhythm. Searing pleasure tore through me with the destructive power of white-water rapids. In under ten seconds, I was writhing beneath Cerulean as I screamed my release.

When I lay still beneath him, my body coated in a fine sheen of sweat, Cer brushed the hair from my face.

"How are you so beautiful?" His chest rattled with the odd clicks again.

"How can you make me so sensitive?" I blurted out before I could close my mouth.

His eyes sparkled with interest. "I had you pegged for a woman who'd be very passionate in the bedroom. Are you telling me this isn't the norm for you?"

I gave a breathless laugh. "Cer, I'm no virgin, but somehow you have me falling apart at a simple touch."

"Maybe our bodies were made for each other," he teased, a gorgeous smile spreading across his face.

That suggestion sent a shiver racing down my spine. If I was this sensitive to his touch, what would happen when we consummated our mate bond?

Cerulean leaned down and placed a tender kiss at the base of my throat. "I'm going for a swim now, darling."

The term of endearment did weird things to my already rattled insides. I'd never gotten close enough to a sexual partner to be given a pet name.

"But I haven't returned the favor—" I reached for Cerulean, but he evaded me with an agility that would have impressed me if it hadn't annoyed me.

I was a vampire. Few creatures were faster than my species, and I wasn't sure how I felt about my slippery mate's speed.

"Beryl, if you touch me right now, I won't be able to keep from burying myself inside you. Our first time should be in my other form, not this form." He motioned at his tentacles.

Two moved as he spoke like an extra set of hands that were mocking him. He used the remaining four to stand and stay balanced. His tentacles were thick and long, so he stood slightly taller in this form than he did as a human.

The tentacles were a pale, buttery yellow that periodically flashed with hints of blue. My fingers ached with the desire to touch him, to feel his slick skin beneath my palm, and to study the shifting colors. But he was out the door and launching himself into the ocean before I could say another word.

Cursing under my breath, I made my way to the bathroom and took a freezing shower to wash away the sweat and ease the heat of my arousal.

STEPPING FROM THE SHOWER, I towel-dried my hair and slipped on a pair of white shorts and a flowy crimson top. Not wanting to appear like I was trying too hard, I decided to forgo any makeup other than swiping gloss on my lips.

Before leaving the bathroom, I stared at my reflection in the mirror, studying my vampiric form. This was the longest I'd stayed in my natural form in years.

My skin possessed a dewy shimmer in the morning light, and my shirt fit a little more snugly thanks to the extra swell of my breasts. Even my eyelashes were lengthened, and my lips had a puffy, well-kissed look.

This was a form built with one job in mind—arousing and luring my prey.

Everything about this body was supposed to help me seduce humans into dropping their guards and coming close enough for me to feed.

The fact that I didn't want to lure anyone to me didn't seem to matter. And it was why I'd avoided this form for all of my adult life. I hated the attention it brought to me as a woman.

My mother had loudly bemoaned the fact that I hid my 'true beauty,' but it was the only way I could navigate a world filled with men who were looking for conquests or trophies.

Standing in front of the mirror, I found myself torn for the first time.

It was easy enough, even in my human form, to find someone to sleep with when my biological needs grew distracting. So it was odd to realize I wanted Cerulean to be attracted to me... and that I enjoyed watching the effect I had on him.

I wanted to drive him wild and arouse him.

I wanted him to look at me and lose control.

"What is wrong with you, Beryl? Get it together!" I snarled at my reflection.

Frustrated with my raging sex drive, I closed my eyes

and shifted back to my less provocative human form. It was time to focus on the important things in my life.

Moving to the desk, I flipped open my laptop and began scanning the list of emails I'd received since I'd fallen asleep.

My assistant, Sara, was doing an amazing job of keeping up with them, but that didn't stop my anxiety from flaring to life. Why had I thought I could sneak away for a week in the middle of handling multiple company acquisitions?

Oh yeah, because this was the week I'd been assigned to meet my mate, and P-Harmony had a nonnegotiable policy when it came to those dates.

I had to admit, it was going to be a relief to attend the after-signing celebrations with a plus one. But at that moment, I was questioning my priorities.

My phone chimed with a new message, and I flicked the screen to read it. It was Sara confirming that everything was being handled, and she knew my phone number if something popped up.

Still feeling off balance and as though I should be doing something productive, I slowly closed my laptop.

My eyes drifted out the open patio doors to the azure blue sea. What was I supposed to do now?

The growling of my stomach reminded me it was time to eat and find some caffeine before I did anything else.

Grabbing my room key and slipping into a pair of low-heeled sandals, I left the room in search of sustenance and the only thing vampires liked more than blood...*Coffee.*

Chapter 8

CERULEAN

room 88

My body hummed as I propelled myself through the water. Just the small taste of Beryl's blood had energy flowing in my veins as though I'd injected myself with pure caffeine.

I wanted more... and I wanted it with a craving so powerful I feared myself.

Octopus shifters didn't drink blood, nor did our bodies need it to survive like a vampire. However, we were known for our intense curiosity. My species was driven to touch, taste, and explore anything we could get our tentacles on.

I'd been captivated by the bright red drop of blood that had beaded on Beryl's lip. When she'd smeared it with her finger, the desire to taste it had been irresistible.

If it had tasted like normal blood, my curiosity would've been sated.

But when I discovered her blood was spiced with cinnamon and honey... I'd wanted more. I'd lost myself in her taste, and the feel of her body pressed against mine, and my beast had taken advantage of it. He'd surged forward with a strength that made it impossible to hold back the shift to my split form.

When the little minx had purposefully cut herself a second time, and her crimson nectar coated my tongue, I'd nearly mounted her on the spot.

Little did she know how close I'd come to impaling her on my mating tentacle. Only by pinning that tentacle to the bed had I managed to stop myself. My actions—or lack thereof—had annoyed my beast, but he'd turned his attention to exploring her body.

And oh, what a body it was!

In both human and vampiric form, she was completely and utterly built for mating. I'd met more than a few sirens over my long life, and they had nothing on my sex-kitten mate.

And her taste....

My body slowed to a stop at the memory. Did Beryl know that octopuses possessed the ability to taste through their suckers?

This morning had been more erotic than anything I could have imagined. Her blood had coated my tongue, tasting like fine red wine from Poseidon's table, while the suckers busy between her legs discovered the sweet nectar hidden there.

Would it taste the same on my tongue as it had on my suckers?

The beast in my mind stirred, his curiosity roused.

This is vital information. We must return and demand to taste her.

No, I was not returning to the room until I wore out my muscles and felt sure I was too tired to get us into trouble.

I desperately wanted to give Beryl time to adjust to having a mate. She'd been clear that she was open to attending to all my biological needs, but just hearing her refer to intimacy in such cold terms had reinforced my resolve to not take things all the way until she could view it as I did... that we were making love.

Resisting my alluring mate was painful. I wanted to take her gentle and rough, slow and fast, tender and hard. But not until I knew it would mean something to her.

Because right now, she still viewed our marriage as a business transaction.

A smile curved my lips. Her walls were already crumbling.

Beryl had kissed me this morning. All on her own.

I'd slept very little the previous night thanks to the rigid erection that had refused to go down, thanks to the naked woman snuggled against me. It hadn't helped matters when the sheet had slipped down to her waist, putting her bare breasts on full display.

Lying beside her was agony... and I wouldn't have changed it for anything.

When her breathing had changed, I knew Beryl had awakened. She'd thought I was asleep, and I'd remained motionless, curious to see what she would do.

I hadn't expected her to kiss me, and the touch of her

pouty lips sucking my bottom lip into her mouth had nearly been my undoing.

Instead of reaching for her phone, she'd reached for me.

Yesterday, she had planned to hire someone to show me around the city, but this morning when we spoke of my need to swim, Beryl had said she would sit on the shore and watch me.

They weren't declarations of undying love, but they were signs of growing affection. It was a start.

She was willing to open her home, her wallet, and her body to me… but I wanted her to open her heart. Still smiling, I began swimming again.

When I finally headed toward shore, it was almost lunchtime.

"No, thank you. I'm not interested in playing," Beryl's voice carried through the water.

Who was she talking to?

"Come on! What could it hurt to play one game?" an unfamiliar male voice echoed through the water.

"I don't want to be rude, but I'm not comfortable having you pick me up. Maybe if my mate wants to play when he returns, we can join you guys." Beryl's words carried a note of strain.

Whoever the guy was, he was making her uncomfortable. My jaw clenched in agitation.

"Come on, Beryl! You were so good at volleyball on land. I bet you'd be amazing in the water. Please come play!" a female's voice pleaded.

Forgetting that I was tired, I pushed my limbs to move

us faster through the water. I reached the shallow area near shore where Beryl and several others were standing on either side of a net.

What game were they wanting Beryl to play?

From beneath the rippling surface of the water, I watched as a man—a werewolf shifter by his scent—took a step toward Beryl, his hands reaching for her beneath the water. The rest of the group had paired up, the men lifting the girls on their shoulders, and he was trying to do the same with Beryl.

I realized with dawning horror that this man wanted to put his head between my mate's thighs. Just the thought of him being so close he would smell her sweet scent had my blood boiling and my rings flashing in anger.

Jettisoning myself forward, I wrapped my tentacles around Beryl's long legs. I kept her balanced as I stood, lifting her from the water on my shoulders.

"Ah!" Beryl shrieked in surprise.

Then she looked down, her eyes meeting mine, and joy flashed through her green irises.

My heart melted.

She's happy to see me.

Her fingers brushed the loose blonde hair off my forehead.

"Hi, mate," she whispered, bringing her lips to mine in a sweet upside-down kiss.

"Is that your mate, Beryl?" the female gushed. "What a hottie!"

Beryl's thighs tightened around my head, and I fought

the urge to spin her around on my shoulders so my mouth would be pressed against her sweet—

That isn't difficult to accomplish, my beast answered matter-of-factly. *I like this idea.*

It was hard enough to resist temptation without having an inner voice to encourage it. *No, we can't take her right here on the beach in front of a crowd. This is a paranormal establishment, but they still have rules.*

Your world has pathetic rules. Keeping a mate satisfied is a thing of honor, not a thing to hide behind closed doors. I could have sworn the beast rolled his eyes.

That's just not how things work, I growled at the unreasonable creature.

I could admit I did find a particular charm at the thought of carrying the beauty on my shoulders to shore and pleasuring her without a thought over who might be watching. That gave me an idea, and my tentacles twitched in excitement while my rings darkened.

I just needed an opening…

"Well, are we playing or not?" the girl ordered. "Nick! Go grab one of the girls on the beach. Two of them are practically panting at you, so I'm sure they'll agree to play."

Nick, the werewolf, shot me a nasty look as he made his way toward the shore. I resisted the urge to smirk. He could sulk all he wanted… he wasn't getting my girl.

"Beryl, since your mate can breathe underwater, it's only fair you play in the corner where the water is deeper." She turned her attention back to us.

And that is exactly the opening I was looking for…

I waded in deeper until only my eyes were above water and waited, my tentacles curling in anticipation under the water.

Beryl's fingers combed through my hair. "We don't have to play. I was only out here waiting for you when they roped me into a game of volleyball."

With my mouth underwater, I couldn't answer. Instead, I turned my head, and I pressed a kiss to her bare thigh, reassuring her I was happy to be with her.

The game began, and I let Beryl hit several balls before I started playing my own game.

One of my tentacles crept up and slipped under her butt. It wiggled its way between where the apex of her thighs pressed against the back of my neck.

My hearing allowed me to hear the acceleration of her pulse as the tip of my tentacle worked its way between our bodies.

"What are you doing, Cer?" she hissed.

Lifting myself on the tentacles anchoring me to the sandy ocean floor, I moved my mouth above the water's surface.

"Calm down, darling. The water is covering everything. Besides, my neck and head prevent anyone in front of us from seeing, and your body blocks anyone from seeing what is going on from behind us. No one will know what is happening unless you announce it."

"But—" Her protest turned to a gasp as my tentacle pushed aside the tiny scrap of fabric between her thighs.

My suckers were made up of two main parts, both of

which were surrounded by different shaped muscles. The outer part had grooves and ridges that helped me form a watertight seal on all surfaces.

A wicked grin spread across my face as I pressed the sucker-covered side of my tentacle along the length of her slit. The delicate taste of her arousal rippled through my body, forcing me to tighten the grip on the beast, who wanted to take our mate right then.

Taking a deep breath, I waited.

As the ball flew at us, I moved toward it, and Beryl threw herself forward, her fist slamming into the ball and sending it sailing back over the net.

Our quick movements had thrown her forward and caused her to grind against my tentacle. Beryl's sharp intake of breath and the clenching of her thighs around my head told me exactly what it was doing to her.

Nicole sent the ball sailing straight back toward us and, a little rougher than necessary, I lurched toward it, loving the slick heat of her core sliding against my suckers.

Beryl growled under her breath, but even with me distracting her, she managed to send the ball flying back to the opposing team.

Nicole missed, giving our team a point. For the next couple of minutes, there was laughing and splashing as her partner worked to balance the feisty redhead on his shoulders while she blamed him for their lost point.

The grin on my face had nothing to do with their antics.

To my absolute delight, my mate was gently rocking her hips against my suckers. Beryl was careful to keep the movement slow and gentle so it was imperceptible to everyone around us.

"I can't believe I'm acting like a horny teenager. Heck! I don't even remember acting like this back then!" she grumbled as her breath quickened.

Sinking a few inches lower in the water, I kissed her inner thighs, desperately wishing my mouth was somewhere else. Beryl's fingers tightened in my hair, and her thigh muscles trembled.

When her muscles stiffened, and she let her long hair fall around her face, I knew she'd found her release. I loved the way her body quivered as she rode the waves of pleasure, and the way her cream sweetened the water around my head.

I wasn't finished, though.

Far from it.

As the game started up again, I kept the tip of my tentacle wedged between us and found as many opportunities as I could to throw her weight forward, grinding her against me... hard.

I counted seven orgasms.

When her legs quivered, and her trembling hand rested against my jaw, I knew she needed a break and food.

My tentacle shifted her bikini bottom back into place before dropping back into the water.

I lifted my head above the water's surface. "All right, I'm hungry. It's time for lunch and a nap."

Releasing my hold on Beryl's legs, I allowed the shift to ripple over my lower half, turning my tentacles to legs.

Using the special cells covering my skin, I created the appearance and texture of swim shorts.

"Dang, girl! He's even hotter than I thought!" Nicole whistled in appreciation, and Beryl's legs clamped tighter around me.

Chuckling, I moved up the beach toward the resort.

My girl might have been a vampire, but she had the grip of an octopus.

Chapter 9

CERULEAN

room 88

I felt, rather than saw, her shake her head.

Stepping onto our patio, I sat her gently in one of the plush chairs and kneeled in front of her.

"You could put me down," Beryl offered.

"I could," I agreed. "But I don't want to."

She continued to run her fingers through my hair. It was soothing, and I wondered if she would consider doing it while we napped… if I could get her to nap instead of going back to her laptop.

"I'm not exactly tiny. It can't be comfortable carrying me on your shoulders for so long."

"Darling, you weigh nothing to me."

"Liar." Beryl's laugh warmed my insides and sent blood rushing straight to my cock.

I tried to clear the lust that threatened to choke me. Maybe I should've taken care of my needs while taking my morning swim, because the continued denial was on the verge of becoming an issue.

"You're a vampire, so you understand inhuman strength. Octopuses are among the strongest of species, capable of lifting forty times their body weight… and that is an ability that the octopus shifters received. I could carry you all day and feel no strain."

"That's incredible," Beryl breathed. "You're incredible."

My circles flashed in pride at her praise, and she brushed a finger across my shoulder. "Your markings can show even in this form?"

"Yes, my skin is unique. It looks human, but it retains the special color-shifting cells of the octopus. They shift colors and textures to help me to blend in with my surroundings if danger is nearby."

"Do the blue rings mean something? I notice they flash periodically."

I nodded. "Intense emotion triggers them. Anger, fear, sadness…"

"But you weren't feeling those just now, were you?" She hesitated before continuing, "Or this morning when they flashed?"

"This morning, it was arousal, and just now, it was happiness from your compliment," I answered honestly, my chest tightening.

She had brushed off the talk of my venom this morning, but I needed to tell her everything.

"Beryl, did the agency tell you exactly what I am?"

Her gaze slid from mine. "I didn't read the file. It didn't matter what you were, only that you fit into my plans."

Something akin to shame flitted across her face, but it happened so fast I thought I might've imagined it.

I patted her thigh, trying to reassure her I didn't mind. "Octopuses are incredibly adept at squeezing themselves into tight places." Realizing it might have sounded like I was talking about certain parts of her anatomy, I added, "I mean, like your schedule."

"I still don't understand why you were so incredibly agreeable to my demands," Beryl murmured.

"You were clear about your needs and expectations. I appreciate that." Catching her chin between my fingers, I lifted her head. "If you didn't read the file, then you don't know what I am."

Her eyes met mine, and her brow creased in confusion. "Yes, I do. You're an octopus shifter. You told me that last night; it was kind of obvious in the pool and this morning."

"There are multiple species of octopus shifters. I'm a blue-ringed octopus." Holding my breath, I waited for her reaction.

When Beryl remained silent, waiting for me to elaborate, I rocked back on my heels.

"Do you know what that is?" I questioned.

Beryl sniffed indignantly. "Of course I do. I'm not an idiot, unlike the tourists who film themselves holding the tiny blue-ringed octopuses. One of the most venomous creatures on earth, capable of killing twenty-six adult men within minutes, blah, blah, blah—"

I couldn't help it.

I snickered.

Her eyes narrowed on me as I tried to hide my smile behind my hand. "I swear, if you make a Dracula joke right now, I'll drain your blood… venom or not."

"But you said, 'blah, bla—'" My terrible attempt at a Dracula-like accent was cut off when she shifted forms.

She lunged toward me, her fangs digging gently into my skin but not puncturing it. "Another word, and I'll bite…"

Her hot breath blew across my skin, sending a shiver down my spine.

Unfortunately, Beryl's threat didn't have the effect on me she was aiming for, and my body was instantly hard.

"Promise?" My single word came out as a husky growl.

Without hesitation, her fangs pierced my skin. I groaned, locking my arm around her waist and pulling her tight against me.

Beryl stiffened with her fangs embedded in my skin. I could feel the erratic pounding of her heart against my chest.

First… time…

The two words drifted into my mind, and my beast surged forward in delight.

I was hearing her voice in my mind.

Because you drank her blood, and now she's tasted yours. Blood exchange, my beast purred.

This was a common practice among octopus shifters. Pricking a tentacle and pressing it against another octopus shifter's tentacle gave us the ability to speak telepathically to each other beneath the water. It was temporary, the effects lasting only a few hours.

We were trained in the art of mental links and barriers from birth, giving us the ability to control which thoughts we shared and which we wanted to keep private. But I'd never heard of an octopus shifter being able to communicate telepathically with a land-dweller.

My heart swelled, delighted to have a familiar type of communication to share with my mate.

Want.

Don't do it.

Hungry.

Might not stop.

Hurt him.

Her thoughts were broken, spilling over into my mind.

Beryl had said she'd never drank from a living being before.

So did that mean I was the first blood she was tasting from a vein? And that I was the first she'd ever bitten?

My cock engorged to a point it was excruciating, and unable to stop myself, I bucked my hips against her bikini bottoms.

The friction was torture and paradise all at once, and my groan was followed by an adorable whimper from Beryl.

Slipping my fingers into her hair, I cradled the back of her head, holding her mouth tight against my skin. "Drink."

Her breathing came in fast pants, and I worried she was on the verge of hyperventilating.

"Let me feed you," I growled. "Stop fighting it."

Her arms wrapped around my torso, and her pointed nails dug into my skin, much like a predator guarding its prey.

Then her beautiful mouth sucked against my skin, pulling my blood into her mouth and sending pleasure surging through every cell of my body.

Each time she drew a mouthful of blood from my neck, my hips jerked, grinding against her, my body instinctively seeking a release for the dark lust and need I was drowning in.

Bold, royal-blue rings were visible across my skin, a warning that I was nearing my breaking point and close to losing it.

Beryl sucked faster, and the fragrance of her arousal grew thick in the air. Her sweet whimpers and muffled moans were turning my blood into molten lava.

Taste… like… heaven.

Need… to stop.

Mine.

I closed my eyes, fighting against the burn of unshed tears, as her last word drifted through my mind. Beryl was in the throes of feeding and lust, but a primal part of her mind had called me hers…

And not because a piece of paper said so.

But because her heart had claimed me.

Easing the tight grip I had on her hair, I tilted my neck to the side, giving her better access and cradling her head as she drank.

"That's it. Good girl," I praised, encouraging her to take what she wanted.

She moaned, and her thighs clamped tighter around me.

Grabbing her waist with my free hand, I held her still as I thrust my hips upward. My erection slid along the fabric of her bikini bottoms, and with each rock of my hips, the rough friction continued to drive us both ever closer to the edge.

Beryl froze, her back arched, and her fangs released my neck.

"Cerulean!" she screamed my name, her body trembling with waves of pleasure.

Gritting my teeth, I thrust against her three more times before my muscles tensed, and I roared as I found my release.

My cock was still spasming between us when Beryl began lapping at my neck like a kitten drinking warm milk.

"You're going to kill me," I rasped.

"I needed to stop the bleeding," my kitten practically purred. "And you taste delicious…. I don't want to waste a drop."

Tucking an arm under her butt, I rose and carried her inside the room.

Keeping her arms circled around my neck, Beryl leaned back to glare at me through thin, catlike pupils.

"I hope you learned your lesson. No vampire on earth has ever used that idiotic phrase." She tried to scowl, but the corners of her mouth twitched.

"Oh, yes. I learned a valuable lesson today." I was careful to keep my expression serious.

I'd learned that saying 'blah, blah, blah' three times would summon a sexy little succubus who'd rock my world.

And I was *definitely* adding it to my vocabulary.

Chapter 10

BERYL

room 88

We spent the rest of the afternoon eating snacks, splashing in our private pool, and sunning on the patio. Each time I tried to sneak off to check my phone or computer, Cerulean would wait thirty minutes before coming inside to pull me back into the pool or swing.

I didn't know if I'd ever experienced such a relaxing afternoon... and it was enjoyable. Was this what people called having a work-life balance?

As we prepared for bed, my stomach fluttered wildly, and my heart thundered in my ears.

Cerulean hadn't pushed for sex the previous night. Probably because it was our first night together, and he wanted to give us a chance to get to know each other a little more. Something I'd appreciated.

But this was our second night sharing a bed.

Which meant he'd likely want to consummate our bond tonight.

I hadn't been this nervous over sex since I was a virgin planning my first time... which had been a long time ago. So why were my palms sweaty and my heart beating so erratically?

Because this is more than sex, and you know it.

I shushed my inner voice, not ready to face what it was hinting at... that I might already be falling in more than 'like' with a certain octopus shifter.

I took my time in the bathroom, letting Cerulean get into bed before me.

Clutching the sink, I stared at myself in the mirror, questions swirling in my mind. Should I sleep in my natural form again? Should I wear the lingerie I'd bought? Should I go out there nude?

It took longer to decide than I would have liked, but eventually, I settled on shifting to my natural vampire form. Reaching for the lingerie, I hesitated, a flush burning my skin.

I wasn't opposed to sex with Cerulean if he initiated it, but something had shifted inside me. There was no way I could strut out with the casual confidence I possessed with one-night stands.

Maybe tomorrow, I'd wear my stringy lingerie. I grabbed the worn, oversized t-shirt I loved to sleep in at home and slipped it over my head. The hem fell just past my butt, making it just long enough to cover my cheeky underwear.

Opening the bathroom door, I made my way to the bed.

It was a breeze to navigate the darkness, thanks to my vampiric abilities.

Without a word, I lifted the blanket and slid under the covers. Cerulean's arm wrapped around my middle. He hauled me toward him and crushed me in a bear hug.

"How are you so cute?" Cer brushed a kiss on my cheek.

I allowed myself to relax and enjoy being surrounded by his scent.

"I don't know. How are you so sweet?" I teased, trying to get used to bantering with a partner.

"I'm not sweet—I'm venomous," Cer growled, nipping at my neck. "Now stop insulting me and go to sleep."

Sleep?

We weren't going to have sex? To my shock, the relief washing through me was tinged with more than a touch of disappointment.

"Cer, we can have sex if you—"

His arms tightened, and he threw a leg over me. "Go to sleep, woman."

The man was invading my personal space in a way no one had dared to attempt before...

And I *liked* it.

Ignoring the dissatisfied aching in certain parts of my anatomy, I scooted back against Cerulean's chest and closed my eyes.

"RISE AND SHINE, my little creature of the night."

Blinking hard, I scowled at Cerulean's smiling face. "Vampires aren't creatures of the night anymore. That nickname was solely based on the past when we needed the cover of darkness to feed—"

"Yeah, yeah. All I'm hearing is blah, blah—"

I sat up, raising a brow, and pinned him with a warning glare. "I'm going to wake up and choose violence if you even think about finishing that."

Before he could respond, I caught the mouth-watering scent of a cheese omelet and rare steak. It was wafting in my direction from the tray Cerulean was holding.

My murderous desires were instantly forgotten. Scrambling to my knees, I watched hungrily as he placed the tray on the bed in front of me.

"Is that for me?" I couldn't hide the note of pleading from my voice.

"Yes, it is. I woke up thinking a werewolf was attacking us… it turned out it was just your stomach growling in your sleep." The rich, velvety sound of his laughter sent heat washing through my body.

Sitting down on the edge of the bed, Cerulean held out the steaming cup of coffee to me. With a grin of appreciation, I downed it with embarrassing speed.

"Careful! You'll burn yourself." He reached out and tried to take the mug from me but changed his mind at my warning hiss. "Fine, keep it. I thought vampires only chugged blood with that much enthusiasm?"

I sipped the dark brew and shrugged. "Most vampires

might prefer blood. But as far as I was concerned, other than the taste of your blood, coffee beats blood every time."

We fell silent, and picking up a fork, I began to eat.

As I chewed a bite of perfectly seared steak, Cerulean cleared his throat. "Would you mind if I go stretch in the ocean for a bit? I won't stay gone long."

"You don't have to ask permission, Cer." I leaned forward to brush my fingers along his jaw. "I understand you need time in the water, especially after staying on land with me all night."

The faint worry lines eased from his face. "Thank you, darling."

"I'll finish eating and check my emails. Then, when you return, maybe we could explore the resort together?" I suggested.

Cerulean placed a kiss on the top of my head. "Sounds like a plan. Be back soon!"

I watched him stride out onto the patio, enjoying the play of muscles beneath his skin. With breathtaking agility, he dove into the water without so much as a splash.

A faint spasm shot through my chest, and I rubbed my palm against it. What was wrong with me?

You don't like to be away from him.

I shushed my ridiculous inner thoughts. I barely knew him!

Besides, how would I be able to work full time once we returned home if I became so clingy I couldn't stand to be separated from him?

Shoving those thoughts into a dark corner of my mind, I finished eating so I could focus my attention on work.

Opening my laptop, I was relieved to have the familiarity of a routine to help ground my spinning thoughts.

My relief turned to concern as I read the top unopened email. It was from Sara, and the subject line read: URGENT.

That single word had my blood pressure skyrocketing. Sara had worked with me for several years and could handle my company almost as well as I could. So, what could she need urgent help with?

I clicked the email.

BERYL, I'm sorry to disturb you, but Timothy has called half a dozen times in the past twenty-four hours. I've explained that you're away on a personal matter, but he's become insistent that he needs to speak with you. Is there any chance you could sneak away for a quick video call with him today?

WITHOUT HESITATION, I messaged Sara back, telling her to set up a time and then forward me the link. Clicking send, I checked the time and decided I should clean up so I'd be ready for the call.

I took a quick shower and blow-dried my hair. Out of habit, I began twisting my long, light brown hair into the tight bun at the nape of my neck.

The memory of Cerulean's eyes when he'd let my hair fall free flashed through my mind.

I liked the way he'd looked at me.

Releasing the twist, I let my hair fall around my face.

Grabbing my makeup bag, I brushed a thin coat of mascara on my eyelashes and dabbed gloss on my lips.

My phone chimed, and I glanced down to find a text from Sara. Flicking a finger across the screen, I read the message and cursed.

Timothy wanted to speak right then.

Scrambling from the bathroom, I rushed toward my computer but stopped. I was dressed in only my cami and thong.

Rushing to the desk, I grabbed the suit jacket I'd worn to the resort. I slipped it on and quickly buttoned it up. My underwear wouldn't show on the video call, so I didn't bother finding pants.

Sitting down in the desk chair, I summoned the cool exterior I relied on for my business dealings.

Taking a last calming breath, I clicked the link to join the call.

Chapter 11

CERULEAN

room 88

My body shifted forms the moment I disappeared beneath the surface of the water. I had three forms: human, full octopus, and my split form.

When I shifted to my split form, my lower body turned to tentacles, but my upper body remained mostly human appearing... if you ignored the oddly shaped pupils and the gills on either side of my neck.

I kept many of my inner beast's abilities in all three forms, but my human form lacked the superior swimming skills that came with having tentacles.

Sinking to the bottom of the sea, I closed my eyes, breathing in deep gulps of the salty seawater. It was far harder than I'd imagined staying on land through a full night.

With time, I knew my body would grow used to the air drying my skin and lungs. But right now, it was excruciating. The only thing making it bearable was lying close to my mate-to-be, watching the moonlight kiss her skin, giving her an otherworldly beauty.

The water vibrated and hummed around me.

Another octopus shifter is nearby.

I ran my fingers through the rippling energy waves, gathering information like a spider feeling its silken web.

My eyebrows rose in shock. Why was my sister here, so far from our home?

I lay still, waiting for her to appear. It didn't take long, and less than ten minutes later, she appeared, dropping to the sandy floor beside me.

Pricking her tentacle, she held it up. Mouthing a complaint, I did the same and wrapped the tip of my tentacle around hers. It was similar to a human handshake —if humans had tentacles and shared blood to talk.

"Brother! It is good to see you well!" She was in her split form as well, and her face lit with a genuine smile.

"Little sister, I've not been gone long enough for anyone in our family to miss me. Are you stalking me?" I narrowed my eyes, suspicious of her true motives.

"I decided I needed a vacation, too." Her eyes didn't quite meet mine, sending worry shooting through me.

"Everyone is healthy?" I asked, pushing up from the sandy seafloor.

Azurea waved a tentacle. "Stop fretting. Everyone is just how you left them, and before you ask—yes, the business is flourishing as usual."

I lay back down on the seafloor. "Okay, then. Start talking, Azurea. You wouldn't have traveled halfway around the world without a purpose."

Azurea flopped onto her back next to me, sending a cloud of sand billowing up around us. "When you announced you were moving to the US, it wasn't a surprise since you've been doing most of your work remotely. But after you left, word on the currents was that you're actually taking a mate."

She lifted a crab from the seafloor, petting the cranky creature until it cuddled against her tentacle. Azurea had always had a soothing effect on most creatures of the sea.

"At the same time, a rumor began drifting through the investment world that a certain hot-shot businesswoman in Boston has gone silent." Azurea fell silent, waiting for me to say something.

When I didn't speak, she huffed. "Listen, it didn't take a lot of work to figure out that she's here as well. Are you telling me that's just a coincidence? A little more research revealed that the Last Shot Resort is rumored to help para-normals find a mate."

She fell quiet again.

Taking a deep breath of water, I blew it out a long, bubbling sigh. "It's not a coincidence."

Azurea's tentacle squeezed my shoulder. "Are you so desperate for a wife that you'd leave the sea? Hundreds of sea-dwelling women throw themselves at you every year. If you'd quit hiding from them, you'd already be mated and have a dozen hatchlings clinging to your tentacles."

She was right... but that's not the life I wanted.

I'd wanted to leave the sea and the expectations that had been placed on me since I was young. And by moving to land, I'd be free to explore and do what I wanted without being recognized. I could just focus on being Beryl's husband.

Reaching out a tentacle, I ruffled Azurea's pale blonde hair. "I love our family, and I swear I won't turn my back on the business, but I want something different for my life. Sis, I've spent years in the sea hoping to meet my mate—hoping to fall in love. But it never happened. It's time for me to try something different."

"But a land-dweller, Rule?" She'd reverted to my childhood nickname, which meant Azurea was getting emotional.

"She's amazing, Az." A smile spread across my face just thinking of my mate.

Azurea studied my face for several minutes. "You've let her bite you."

Her fingertips brushed the tiny marks left by Beryl's fangs. "You need to be careful. If you lose control—"

"I won't," I snarled, then seeing the hurt in her eyes, I softened my tone. "You know I've never lost control before, and I wouldn't risk it now."

My sister looked dubious but said nothing else about it. "Does she know who you are?"

This made me chuckle. "I don't think so. The agency didn't hide my identity, but I think she's been too distracted by work to put two and two together."

Azurea choked, bubbles bursting from her mouth. "Are you serious?"

"Az, I'm pretty sure she believes I'm a broke-arse beach bum." I started laughing.

After a moment, Azurea joined me. We laughed until tears leaked from our eyes, and our tentacles slapped at the sand.

When our laughter finally died down, we lay on our backs, staring up at the surface. A small shark moved lazily through the water, sending a school of shimmering fish darting around us. We watched the show in companionable silence.

After a while, I sat up and stretched my tentacles. "I should head back."

Az wrapped me in a tight hug. "Don't get hurt, big brother."

Chuckling, I squeezed her tight. "In case you've forgotten, I'm venomous. It would be a challenge for someone to hurt me."

"I'm not talking about your hulking body, Rule. It's your heart I'm worried about. Your future bride is known for her incredible business skills—not her warmth."

"That's because she has to keep a tough exterior. Underneath, she's a completely different person." I paused, then added, "A person I'm falling in love with."

Azurea reluctantly pulled away. "Then there is one more thing you should know. A CEO in Boston has been spreading the word that Beryl is his, and he intends to marry her. He's been warning the other land-dwellers in their business circles to keep their hands to themselves when it comes to her."

My anger flared, and my blood boiled.

She is ours, my beast snarled, releasing a cloud of ink.

The sea grew dark as ink swirled around us, blocking out the light from the sun. Ink wasn't just a tool to help an octopus escape a predator... no, it was also an effective tool we used to hide our presence as we stalked our prey.

"Calm down, Rule," Az warned. "Beryl is here with you, not him. I'm only warning you because if I could find you two, people might find her as well."

I swallowed back my fury long enough to smile at Azurea. "Thank you, little sister. I hope you will visit us in Boston."

"Of course I will! But only after you guys get through the honeymoon sex for breakfast-lunch-and-dinner stage." Azurea fake gagged. "Now get back to your mate before someone else swoops in—"

I was jetting through the water before she could finish her sentence.

As I broke the water's surface near the pool's edge, a male voice drifted from our room. I bit back a growl and lifted myself from the water and onto the stone patio.

Not bothering to dry or shift, I moved silently toward

the open doors. As my eyes took in the scene in front of me, I stumbled to a stop.

Beryl was sitting at the desk, focused intently on the laptop. That wasn't exactly surprising, since my beautiful little mate was a self-proclaimed workaholic.

The part that had my jaw dropping was her wardrobe choice—or lack thereof.

A low-cut, hot pink shirt peaked from beneath her perfectly tailored suit jacket. From the waist up, she was every bit the edgy businesswoman.

But from the waist down, she was wearing nothing but the tiniest thong I'd ever seen. She looked sinfully sexy, but I still couldn't understand why women insisted on wearing those things.

I couldn't imagine it would feel comfortable having my butt flossed with every step I took all day long. Besides, Beryl would be mouth-wateringly gorgeous in granny panties from the 1800s, so she didn't need to be uncomfortable on my account.

Heck, last night she'd worn a t-shirt to bed, and I'd never seen her look better. Better yet, it had ridden up over her hips during the night, giving me a fantastic view of her curves. The only thing that would've made it better was if she'd been wearing my shirt.

I wasn't proud of the territorial instincts growing inside me. But hopefully, once we completed the bond, my beast would settle. With each hour I spent in Beryl's company, it was becoming harder to separate my emotions from my shifter instincts.

My suckers ached with the desire to cover her in hickeys, and I longed to cover her in my scent. The desire to pin her beneath me had my body granite-hard.

I wanted to mount her as the man... and then mate her as the beast.

I wanted to slip my ring on her finger even as I thrust my mating tentacle deep inside her beautiful body... marking her as my wife and mate.

More than anything, I wanted her to claim me as hers. I wanted to belong.

It was why I'd agreed to her terms. I was more than willing to be her pet.

After spending decades alone, with women throwing themselves at me for what I could do for their status, I was tired.

I longed to be desired for what my heart could offer... and for how willing I was to worship my mate's body.

Beryl was unimpressed by status and wealth. I'd already figured out she wasn't materialistic. She enjoyed the challenge of her work and was driven by the need to always improve herself.

Since she couldn't care less about my status, it gave me a chance to win her love... without worrying if she was just pretending until I put a ring on it.

But now I was struggling to hold back the tide of joy, desire, and love I'd been storing up for decades to pour on my future wife.

Beryl wasn't ready for that, and I didn't want to scare

her. Nor did I want her to think I was only interested in my 'biological needs,' as she liked to refer to it.

"I can't believe this will be settled in just two weeks' time," the unfamiliar male voice said from the laptop.

Some of the tension eased from my body. There wasn't a strange man in our room... *our nest*.

"Yes. We are very close to the finish line. You needn't worry about anything. My team and I have it under control." Beryl appeared calm, but her foot twitched under the desk.

"That's not the only thing I'm looking forward to in two weeks." The guy's voice dropped to a pitch usually reserved for seduction, and instantly, the tension returned to my body.

Even though her body was angled toward the ocean, Beryl was so focused on the video call she hadn't spotted me yet.

A wicked thought drifted through my mind.

One I immediately decided to act on.

Chapter 12

CERULEAN

room 88

L etting my skin shift colors, my body disappeared into the patio decor. It wasn't good enough to trick a human eye that was diligently searching for me. However, most people took things at face value— meaning they didn't search for an octopus where they didn't expect to find one.

Moving slowly, I crept across the stones, using my tentacles to stay low.

"I'm sure everyone will be ready for a long vacation after the final paperwork has been signed." Beryl had a smile on her face, but it didn't reach her eyes.

The man laughed. "Of course, of course! But what I'm looking forward to most is taking you on a date. So, dinner at Miguel's, the night after the signing? I've already made the reservations."

A soft growl rumbled in my chest, and I did my best to swallow it. Without a sound, I slipped beneath the desk before Beryl even had a chance to answer the arrogant man's question.

Her foot was tapping impatiently against the carefully laid mosaic stone floor, but her upper body didn't so much as twitch. She was an impressive business woman, and although the land-dweller investing scene hadn't interested me in the past, I found myself wishing I could watch Beryl handle a room full of businessmen.

I knew in my gut she'd be magnificent, and I had a feeling it would be like watching an orca hunt with cunning efficiency.

"Mr. Hillar, I thought this was a business call?" Beryl brushed the invitation off, keeping her tone relaxed, but professional. "You said you had another question your attorney wanted clarification on?"

"Timothy. Call me Timothy. We've worked together for months on this. There's no reason to revert to last names." The guy chuckled but took her hint and his tone switched to business matters. "Yes, do you have the document in front of you?"

"I do—" Beryl's voice rose at the end.

It probably had something to do with the tentacle slithering its way up her inner thigh.

"Everything okay?" Timothy asked.

"Of course, just a slight chill in the room. Which part should I open?"

Two of my tentacles coiled around her ankles. I gently pried her legs apart, showing her I wanted her to open to me... and to me only.

"Page sixty-nine, clause eight," Timothy answered.

The tentacle between her legs teased the edge of her thong, while the other two pulled her legs open until the scrap of silk fabric was barely covering her.

"Did you find it?" Timothy asked.

I could hear clicking on the laptop keys.

Keeping my voice low, I murmured, "Can I?"

I longed to pull the fabric aside and delve into her tight heat, but I waited.

"Yes." Beryl cleared her throat, and I tried to figure out if she was speaking to me or Timothy.

My question was answered when Beryl shifted positions, scooting forward on the edge of the seat and straddling the chair. She was giving me permission... and better access.

With the sweet fragrance of her arousal so close to my nose, I couldn't resist the urge to taste her. Not with a sucker this time, but with my mouth.

Leaning forward, I pressed my mouth to the tiny damp spot on the fabric and breathed deep. With my tongue, I stroked her through her thong.

Beryl's fingers brushed through my hair and I wondered if she was going to push me away, but her hand remained still.

"Should I read it?" Timothy asked.

"Please. Go ahead." Her words were stilted, but he didn't appear to notice.

Her fingers tightened in my hair, and she shifted her hips, making it clear she wasn't talking to him... but to me.

As Timothy began reading about stock options, I pressed my mouth harder against her. I sucked the strip of fabric into my mouth, determined to get every drop of her sweetness from it.

Beryl's hand trembled, a delightful sign of the effect I was having on her. Wrapping a tentacle around her waist, I lifted her just enough to slip the thong over her hips and under her butt.

My eyes followed them as I worked them down her legs. Once they fell from her ankles, I pulled them off.

Mine. The beast snatched her thong with a wandering tentacle.

That could be a problem, because Beryl wasn't likely to get them back without fighting him for them.

I slid my tongue along the length of her slit, and my eyes instantly rolled back. She'd tasted incredible on my suckers, but it paled in comparison to tasting with my mouth.

Beryl would be lucky if she ever managed to pry me from between her legs... I was an octopus, which meant I definitely had the advantage when it came to suction power.

"It's the wording of that sentence that worries me." Timothy reread a sentence. "I just don't want anyone to get screwed because of this deal."

I hummed in amusement at his choice of words. The vibrations traveled from where my mouth was pressed to Beryl's slick heat, and traveled through her body.

"Oh!" she exclaimed, then turned it into a breathy laugh. "No, we wouldn't want that."

Her fingers clicked across the keys. "I'll make a note to clarify the wording on that clause to ensure there is no misunderstanding."

As she spoke, her hips rocked a fraction against my mouth. My heart swelled at that sexy little confirmation of her enjoyment.

Beryl broke down the clause with a simplistic explanation that was both elegant and concise. It amazed me how she simplified many of the complicated terms while not making the other party seem stupid.

Her unbreakable professionalism was impressive. Even with my tongue delving inside her, lapping and sucking, she kept her voice steady.

If it hadn't been for the way one of her hands moved back beneath the desk to tangle in my hair, or the way her tight channel clenched around my tongue, I would have thought she was unaffected.

"Are there any other questions or concerns you'd like to go over?" Beryl asked. "Or perhaps you have other business to attend to and we should pick this up later?"

I couldn't help my soft chuckle at the almost hopeful note in her voice. Her body responded to my rumble with another wash of cream.

"Now that I have you, I don't plan to let you go," Timothy laughed, and there was no way to miss the flirting in his tone.

We need to mount our mate. Mark her so the male will back off, my beast snarled.

I wanted to remind him that it was called making love, not mounting, but I couldn't find those words... because a primal part of me wanted to do exactly as he suggested.

Beryl might not wear my mark on her skin, and I might not wear hers, but on paper—and more importantly, in my soul—she was mine.

And I wanted to remind her of that.

I pulled my mouth away, and without preamble, thrust my tentacle into her heat. On instinct, Beryl's legs tried to close, but I curled two tentacles around her thighs and held them apart.

I held the tentacle inside her still, giving her time to adjust.

"We have a couple more minutes. Which clause should I flip to next?" Beryl asked Timothy, once again ignoring his suggestive comment.

She was wrong.

Because if she thought she would last a couple more minutes before falling apart on my tentacle, she'd definitely miscalculated.

"It's all work and no play with you, isn't it Beryl?" Timothy huffed.

His annoyance delighted me and my tentacles flexed and curled in delight... even the one buried between her legs.

"That sums me up." Beryl's hands moved to grip the

sides of the chair, as though trying to keep herself from squirming. "Which page?"

After a bit of mumbling, he called out another page number, and he started reading it out loud. With my would-be rival focused back on monotonous business jargon, I was free to focus on exploring Beryl's body.

My tentacle between her thighs flexed, and again I curled it slightly, studying Beryl's body for signs of discomfort or pleasure. When the tip of my tentacle pushed deep and bumped against her G-spot, Beryl's breathing came to a halt and her heart skipped several beats in a row.

Bingo.

Kissing the delicate skin of her inner thighs, I locked a sucker on her clit, then began a rhythmic sucking and rocking, stimulating each of her pleasure spots... all at the same time.

I alternated my pace. Fast, slow, then fast again.

Beryl's fingers turned white on the sides of the chair, and while she kept her upper body rigid, her hips would periodically rock against me.

"Those are the last two questions, I believe," Timothy's voice drifted from the laptop, but I didn't care.

I was too focused on the way Beryl's body squeezed my tentacle and imagining how it would feel on my cock—or mating tentacle—to care.

Just as she prepared to speak, I released my sucker from her clit. Pressing my mouth between her legs, I worked my tongue against it in fast strokes.

"To answer number one, ah... ah—" Beryl pretended to cough, trying to cover her surprised gasps.

She wrapped her legs over my shoulders. I couldn't tell if she was trying to close them, or keep me prisoner between her thighs. Since she made no move to stop me, I decided it was the latter.

Beryl was soaked, and the scent of her arousal was the only thing I could smell.

Her body wishes to be bred. Breed her or I will take control. It was an empty threat from my beast. He was strong, but I'd never been weak enough to be pushed aside.

Even with her body on the edge of release, Beryl explained the first question and moved to the second.

And I was ready.

Using the texture-altering abilities of the papillae in my skin, I shifted the surface so that rows of short, rounded spikes spread across the tentacle inside her heat.

It was more difficult, but with focus, I did the same to my tongue.

When Beryl spoke again, I licked. It created a friction against her clit as my tentacle rocked back and forth.

"As for number two, ah... ah—" Again she began coughing and finally wheezed out, "One minute."

She bent over as though covering her cough, but I caught a flash of her face. Her cheeks were red.

And it wasn't from the embarrassment that she'd suddenly started counting like a certain vampire puppet. No, her reaction had everything to do with the fact that the rough friction between her legs had pushed her over the edge.

I had to hand it to her. She was an incredible actress.

Beryl quickly recovered and was answering the last of Timothy's questions… even as her muscles spasmed around my tentacle, milking it and driving all reason from my mind.

Mate, my beast demanded again.

Not yet. I grit my teeth, fighting my shifter instincts. She needs to want me.

Her legs are holding us between her thighs with a stronger grip than we have with our tentacles. And if not for your licking, the chair would have been wet with her cream. Are you too stupid to understand the signs of our mate's desire? My beast paced, pushing against the walls that kept him from full control of our form.

Her body wants us, but it doesn't mean her heart does, I snarled back, sweat beading my brow.

If you are worried you can't satisfy her, then release me. I will ensure a more than satisfactory performance. The beast pushed his full weight against the barrier, causing it to shake.

While I had been arguing with my beast, I'd not paid attention to the workings of my tentacles.

And it wasn't until Beryl's nails dug into my shoulders that I realized my tentacles had been twitching like an angry cat's tail. A second tentacle found its way to tease her clit, and with her body already overly stimulated, she climaxed a second time.

See? Her body responds to ours. We were made to please her. Just think how much she will enjoy having our mating tentacle insert—

I stopped listening. If I imagined what he suggested, I'd lose control, rip her from the chair, drag her to the bed, and mount her until she screamed my name.

No. I refused to give in to my animalistic instincts. It was her heart I wanted most.

However, the moment Beryl showed signs of emotion for me and made the first move... the floodgates would open.

I hoped she would be ready.

"Thank you for reassuring me." Timothy's voice sounded a thousand miles away.

"It was no problem. I hope you feel better about things." Beryl sounded confident and slightly breathless.

Unable to resist, I pressed my mouth to her inner thigh and trailed kisses upward.

"Just seeing your beautiful face made this a better day." His voice dropped low as he tried again to flirt with her. "I can't wait for our dinner together. Write it down. Monday after the signing."

"I," Beryl started, struggling to keep her breathing even, "can't come."

But she'd come for me twice already, and I wasn't finished yet...

I slid my tentacle from her silken heat, then slowly pushed back in.

"I'm not a man who takes no for an answer, Beryl. You

should know that by now." His tone was teasing, but irritation lurked under the surface.

I thrust the tentacle slightly faster, causing her legs to quiver.

"I'm afraid that isn't going to work for me. You see—" Beryl tried to explain, her hands clenching the sides of her chair again.

"No excuses. I've honored your policy of not spending personal time with clients during a deal. Afterwards, you are mine—"

My control slipped at his use of the word mine. My suckers latched against both her clit and G-spot, massaging. Faster and faster, I thrust the tip of my tentacle inside her, as deep as I could without pulling the suckers free.

Her walls clenched around my tentacle, and her legs tightened around my neck again.

"My apologies. There is a matter I need to attend to." Her voice cracked slightly. "Please feel free to email any other questions you may have regarding the documents. Sara is watching for your emails and will get back to you immediately."

Beryl slammed the lid of her laptop down without giving him a chance to respond. "If you cost me that deal, so help me—"

I was on her faster than she could blink.

Lifting her from the chair, I pulled her down onto my lap. My tentacles worked with swift precision to unbutton her jacket and slip it from her shoulders. They moved on to her shirt, grabbing the hem and pulling it over her head.

All the while, I continued to thrust and flex the tentacle between her thighs. Her breathing grew ragged as another release neared the surface.

"Cerulean," Beryl whimpered, her body shifting to her vampiric form.

Her arms wrapped around my neck, her bare breasts pressed against my chest. We were skin to skin, with no clothes between us. I growled into her hair, overcome by the erotic sensations racing along my skin.

I don't think she realized she'd switched forms... at least not until her frenzied kisses on my chest caused one of her fangs to slice my skin. Her body went rigid in my arms.

"It's okay," I growled, frustrated that she'd stopped kissing me. "I love your fangs."

Her body trembled. "We should stop... I should stop... before I can't..."

She lifted a hand to push against my chest, but my tentacle wrapped around her wrist, pulling her close. "What if I don't want you to stop?"

The pupils of Beryl's glowing, green eyes had become the razor-thin slits of a predator.

"Cer." Her bottom lip quivered. "I just drank from you yesterday, so I shouldn't need to feed. But I'm so hungry— No, that doesn't describe it. I'm ravenous and my craving for your blood is so powerful it is almost painful."

"You're a vampire, darling. Drinking blood is sort of your thing," I teased, trying to ease her anxiety.

"You don't understand!" Beryl panted, her arm wrapping around her stomach as though to ease a cramp. "It shouldn't be like this! I should be able to drink from a vein without becoming addicted."

What did it mean? My heart pounded against my ribcage, hope flaring in my chest. Was it possible her body had accepted me as hers?

Chapter 13

BERYL

room 88

Cerulean wasn't grasping what I was saying.

This wasn't a normal hunger, nor was it simple arousal. It was both and neither.

I wanted him to fill me… with blood and body.

Cerulean's hand cradled the back of my head, pulling me forward until my closed lips pressed against his chest. His tentacle buried between my thighs rocked gently, sending fresh chills across my skin.

I swallowed back my moan of desire, afraid if I opened my mouth, my instincts would take over. What would happen if I lost control?

"Give in. I want you to use my body for your pleasure." Cerulean's tentacles curled and coiled around my body.

"But what about your pleasure?" I mumbled against his skin, desperately trying to keep my fangs to myself.

My body was shivering violently, as though I were burning up with a raging fever.

I was always in control. It was something I took pride in.

Battling against my vampiric nature wasn't something I'd ever experienced, and the struggle was costing me dearly.

"Tasting you, touching you, holding you, feeding you… those things give me pleasure. Now stop depriving us both."

"What if I can't stop? This isn't a craving I've experienced before."

"You will. Stop stalling." One of his tentacles curled around my neck, not squeezing, but showing me he could stop me if I lost myself. "Is that better?"

"Yes—" I began, only to have the tip of his tentacle slip into my mouth.

My mouth widened in shock, and Cer took advantage of it by delving slightly deeper. Before I could figure out what he was planning, the tentacle pushed against my fangs.

And like a hot knife through butter, my fangs sank into his tentacle.

His blood poured into my mouth, and on instinct, I sucked, drawing him deeper into my mouth. We groaned in unison.

As I drank, my tongue worked its way along the underside of his tentacle, stroking the edges of his suckers. Cerulean reacted by thrusting the tentacle between my thighs deeper into my heat.

The rest of his tentacles moved across my skin, his suction cups leaving hundreds of kisses on every inch of my body. And with each pull of blood into my mouth, Cerulean responded with a thrust of his tentacle in my heat.

His blood tasted nothing like the blood I'd sipped from blood-bags or wine glasses. That had been like drinking a healthy smoothie that you knew your body needed, and it didn't taste awful, but it wasn't something you particularly enjoyed.

Cerulean's taste was like the sweet spiced chai I loved sipping in the evening while reading through spreadsheets.

Moaning, I sucked harder, rocking against him.

"That's it," Cer rumbled. "You're so, so beautiful."

This made no sense. I'd made it clear to Cerulean that I would take care of his needs whenever he desired it, but the stubborn man was more focused on pleasuring me.

He was a man, and in my experience, they thought with their dick more than they did with their brain.

Cerulean wanted me. I'd felt his erection pressing against me when he was in his human form, and I'd scented the pheromones on his skin that signaled arousal.

So why hadn't he taken me up on my offer?

Because he wants your heart more than he wants your body.

In my mind, it was as though a key was being turned in the lock of a door I'd kept closed.

Mentally, I scrambled away from the door, not ready to find out what lay behind it.

I ignored my inner voice, and I gave my full attention to the delicious liquid sliding down my throat. But each time his tentacle sucked against my clit, my lust grew, and that dang key turned a fraction more.

My belly grew heavy, and my need clawed at my insides, fighting for release. The pleasure mixed with pain until I couldn't tell them apart and a tear leaked from the corner of my eye.

Still, I fought against my impending climax. I knew the moment I let go of control, the mental door would swing wide open and I was terrified to face what was behind it.

Cerulean's thrusts became rough, creating a friction that drove me wild and pushed me toward the edge of a cliff. His tentacle around my throat tightened, and the one between my thighs ground hard against me.

"Stop fighting it." Cerulean's voice turned harsh and demanding. "Come for me."

I was used to giving the orders, but there was something thrilling about being told what to do... at least in my current position. And without stopping to ask my opinion on the matter, my body gave him what he wanted.

I came hard.

My body jerked with each wave of orgasmic bliss that ripped through me. Cerulean held me as my world shattered and my vision blurred.

The door in my mind flew open with enough force to nearly rip it from its hinges. An avalanche of raw emotion slammed into me.

Emotions were something I'd avoided like a wooden stake after realizing they severely complicated everything and eventually led to heartache.

But suddenly, I was drowning in them. I gasped, sucking in harsh gulping breaths.

As the emotions swirled, another unfamiliar thing paced

in my chest... and with his body supporting me, I faced it head on.

My heart tripped over its beat as I recognized it.

Love.

A tiny seedling of love had taken root.

It wasn't the mighty oak it would grow to be after spending years together... but it was there.

Its warm glow radiated through me, beginning the work of dismantling the walls I'd built to protect myself from hurt and disappointment.

A second strange emotion followed on the heels of the first.

Passion.

Sex had been a means to satisfy my hormones. And since I always left my partners begging for more, I knew I didn't suck at it. Pun intended.

But passion had never been a factor in my bedroom romps.

Now it was surging through me with a hunger that rivaled the strength of my lust for Cerulean's blood.

My nails dug into his skin. Raising my chin, I stared into his worried blue eyes. I could tell him what I felt, but I'd finally realized he was a man who preferred acts of love rather than words.

So I was going to show him.

"On the bed," I panted, my body struggling to cope with the effects of his blood in my veins.

Overwhelming emotion pounded inside me like a battle cry.

But I was a warrior ready for war... even if that battle was against the self-imposed rules I'd forced on myself.

Cerulean surprised me by shifting to his human form. Then, without a word, he lifted me in his arms and carried me to the bed.

He sat, resting his back against the headboard. I wrapped my legs around his waist and locked my arms around his neck.

His erection bumped against me, and my breath caught. If I shifted even a fraction, he'd be pressing against my entrance.

"Mmm. I like this," Cer murmured, making no move to take advantage of our position.

With my vampiric instincts and emotions roaring out of control, I knew this was the calm before the storm. I either gave in and let my instincts take over, or I needed to climb off his lap and lock myself in an ice-cold shower.

I brought my mouth toward his, but stopped just before our lips touched. "Cerulean, I want—"

"Do it. Whatever you desire." His blue rings flickered. "Beryl, your eyes, they're—"

"What about my eyes?" I asked, tightening my legs around him and licking my lips.

"They're black with tiny flecks of silver. It's like looking at stars in the night sky." Cerulean caught my chin, angling my head so he could study them closer. "It's mesmerizing."

My blood was scorching hot, but a chill licked down my spine. If my eyes had gone dark, then the stakes had just been raised.

I was in predator mode.

"You should run." I hardly recognized the husky voice that came from my mouth.

"I'm in danger." Cer gave me a cocky smile and pulled me tighter against him. "And I like it."

Well, I'd warned him. Whatever happened next wasn't my fault, right?

My lips found his in a searing kiss that stoked the flames of my desire to a temperature on par with the fires of hell.

His hands trailed across my skin, exploring every part of my body.

Releasing his mouth, I slid down his body. Rather than leaving a trail of kisses, I left a path of tiny pinprick fang marks. I tasted and teased… and marked his body as mine.

Cerulean didn't make a sound, but his blue rings danced across his skin. I knew in nature it was a warning of impending death, but it only served to send a thrill of excitement sizzling through me.

We were both paranormal species known for our skills as predators. It was like fire playing with gasoline, which made this an exhilarating dance.

Right now, Cerulean was happy to let me have my way, but if he lost control, things could become dangerous.

Another chill traveled down the length of my spine, and I licked my fangs. Why did that sound like fun?

I was partial to Cerulean's split form, but there was no denying his human form was equally impressive. Shimmying my way down his body, I didn't stop until my mouth was inches from his hard length.

"Last chance," I whispered, running my tongue around the head of his cock. "You really should run."

Cerulean propped an arm behind his head, watching me. "Not a chance in Hades of that happening."

Sifting to my human form so my fangs would disappear, I took him deep, swallowing hard once he hit the back of my throat. Cer must have been expecting more teasing, because his entire body jerked at my sudden movement.

He released a long hiss, but not giving him a chance to recover, my mouth devoured him. I sucked and swirled my tongue as I bobbed on his cock. Each time he slid down my throat, I'd swallow hard, squeezing his length.

"Beryl!" he growled, his hand tangling in my hair. "I don't know how much I can take—"

I snorted and shifted back to my vampiric form.

Silly boy.

I was just getting started.

My body flushed from head to toe. Once. Twice.

I sniffed and was unsurprised to smell the intoxicating scent of vampire pheromones... an alluring fragrance that was far more effective than a witch's love spell.

"What's that scent?" Cerulean gasped, his breathing becoming ragged. "Oh, frick."

His cock swelled, becoming impossibly hard in my hand.

Cerulean might as well have been an insect caught in a spider's web... He couldn't leave if he wanted to now.

I licked my tongue up the length of his rigid erection, barely resisting the urge to take a little taste from the hot blood pumping beneath his skin. A pang of lust-filled hunger seared through my stomach.

Enough teasing.

I wanted him inside me.

With vampiric speed, I slid up his body until my hips straddled his. Rising on my knees, I gripped his length and prepared to impale myself on him.

Chapter 14

BERYL

room 88

With painstaking slowness, I slid down his length.

"Beryl." Cerulean drew out my name on a groan.

I couldn't respond, because my lungs had ceased to work as his erection stretched me.

I paused, fighting the powerful need that demanded no talking and more action. But there was something I needed to make sure Cerulean understood.

"Cerulean?" The head of his cock was pressing against my heat, making it hard to think.

"Yes?" His breathing was harsh, and his eyes burned with a desire that matched my own.

"I'm not good with emotions, but I need you to know I want you." My whisper was barely audible. "Your body and your heart."

He opened his mouth, then closed it, his throat working as he tried to speak.

My legs trembled. I'd said what I needed to say, and I could no longer fight the instincts driving me.

We moaned as I slid down his length. My body stretched to fit him, and I was thankful I was already wet; otherwise, he might not have fit.

When our pelvises pressed together, I took a second to breathe. After a moment, Cerulean began a gentle rocking of his hips, and his thumb rubbed between our bodies, sending little ripples of pleasure rippling through me.

I moved on top of him, grinding down and enjoying the tiny shocks of pleasure that zapped through me.

My hips rocked faster and faster, my release building and coiling like a living thing. My breath came in little gasps as I rode him toward the edge.

"You're the most beautiful woman I've ever seen." Cerulean's soft compliment gave me the final push.

Collapsing on top of him, I let him hold me as my orgasm stole the air from my lungs. My relief lasted for about twenty seconds before fresh hunger pangs cramped my stomach. I wanted—no, *needed*—more. So much more.

I grabbed his shoulders, rolling onto my back and pulling him on top of me. Hooking my legs around his waist, I pulled him deep inside me.

Cerulean needed no further encouragement and slowly slid back until he almost slid free before burying himself deep.

"Oh…" I moaned, my eyes rolling back in my head at the exquisite sensations he was causing.

"I knew you would feel amazing, but this is beyond my

wildest dreams." Cerulean's voice held an awe that did weird things to my chest and stirred up the new emotions I was still coming to terms with.

He continued his torturously slow pace until I was writhing beneath him. "Cerulean, we have many years to have slow, passionate sex. Right now, my vampiric nature wants to claim her mate... and we aren't known for our gentleness."

Sucking my bottom lip into my mouth, I sliced it with my fang. It took all my control not to gag at the taste, and was again surprised that Cerulean enjoyed it.

I caught his mouth in a kiss, letting his tongue stroke the small injury. I knew the instant he realized what I'd done. Cerulean's chest rumbled with a growl, and my body responded by coating his length with more wet heat. Which was good, since he thrust into me with a force that caused my teeth to rattle.

I squeaked in surprise, but the rest of my words were devoured by his mouth on mine. He sucked and licked as his body pounded into me, driving me into the bed.

It was about fanging time! This was what I'd wanted. Wrapping my arms around him, I clung to him as his thrusts became frenzied, and our bodies became slick with sweat.

Blood roared in my ears, and my heart galloped in my chest. He pushed us higher and higher until I was dizzy and slightly terrified of letting go.

Needing to anchor myself, I bit down on his chest. The

moment his blood touched my tongue, my orgasm tore through me like a wild thing seeking freedom.

My body clamped around his cock, milking him and bringing him over the edge with me. Cerulean shouted my name, his hand curling around my lower back to cradle me to him as we convulsed.

Pulling my fangs from his chest, I lunged for his neck. My fangs sank deep, and I released the fire burning in my chest into him. A normal vampire bite would heal like any other animal bite and rarely leave scars.

But the claiming bite was like a brand burned into the skin.

A permanent sign that he had been claimed.

He is mine.

If I thought that by claiming him, the fire inside me would ease or that my vampiric nature would be sated... I was sorely mistaken... in all the best ways.

My hunger tripled. And it wasn't just me who was struggling. Cerulean groaned, and the muscles in his jaw clenched.

"I can't hold my shift back."

"Stop holding back," I snarled. "Take me."

Cerulean closed his eyes. "I can't. My beast is pushing, and I'll hurt you. Let me gain control."

Cerulean shifted, and his tentacles slid across my skin. I caught one of his tentacles and sucked the tip into my mouth, stroking my tongue along the row of suckers.

"I don't want you in control."

A shiver traveled through his body, and the inky black

of his beast's eyes pinned me. "You don't know what you're asking... what you're risking."

I bared my fangs. The primitive drive to have him complete our mate bond was stealing all thoughts from my mind.

No one had told me claiming could be like this... with pleasure verging on pain. It was becoming harder to breathe, and my stomach spasmed.

More. I needed more from him.

"Let your beast out to play." My seductive purr caused his rings to flicker and darken to a navy blue.

"Beryl..."

Later, I would wonder where I'd found the boldness to do what I did next.

Grabbing one of his tentacles, I guided it between my legs and ground myself against it. I was so sensitive I nearly came.

Cerulean's face had taken on sharper angles, the gentleness gone. Heat rushed between my legs when I realized a predator was staring back at me.

"If you are afraid to take care of me, I'm sure I can do it myself..." I slid my heat against his tentacle and moaned, purposely goading him.

"Behave." His voice was an order and a plea. The man and the beast were sharing his body, and the man still wanted to save me, while the beast wanted to...

I wasn't sure, but I had a guess and couldn't wait to see if I was right.

"Make me." I guided the tip of his tentacle inside me

and ground against it. My breathing came in tiny gasps. I was getting close…

The lines of strain disappeared from his face, leaving only raw hunger. He'd accepted my challenge.

A tentacle wrapped around my waist and lifted me off the bed. Cerulean caught me in his arms and carried me to the pool.

I clung to him, slightly dizzy from his speed, which was saying something since I was a vampire.

"Where are we going?" I murmured, licking and sucking up his neck.

My tongue teased across the two indentations left by my fangs, and Cerulean's chest made that adorable clicking sound.

"The pool. You'll need the water to take my mating tentacle without being injured."

My legs were clenched around his waist, eager to find out what that meant.

We sank beneath the water, and Cerulean pulled me toward the deeper end. He stopped when the water reached his shoulders… which meant it was over my head.

I'd thought he would do more kissing and talking, but apparently, Cerulean's beast was more into doing—something my impatient vampire nature appreciated.

A tentacle wrapped around my wrists, pulling them over my head and lifting me from the water.

"What—"

His mouth pressed between my thighs, and his tongue

slipped inside me. I twisted in his grasp, my overly sensitive body threatening to burst into flames.

"Be still." He growled out the order.

I shivered in excitement. How far could I push him with his beast at least partly in control?

Not bothering to hide the challenge in my eyes, I squirmed harder.

A tentacle wrapped around my waist. It coiled around my middle, and the tip rested over my breast. When the sucker attached to my hardened nipple, I whimpered.

Lowering me, his mouth found my other breast and lavished attention on it.

"Cerulean!" I cried out his name, arching and bucking as he fanned the flames inside me.

My legs kicked out as I tried to get away... or was I trying to get closer? I didn't know because the man was driving me crazy.

A tentacle wrapped around each of my ankles, and I sucked in a ragged breath.

He slowly turned me in his arms, kissing his way across my ribs to my back. Goosebumps skated across my skin.

Slowly, but with an unyielding grip, he parted my legs.

The tentacles coiled and placed suction kisses up my legs while the one around my breast continued to knead and stroke.

Even with the breeze and the cool pool water, sweat dripped from my body. I was overheating, my need for release and his claim reaching a boiling point.

He slowly lowered me a few more inches, and something teased my slit. Desperate for stimulation, I rocked my hips.

His hands dug into my thighs, holding me in place. "This is going to feel strange, and I don't want to hurt you. You need to hold still."

"I don't know if I can. My body is too sensitive," I whimpered between breaths.

"We can stop. You don't have to do this." Cerulean sounded like he was speaking through a clenched jaw. Was his need driving him insane, too?

"I want this. Please," I begged, my eyes blurring with tears at the thought of him stopping.

"Then I can force you to be still, but you need to tell me you want it." His mouth sucked and nipped my neck.

"Yes. Yes." The idea of him holding me and taking me sent a fresh wave of arousal rushing south. "Hold me. Pin me. Take me."

His tentacles tightened on my body, and another tentacle slid up my back and curled around my throat. The tip slipped down between my breasts, finding the breast that had been neglected since he'd turned me around.

"If you say stop, I'll stop," Cerulean swore, even as the thing between my legs pushed upward.

"Don't you dare stop," I snarled, snapping my fangs.

Without a word, he slowly lowered me onto his mating tentacle while simultaneously pushing it upward.

Inch by slow inch, it pressed inside me. He hadn't been kidding. It was a tight fit. His hand slid between my legs, and his finger stroked me.

"You need to be relaxed. Come for me." His husky words, combined with the friction I'd desperately craved, were all it took.

I cried out, my muscles spasming with my release. With each spasm of my muscles, Cerulean pushed deeper inside me.

He wasn't done. I was still riding the waves of the last climax when he resumed stroking. "Again."

"You're going to kill me."

"Maybe." He chuckled. "Now show me you want me. Come for me."

My body obeyed, and I closed my eyes against the fireworks sparkling in my vision.

"Good girl," he praised, his tentacle slipping deeper. "Almost there."

Almost? He was going to split me in half if he kept going. "I don't think you're going to fit."

"I will. And you will love it." He held me still, letting me catch my breath before he moved again. "I could make it easier for your body to accept me, but it is dangerous."

"Do it." I was tired of waiting. My body longed for the finale where he would claim me.

"If I bite you and give you a touch of my venom, it will relax your muscles. You've kissed me and have been getting the broken-down version of my venom. So your body should be able to handle a bit."

I heard little after the part where he mentioned biting me. Someone should have told him to never threaten a vampire with a good time.

"Bite me. Please." I could barely breathe past the new desire he'd unlocked in me.

His teeth sank into my neck. They weren't sharp like mine, so there was a prick of pain. It was followed by the sharp burn of his venom.

I hissed in pain, and he started to pull away.

"Don't you dare," I growled.

It took only a matter of seconds for a warmth to travel through my limbs, and with a sigh, I relaxed in his hold. My body was still screaming for release, but my muscles were no longer tense.

With one last thrust, the bulbous end of his tentacle nestled inside me.

"Ready?"

For what? I wanted to ask, but couldn't.

He rocked the appendage, and the texture of the skin rubbed against erotic zones I didn't know I possessed.

"Oh…" I moaned.

Was it just my imagination, or was the tip growing bigger? Swelling to fill me?

"Claim me. Please." I was desperate to know I was his. It had become more important than anything else in my life. "Make me yours."

Cer sighed. "I want to claim you. But if I do it now, it will leave a mark everywhere a sucker is touching your skin. They will be like invisible ink that is visible only beneath a black light. Black lights and my venom are the only things that will make them visible."

"I love that. I want to remember how you claimed me for the rest of our lives. Mark me as your mate," I purred.

And so he did. His mouth found my neck again, and the burn of venom moved through my blood once more. There was a wave of nausea, but it was quickly forgotten as I felt the kiss of each sucker teasing my skin.

The pressure inside me eased as my vampire was finally satisfied the bond was complete.

Cerulean's finger moved to stimulate my clit as the mating tentacle heated me from the inside out. I couldn't take much more without passing out.

"Cerulean," I panted, "I need…"

He ground his palm against me, and I screamed as a final orgasm flipped my entire world upside down. Cerulean stiffened behind me. With a roar, the mating tentacle I was impaled on began to pulse, and my mate joined me in erotic bliss.

"Mine," I whispered, my mouth dry.

"Mine," he answered, his tentacles cradling me to him.

We spent the next two days devouring room service... and each other.

My laptop remained closed, and I tossed my phone in my bag. Rather than leaving me to swim in the ocean, Cerulean used the pool, and my body, for his morning stretch.

Sitting on the patio swing, I snuggled against my mate, relaxed and content. I knew I should check in with Sara, but I struggled to pull myself away from his side.

He was the octopus shifter... shouldn't that make him the clingy one?

Cer made a strange choking sound, and I twisted my neck to look up at him. "Are you okay?"

"Yes, fine," he wheezed. After a minute, he pulled himself together. "I was thinking we should eat in the restaurant tonight."

"That means we'd need to find clothes," I whined.

I'd spent years in restrictive business suits, uncomfortable heels, and tight buns... now I was enjoying the freedom of being naked and not worrying about what I should wear.

Maybe we should join a nudist colony?

Cerulean coughed again.

I pressed my hand to his forehead, checking for a temperature. "Are you getting sick?"

Catching my hand, he brought it to his lips for a kiss. "Stop worrying. I'm fine. Just thinking about amusing things."

I side-eyed him. He was being evasive, but why?

"So, dinner?" he prompted, running his fingertips down my bare leg and completely distracting me.

"We could stay in and have the restaurant bring the food here. We don't have to go there," I pointed out.

Cerulean's tentacles wrapped around my body, pulling me against his chest. "Maybe I want to show off my beautiful mate."

I was shocked to find my cheeks heating. How could we do everything we'd done in the last two days, and yet I could still be embarrassed around him?

"Okay. Let's do dinner. I'd like to show you off, too." I kissed his cheek. "But I better get ready. It's probably going to take two hours to get the tangles from my hair."

"If it's okay, I'd like to take a quick swim."

"You don't have to ask for permission, Cer. Enjoy your swim!"

I tried to push out of the swing, but his tentacle wrapped around my waist and pulled me back. Catching my face between his warm palms, he kissed me until I was breathless.

"What was that for?" I brushed my hand across his cheek.

"Just wanted you to have something to think about while I'm gone."

I was ready to cancel our plans and eat him for dinner instead, but Cerulean's tentacle lifted me to my feet. "Stop looking at me like that and go enjoy your shower."

"But—"

He cut me off with a soft swat on the butt. "Be a good girl and go shower."

Biting my lip, I reluctantly headed for the shower.

I was going to need a cold one.

NINETY MINUTES LATER, I stared at the full-length mirror. I hardly recognized myself. After years of downplaying my looks, this was the first time I'd taken the time to enhance my features.

A bit of contouring, highlighting, and a touch of blush showed off my high cheekbones. I'd gone with a smokey cat eye makeup, and it had done wonders to make my green eyes pop. The final touch had been the brilliant red lipstick for a pop of color.

I was wearing a floor-length, skin-hugging gown with a

sweetheart bodice... except there was nothing sweet about it. Nope, this dress practically screamed 'take me to bed for a good time.'

The dress was low-cut, and by low, I mean the fabric had a cutaway strip that traveled between my breasts, down my stomach, past my belly-button, down to my pelvic bone and only missed showing my privates by a mere three inches. Instead, it curved over to my right thigh and down to the floor.

I'd need to keep an eye on it to make sure it didn't ride up throughout the evening if I didn't want to flash anyone accidentally. Sparkling sheer mesh covered the exposed areas, but somehow that only seemed to draw the eye more than the bare skin would have.

The dress was sucking on to me with the ferocity of a starving vampire with their fangs in a vein. With it being so tight, I couldn't wear any undergarments outside of pasties to cover my nipples.

A slit traveled from the floor to the top of my left hip, this side without the mesh covering. This allowed my black heels, with the thick black ribbons tied around my ankles, to play peek-a-boo when I moved.

It was the type of dress I never would've bought, and the only reason I owned it was because of the designer's stubbornness. She created my tailored business suits and was constantly sneaking various garments into my wardrobe, hoping I'd wear them to the high-profile events I attended for business.

Never in a million years did I think I would wear this

gown, and I'd laughed until my sides ached when I'd first found it in my closet.

But when I walked from the bathroom into the bedroom, Cerulean's jaw dropped, and I was glad I'd impulsively packed it at the last minute.

"I have no words." Cerulean's voice was deeper than the Mariana Trench.

He must have showered on the patio, because he was dressed in a black tuxedo with a royal blue silk shirt beneath it. The color made his blue eyes pop... at least until they turned black and he stalked toward me.

The top two buttons of his shirt were undone, and his blonde hair was dry, but he'd left it down. He looked like he'd walked straight out of a high-end perfume ad.

With each slow step he took toward me, my heart banged harder against my ribs. I stepped backward, unable to stand still while a predator was coming, but came to a stop when my butt hit the wall.

Cerulean closed in on me, his body pressing hard against mine, crushing me between him and the wall. Catching my wrists with his left hand, he lifted them above my head.

I was pinned, and although I was strong, he'd already shown he had more than enough strength to restrain me if he wanted. He pressed his erection against my belly, letting me feel the effect I'd had on him.

"Maybe we should stay in after all." Cerulean's lips teased their way from my neck down toward my breasts.

I whimpered as his right hand slid up my bare left thigh

and slipped beneath the dress. When his finger slowly pressed inside my entrance, my legs trembled and Cer's left hand tightened around my wrists to help hold me upright.

"You're so wet," he purred, stroking and teasing.

When his finger disappeared, I whimpered. He'd left me aching and empty. I lifted my eyes to his face, only to find him licking the evidence of my arousal from his finger, his tongue working with a dexterity that should be illegal.

"Ohh… Cerulean," I breathed, unable to take my eyes from his mouth.

"I have something for you."

I was hoping it was his mating tentacle, and was slightly disappointed when he reached into his pocket. He pulled out a thin black box.

"I have something for you too," I murmured, still working to get my galloping pulse under control.

"You do?" His eyebrows rose.

"Yes, but you can go first."

Releasing my wrists, Cer caught me around the waist and sat down on the nearby sofa, pulling me down so I sat sideways on his lap. There was no way I could have straddled him without pushing the dress up over my hips.

Cerulean held out the box. "Open it."

Lifting the lid, I found a three-strand pearl necklace on the black velvet. But these pearls were unusual. Each pearl glowed as though it were under a black-light.

"Cerulean! It's beautiful. I've seen black, pink, and white pearls, but never pearls like these." I tilted the box to the side, watching how the colors shifted.

"They are from the Deep. There are many things there that are hidden from land-dwellers. Aurora pearls, like these, are one of my favorites." Cerulean took the necklace from the box and placed it around my neck.

"Aurora? Like the aurora lights?" I asked, lifting my cascading hair out of the way so he could latch the tiny hooks.

"Exactly." Cerulean pressed a kiss to my throat.

I fingered the pearl necklace, blinking hard to keep my tears at bay. The man had turned me from a shark to a woman who cried at romantic gestures. Oh, how the mighty had fallen.

And I liked it more with each passing day...

Clearing my throat, I whispered, "Okay, my turn."

I opened my tiny black clutch and pulled out a gold ring.

"The yellow of the gold reminds me of the golden hue of your tentacles, and the ring of sapphires circling the band represents your blue rings." I reached for his hand and started to slip it on his ring finger, but paused. "May I, husband?"

Cerulean swallowed hard, his rings flashing wildly. "Yes."

He watched me push the ring onto his finger, then lifted his hand to the light. "You brought it with you? How could you have known about the gold and blue if you didn't know what I was?

"I didn't know. I'd brought a standard wedding band I'd

intended to give you, but I decided I wanted something different—something personal."

A flush traveled across my skin at my admission. "I acquired a company a few years back from a sweet gentleman who has tried to make me custom jewelry for the past year. When I contacted him, he was delighted to rush this for me. He finished this morning and gave it to the courier I'd hired to fly it down to me. It arrived this afternoon."

"Beryl! If I didn't know better, I'd think you've turned into a romantic." Cer wrapped me in a hug, squeezing until I was laughing and begging to be released. "I love it, darling."

"Maybe." I placed a chaste kiss on his lips, knowing that anything more and we'd never make it to our dinner reservation.

Cerulean's eyes sparkled. "What are we waiting on? I can't wait for the world to see that you put a ring on it."

Without giving me time to respond, Cerulean stood, steadied me on my heels, then rushed us out the door.

Chapter 16

BERYL

room 88

We arrived five minutes before our reservation time. Our table was ready, and the smiling hostess seated us immediately.

I'd have preferred a private booth, but we sat at a four-seat table in the middle of the restaurant. Thankfully, the restaurant wasn't overly crowded, and they spaced the tables apart to give some privacy to guests.

Cerulean pulled out my chair and bent to kiss my cheek as I sat down. As he stood, his gaze fixed on the partially obscured bar area on the other side of the restaurant.

"Darling, I see someone I need to speak with. Do you mind excusing me for a moment?"

"You've been overly patient with my business needs. Take your time." Picking up the leather-bound beverage menu, I perused the list. "I'm going to order a glass of wine."

"Sounds good. Order a bottle and we'll share." He

brushed his fingers across my bare shoulder and strode away.

I watched his gorgeous butt until he disappeared between the monster-sized ferns that created a barrier between the bar and the restaurant. My eyes drifted around the room, noticing quite a few women were staring at the spot my husband had disappeared through.

Husband.

When I'd signed up for P-Harmony's services, the word *husband* had held no special meaning to me. Now, just thinking the word caused my chest to warm and my belly to quiver... because Cerulean meant the world to me.

The server appeared at the table, startling me from my inner musing. I ordered a nice bottle of red wine. A few minutes later, the server reappeared and opened the bottle. After handing me the cork, he poured a little in my glass to sample. Once I'd approved, the server poured more in my wineglass and disappeared.

Sipping my wine, I leaned back in my chair. I stared out the large glass windows that looked out over the sea. Glowing lights from various fishing boats bobbed on the ocean's surface, reminding me of fireflies dancing on warm summer nights.

I was so lost in my thoughts, I jumped when a voice whispered near my ear. "Hello, sister. Fancy meeting you here."

Instincts kicked in, and my body responded to the threat. I straightened my spine, pushed my shoulders back, and lifted my chin a fraction.

Most importantly, I squashed the happy glow that had warmed my body and lit my eyes since Cerulean and I had completed our mate bond.

Within the blink of an eye, I'd reverted to my cold, indifferent business exterior.

Taking on a bored attitude, I sipped my wine, watching as he took the seat across from me. To no one's surprise, my father appeared beside him and sat down as well.

Those two were rarely apart, and they were always scheming together. If they were here, something sketchy was going on, and I needed to figure it out as quickly as possible.

"I don't recall inviting either of you on a family getaway." I swirled the wine in my glass, studying their faces for tells.

"We were worried about you, Be." Stefan was using my childhood nickname he used when teasing me or trying to make me cry.

It meant he believed he had an ace up his sleeve he could blindside me with. If that was the case, I couldn't allow my senses to be dulled with alcohol.

"I find that hard to believe," I laughed.

Setting my wineglass down, I began inspecting my long, black french-tipped nails. From the corner of my eye, I caught the twitch of Stefan's mouth. He always wanted to be the most important person in a room, and by acting as though my nails were more interesting, I was riling him.

Good. His quick temper would help me get the information I needed.

"Batty-Bee, he's right," said my father, speaking for the first time.

Clustersuck!

I'd loved when he'd called me that back when I was an innocent child who believed her daddy would always have her back. He hadn't called me that in years. Not since my company's success had grown to heights that no other Latos vampire had achieved.

If both my brother and father were using the names they'd used back when they felt superior to me, they really must think they had something to use against me.

But what backdoor did they think they'd found to gain a footing in my business?

They didn't make me wait long.

My father straightened the silverware in front of him. "Everyone who is anyone in Boston has been talking non-stop about Chiroptera's acquisition of Tenser Enterprises happening this month. It is the deal of the decade—and one you've worked yourself into a coffin for."

I raised a brow. "I doubt you traveled all the way here to tell me something I already know."

My father continued. "Then, *poof!* You vanish into thin air. Your brother just happened to see a photo of friends on Fangbook playing volleyball on a beach, and you're in the background. You never take a vacation, so I was worried someone had kidnapped you. We immediately booked a flight down here to see for ourselves that you are okay."

My mind dropped the pieces into place, and before my

brother opened his mouth, I'd already figured out their plan.

"Imagine our shock to find you here taking a vacation!" Stefan grabbed the bottle of wine and poured himself a full glass before handing the bottle to my father.

I rolled my eyes, keeping my unruffled exterior in place. "For the record, the acquisition is none of your business. However, everything is finished and simply waiting for a final proofread from the attorneys. We can't sign until the end of the month, so yes, I took a trip to clear my head and take care of some other matters."

A surge of anger threatened to break through my stoic facade. Why couldn't I have a normal family?

A family who showed up to check on me and were happy I'd finally taken a vacation.

No, my family was here to harass me and dig up dirt so they could blackmail me.

"Darling, I leave you for five minutes and you start attracting people to you like sharks to blood."

Cerulean's voice spread across my frayed nerves like molasses, and for a beautiful moment, my anxiety eased and I could breathe.

Then I realized my brother and father were eyeing Cerulean with keen interest.

Stefan didn't bother to hide the evil smirk that spread across his face. "Wow, sis. This wasn't just a vacation, was it? Looks like the other business you needed to do was a married man. Dad, I wonder what Timothy would think to find out the person handling his entire livelihood is down here fanging a married guy while everyone else is stuck in Boston, working to make sure everything is perfect?"

Cerulean's laugh was harsh. "Why would this Timothy care? He isn't married to me."

I choked on a laugh.

Stefan's eyes shot daggers at Cerulean. "And how would your wife feel about you banging my sister?"

Cerulean pursed his lips as though seriously thinking it over. "Hmm. I'm not sure. Let me ask her."

Cer's hands circled my waist and lifted me onto his lap. I couldn't help but notice several people at the surrounding tables were darting curious glances our way.

"How do you feel about me keeping you up all night having wild, passionate sex, Wifey?"

I forgot about my brother, my father, and the strangers in the restaurant.

Only Cerulean mattered.

"It feels great," I murmured, brushing a kiss across his lips.

The jerk of his cock beneath me made it clear how he felt about it.

"Beryl? You're married?" My father's voice cracked.

"I think they're lying so they can cover it up. He's wearing a ring, but she isn't," my brother hissed, a challenge in his eyes.

There was no denying I had more than my fair share of faults—one of which was my inability to back down from a challenge. What could I say? I liked to win.

Turning slightly on Cerulean's lap, I faced my family with my back to Cerulean's chest.

"I wear his rings." Brushing my hair to the side, I presented my neck to my mate. "Show them."

Cerulean's breath caught. "Are you sure?" he whispered, no doubt worried I would experience the side-effects again.

I didn't care if it killed me; I wanted there to be no doubt who I belonged to.

Cerulean didn't argue. Leaning forward, his mouth pressed to my neck.

There was a sharp pang, and fire slowly spread through my veins. It hurt like hellfire, but my anger burned far hotter.

As his venom spread through blood, his mating marks appeared on my skin as small, royal blue rings.

Gasps sounded around the restaurant. Everyone was openly staring, no longer keeping up the pretense.

I knew what they were seeing. Cerulean had marked me during an act of sexy dominance and the pattern of the rings on my skin reflected that.

A trail of sucker rings circled my neck before trailing down between my breasts. The mate marks looked a lot like a collar and leash.

Lifting a hand, I stroked Cer's jaw as he languidly sipped my blood and trickled his venom into me. I rested my right hand on the table, allowing everyone to see the claiming marks that circled my wrists like blue ringed bracelets.

Even without being able to see the line of blue rings that trailed from my hip to my thigh, the rings wrapping around my ankles, or the marks he'd left in far more intimate places... it didn't take a genius to understand that I'd been restrained and at his mercy when he'd marked me.

I hadn't been in control... and I'd loved every second of it.

Cerulean had bound and marked not just my body, but my heart, too.

My hips wiggled on his lap at the memories, eager to have him do it again.

"Cerulean, if you're done showing off, maybe you could introduce me?"

A stranger settled in my vacant chair.

Chapter 17

CERULEAN

room 88

Reluctantly, I pulled away from Beryl's neck. I kept my arms tight around her waist, holding her against my body and nuzzling her neck.

I fought to steady my breathing. It wasn't just the taste of her blood that was driving me insane. The fact she'd wanted to show her rings—the marks I'd left on her while claiming her as mine—had me painfully hard.

My beast wanted us to push her dress over her hips and breed her right there, and I was having a hard time remembering why that was a bad idea.

Beryl seemed unsure of what to do, but allowed me to continue holding her while I tried to calm my pacing beast. This wasn't how I'd wanted our first outing as a mated couple to go.

"Forgive my brother. He's always been on the clingy side—it's an octopus thing." I rumbled a warning as he shook Beryl's hand a fraction too long. "I'm Lapis."

My brother would never make a move on my wife, but

he loved to get a rise out of me. He knew I was newly mated, and therefore slightly unstable, so he was going to see how far he could push me.

"Well, this is turning into quite the family reunion," Beryl blurted out.

I snickered, but she'd cringed in my arms the moment the words left her mouth. Pressing a soft kiss to her shoulder, I tried to ease her discomfort.

Beryl was the type to think her words over carefully before speaking, but I'd noticed in the last few days she was speaking more freely, and not overthinking every word before she said it. I loved her open honesty.

Lapis laughed and leaned back in his chair. "I like her, brother. It's a shame you met her first."

It wasn't until Beryl squeaked that I realized I'd tightened my arms around her middle a little too tight.

"Sorry, darling," I whispered, easing my grip.

"It's a pleasure to meet you, Lapis. Cerulean didn't tell me you would be visiting."

Beryl's smile was genuine, but she'd switched to the same cool, professional voice she'd used with Timothy. No doubt because of the two men seated across from us who watched her every move like wild animals waiting to attack.

Beryl was ignoring the vampire men, so taking my queues from her, I ignored them as well.

Everything was perfect.

Why did they have to ruin it?

Her thoughts drifted into my mind, and my heart ached.

I'd wanted this evening to be wonderful for her, and the vampires' appearance was threatening to ruin it.

I refused to allow that to happen. If Beryl didn't want them here, then they weren't going to stay. I opened my mouth, preparing to tell them they needed to leave, but the older vampire spoke first.

"Married? He's your husband?" His green eyes darted between Beryl and me.

Beryl lifted her chin. "Yes, he's my husband."

"Why haven't I met him? You haven't even mentioned him to me, and I'm your father! Don't you think I should know about these things, Beryl?" The older vampire smacked his palm on the table.

Beryl didn't even twitch at his sudden move. "Apologies, *father*," she said, emphasizing the word. "Maybe if you'd actually taken any interest in my life or tried to see me outside of New Year's dinner, I would have remembered I had a father to share the good news with."

"Talk about a mic drop, sis!" Lapis barked a laugh, but tried to cover it when he caught my sharp look.

I knew him well enough to know this situation was highly entertaining for him.

"Sis? She's not your sister," the younger vampire hissed.

"She married my brother, so yeah, she's my sister. It's the way these things work." Lapis raised an eyebrow.

I could count on one hand the number of times in our lives that Lapis had been rude to someone. Between the two of us, he was the conversational genius. He could read situations and navigate sensitive topics with a skill politicians would envy.

My brother was also quick on the uptake. He no doubt sensed the animosity the vampires radiated toward Beryl, and he was showing support for her… while also goading the vampires into reacting and giving him whatever info he was looking to weasel out.

It still irritated me he'd flown to the opposite side of the world just to stick his nose in my business, but I couldn't deny the joy I felt at the reminder that my brother always had my—and now my mate's—back.

"Who do you think you are?" Stefan's eyes flashed black as his anger mounted. He turned to glare at me. "And who are you to claim a vampire of our family and mark her body?"

I made a move to shove to my feet, ready to throw the vampire out of the restaurant myself, but stopped at the touch of Beryl's hand on my thigh.

"I'm Lapis." Realizing I was struggling with my agitated beast, my brother answered for both of us. "And that's my brother, Cerulean."

Lapis waved down the waiter and ordered a second bottle of wine since the vampires had finished the bottle Beryl ordered.

"No last name?" Beryl's father raised an eyebrow.

"Should we know you? I don't recognize either of you from social events or business meetings." Her brother, Stefan, crossed his arms.

He'd dismissed us as unworthy of his time.

"Oh. You don't know?" Lapis's eyes widened in feigned innocence as he looked between our faces.

I sighed, knowing we were seconds away from Lapis dropping a bomb.

Three...

Two...

One...

"Thalassa." My brother leaned back in his chair, a cheshire grin on his face.

He was enjoying this far too much, and I was tempted to kill him later for it.

That one word seemed to suck the oxygen from the room, leaving everyone at our table and the tables close enough to eavesdrop, gaping like fish out of water.

THALASSA.

Cerulean Thalassa.

Why didn't he tell me?

Why didn't I bother to ask him?

To my shock, Beryl shifted on my lap to look up at me, with tears shimmering in her eyes.

"I'm sorry," she whispered, her voice pitched so low I doubted even the vampires across the table heard her.

For the past few days, I'd imagined multiple versions of what her response might be when she found out who

I was... but I'd never guessed this might be her reaction.

"You have nothing to apologize for, but we can talk about this later." Catching her chin between my fingers, I placed a soft kiss on her lips.

"Thalassa?" Stefan and her father croaked in unison like bullfrogs. "Like the Thalassas who own Trident?"

"One and the same!" My brother swirled the wine in his glass.

"Cerulean and Lapis Thalassa?" Stefan repeated, as though still trying to process the information.

"Yes, those are our names. Don't wear them out." Lapis winked at Beryl.

He'd reverted to grade-school comebacks? I fought the urge to pinch the bridge of my nose.

Stefan sipped his wine, all the cocky confidence wiped from his face.

Her father was the first to recover. "Well done, daughter. You've made me proud."

Beryl laced her trembling fingers through mine beneath the table, seeking comfort and showing me her vulnerability. On the outside, my mate appeared unaffected. Her posture hadn't changed and her breathing was steady.

"I've spent years building my business from the ground up, using the money I earned while working under one demanding boss after another, to fund Chiroptera. Then I spent years re-investing every dime of my profits back into the company. All because I believed in myself when no one else did."

Beryl took a breath and continued. "You offered Stefan a large financial gift when he turned eighteen to get his company off the ground. Most of which he squandered because he cared more about partying than work. Since then, you've poured thousands of dollars into his company every year to keep it afloat. All so he doesn't have to face failure. And so you can parade him around, bragging to the vampire community, friends, and various business associates that your son is talented and takes after you."

Unlocking her finger from mine, she flattened her palms on the table, and her voice rose. "Yet year after year, when I'd excitedly tell you of a promotion or award, you'd shrug it off as unimportant. I'm a vampire. Do you seriously think I couldn't hear the laughter and comments you two made behind my back? The jokes about how many people I must have slept with to move up the ladder?"

Beryl rose to her feet, leaning toward her father as though staring down an opponent. She was breathtaking in her fury.

"And all because you couldn't be bothered to recognize my talents or acknowledge my hard work. For years, I dreamed of the day I'd become successful, and you'd say those five little words to me: *I am proud of you.* Eventually, I realized I didn't need your validation to feel worthy."

Stefan made a move to speak, but shut his mouth at the warning glare I shot him. Or maybe it was the dark rings flashing on my neck and the back of my hands that scared him.

Beryl wasn't finished. "Tonight, I finally heard those

words I craved for so long. Not because my company made the cover of a dozen magazines in a single year. Not because I was nominated for Woman of the Year. Not because Chiroptera ranked among the top 10 investment firms worldwide. Not because I am mother-freaking-fantastic at my job."

She was breathing hard and took a moment to steady herself before finishing. "No. You're proud because you think your daughter finally took your advice to open her legs and her bed to a rich man... a man who you clearly have more respect for than you've ever had for me. You're a pathetic excuse for a father, and I will never call you by that title again."

Every eye in the room was staring in stunned shock at Beryl, and complete silence engulfed the restaurant. There was no sound of silverware clinking against china, idle chatter, or chairs scraping against the wooden floor.

Nothing.

At least until Lapis began a slow clap and stood to his feet. Within seconds, the table beside us joined in, and soon the entire restaurant was applauding.

Beryl jumped in surprise, her glazed eyes taking in the onlookers. She'd been so absorbed in telling her dad off, she'd forgotten where we were.

"That's my sister-in-law!" Lapis proudly told the guests closest to him. "Isn't she magnificent? We're definitely keeping her."

I was tempted to smack him until I caught sight of Beryl's expression as she watched him. A tear trickled down her cheek as she hiccupped a laugh, and she sagged onto my lap.

Lapis' silliness had dispelled her embarrassment at having made a scene, and I was grateful to him. Wrapping my arms around Beryl, I pulled her into a hug.

"Okay, the show part of the dinner is over. Everyone can go back to eating." Lapis laughed as he spoke and settled back into the chair beside me.

The sounds of eating and chatting had barely resumed before Stefan leaned toward Beryl. "Stop trying to distract dad with your tantrum. You're the issue here. It is you who is slacking, and how do you think your investors will react when they find out you married a Thalassa? I doubt they will believe you truly care about Chiroptera and its assets when your husband has more money than you could ever spend. I think they'll worry you might become sloppy and take more risks because you can afford to... even if they can't. It's going to be a real shame when that news gets out..."

It wasn't until that moment that I realized Stefan wasn't just an entitled brat. His mask had slipped, showing the evil soul beneath.

I would have my team find every asset this man owned and sink them. Like the arrogant dick he was, he wanted to taunt Beryl with what he planned to do to her company. He was enjoying the perceived power he held over her.

That was the difference between us.

He had perceived power.

I held real power.

Pulling out my phone, I began texting my assistant with orders.

Stefan Latos would be bankrupt before his flight landed back in Boston.

Putting my phone back in my pocket, I stared him dead in the eye. "Why would anyone jump ship once they find out Beryl owns half my shares in Trident? Land-dwellers have tried for years to create deals with us and we have declined. Once they find out she has an in with Trident, I'd imagine she will be overwhelmed with CEOs trying to get in good standing with her."

Lapis leaned forward, folding his hands on the table. "Exactly. And it will be worse when the news is announced that Trident is expanding to investment opportunities on land, and Beryl is our only liaison on land. She alone will be in charge of deciding which investments and proposals will be presented to Trident."

I stared at my brother's face. Hard lines of anger were etched on his usually easy-going face. Lapis was dead serious about this. My brother had made the decision without talking to either Azurea or me. But it didn't matter. When one of the three heads of Trident made a decision, it was fully backed by the other two.

My brother was defending my mate as fiercely as if she were his blood sister. He had our backs and wouldn't allow her to be intimidated, blackmailed, or bullied by anyone.

That took the wind right out of Stefan's sails, and he dropped back into his seat. His eyes bled to black as rage at losing pumped through his veins.

When the server neared the table, I caught his attention. "I believe these two have gotten lost and can't find their table. Could you assist them?"

"Of course, sir." The server eagerly escorted the scowling pair of vampires toward the front of the restaurant.

"Are you going to allow your husband to speak to your family like this?" her father hissed as they moved past Beryl.

She lifted her chin. "We share DNA, but you are not my family. Until you can understand the pain you've caused me, and change, there is no place for you at my table—not in my home or in my business."

She kept her spine straight until they were out of sight and went limp in my arms.

"Are you okay, darling?" I pressed a kiss to the top of her head.

Beryl blew out a long sigh. "I've never been better. You have no idea how long I've wanted to say that."

Chuckling, I handed her the glass of wine she'd avoided sipping during the confrontation.

She took a small drink, then gulped several mouthfuls. Scooting from my lap, she carefully adjusted her dress and sat down in the chair her brother had vacated.

The server returned and cleared away the wine glasses the vampires had used, and placed clean dishes and silverware in front of her.

Lapis cleared his throat. "Beryl, I flew here after our sister confirmed Cerulean was planning to mate. He's avoided it for so long I thought he was making a massive mistake or he was planning an epic prank. But nothing could have prepared me for meeting you tonight and I couldn't be happier to welcome you into our family."

He turned to me. "Treat her well. I've lived in the sea for a long time, and there aren't many like her out there. Now, I'm going to leave and let you enjoy your romantic dinner together. I only came over to provide backup if needed... and to make sure my brother didn't decide to bend you over the table when you showed off your rings."

"I wouldn't have dreamed of—" I spluttered.

Lapis rolled his eyes. "Brother, I shared a womb with you. It was plain on your face that you'd forgotten you were in the middle of a restaurant. You were ten seconds away from pushing up her dress and taking her."

I mumbled a hollow denial, which my brother ignored.

He grinned at Beryl. "Cerulean wants you to think he's a cultured gentleman, but his beast is strong."

"I know." Beryl's cheeks burned a bright red. "But it's okay. I bite back."

Lapis burst out laughing, and I punched him playfully.

He started to rise, but Beryl stopped him. "Please don't go. I'd love to have dinner with you and get to know you better... and maybe learn more about Cerulean."

I groaned at the sly look Lapis sent my direction. He was absolutely going to dig up every embarrassing childhood memory he could remember.

"Brother?" Lapis raised a brow, checking if I preferred him to leave.

I would have liked a romantic dinner with my beautiful wife, wooing her… and then taking her back to our room to ravish her until sunrise.

But I caught the slight tremble in her hand as she reached for her wineglass and knew that silly bantering and laughter would help to settle her anxiety… even if it was at my expense.

"My wife wants you to stay, so I guess you can stay." Grabbing the wine bottle, I poured a bit more into my glass and leaned back to watch my wife.

Chapter 18

BERYL

room 88

I tapped my nails on the desk and stared at my laptop. Cerulean had gone for his morning swim, and I'd decided to check my emails. But I was struggling to focus, because my mind kept drifting to Cerulean.

Besides, there was nothing that needed my attention. Sara had everything under control, and had even been handling Timothy's whiny emails with a patience I envied. I made a note to give her a raise and schedule a long overdue conversation with her about the potential of taking on a new position with more responsibility.

Opening a new document, I wrote an email to one of the few high school friends I'd remained in casual contact with. I presented an idea that had come to me this morning and explained that I thought it could be mutually beneficial for both of us. I clicked send and received an excited reply less than three minutes later.

I forwarded the message to Sara, describing my plan

and asking her to organize it for the day we returned to Boston.

Clicking back to my business email account, I noticed a couple of new reports waiting to be looked over, but I realized in a moment of brilliant clarity I didn't need to read them.

I'd hired and trained a very competent team who poured over these documents and would send me a summary in a single report with any important things they felt I should see. Maybe it was time I trusted my team a little more and let them do the jobs they were paid to do.

I looked out at the sea, and my heart ached. Cerulean was out there, and with each day we spent together, I found it harder to be away from him. He was becoming my entire world at a frighteningly fast rate.

It was confusing, and turning back to my laptop, I pulled up a website I'd bookmarked. A therapist for vampires.

I'd never wanted to admit there was something broken inside me, and so every time I'd thought about reaching out to the kind-looking therapist, I chickened out.

This time, I gathered my courage and typed out a lengthy email, giving a condensed version of my life. I finished by asking the question that had been burning in my mind for three days.

My finger hit send and I closed the laptop. Pacing around the room, I chewed my lip and worked through the chaos of this week.

The sharp ring of my phone nearly gave me a heart attack, and I quickly checked the screen. Seeing the therapist's name, I answered.

For the next hour, she patiently answered questions I never thought I'd find the courage to voice. When the call ended, I stared, unseeing, at the wall.

My heart felt light, and the confusion had dissipated. Happiness and excitement were bubbling inside me as though I were a shaken soda drink.

I decided it would be fun to snorkel for a few hours. Who knew? I might even bump into my husband, and could tell him what I'd learned.

Hurrying to the storage bench on the patio, I pulled out a pair of fins, a mask, and a snorkel. I splashed around in the aquamarine waters, following schools of brightly colored fish and enjoying the sun, when a boat got a bit too close to me.

Lifting my head from the water, I was surprised to find my father and brother staring down at me.

"Beryl—" My father began.

"I have nothing to say to either of you. Leave," I hissed, flashing my fangs.

It was the vampire equivalent of throwing the middle finger at another vampire, but I didn't care anymore.

Being a good daughter had gotten me nowhere. So I saw no reason to continue to allow myself to be mistreated.

I put my face back in the water. Ignoring them completely, I swam in the opposite direction.

CRACK!

Something smashed into the back of my head.

My body went limp and darkness swallowed me.

"It's forty feet here. That should be deep enough," a disembodied voice drifted into my foggy skull.

"Do you have the weights attached?" a second voice screamed.

Oh, wait. He wasn't screaming, it just sounded like it thanks to the pain jack-hammering my skull.

I hadn't been hungover like this since my college graduation. No one had shown up, and I'd watched my classmates take photos with their parents and exchange warm embraces. They'd all left to eat, and I'd retreated to my dorm room to drink tequila and cry myself to sleep.

So why had I decided to get drunk this time?

"Dad, I think she's waking up." Voice number one sounded oddly familiar, but I couldn't quite place it...

"Really? Then we better hurry. You cracked her skull open. It should've taken her longer to heal an injury like that. I didn't know she could heal as fast as a full vampire." Voice two sounded impressed, which annoyed me, but I didn't know why.

Something cool wrapped around my ankles and wrists,

and the sound of metal chains hitting metal vibrated through me.

My head felt as though it was being torn in half. If they didn't quiet down, they were going to kill me.

"Once we drop her, how long will it take for her to drown?"

Oh crap!

They *were* trying to kill me.

Adrenaline surged through my body, sweeping away the last of my mental fog.

"She will have about fifteen minutes. Maybe less. She lost a lot of blood from that blow. Alright, I've got her hands and feet wrapped. You're going to have to help me throw the weights over, Stefan."

Shock froze the blood in my veins. My father and brother were going to kill me. I'd stupidly believed they could never hate me enough to kill me, and I'd turned my back to them.

My chest tightened with panic and I fought back tears. This week had been so perfect, and I'd thought it was the beginning of a new life with Cerulean. And it was about to be taken from me.

I pulled at the chains around my wrists, trying to free myself, but they wouldn't budge.

"What's wrong, sister? I thought you liked being bound?" Stefan laughed, watching my struggles. "You won't be able to break those, Beryl. They are pure silver."

Ignoring him, I yanked harder, using my full strength in

my effort to free my wrists. If I could get my hands free, I just might have a chance of surviving this.

"Why? Why would you do this to me?" I met their cold eyes.

"Because your husband is right. When word of your marriage gets out, you'll be the most sought-after investment firm in Boston. With you gone, I can offer assistance to your clients. I'll finally get the success I deserve."

Stefan was willing to kill me for his greed, and my father was willing to go along with it to keep the image of his successful son intact.

Their greed and pride were going to cost me my life. The unfairness of it all tore at my insides. This couldn't be the end of my story. It just couldn't be.

"Any last words?" Stefan squatted in front of me.

I wished I had something meaningful to say, but at that moment, I didn't feel particularly inspirational. I felt furious.

"Go gargle garlic," I snarled.

Garlic might not bother us, but the insult was still a wonderfully low blow.

Lunging forward, I sank my fangs into the hand that rested on his knee. Stefan screamed in pain and sent a retaliatory kick into my stomach.

I doubled over the best I could while confined by chains, but refused to cry out. Watching the blood pouring from his hand made the pain worth it.

The two vampires bent and slowly lifted the cement block. Two chains led from it to me.

"The witch wasn't joking about her spell making it heavy," Stefan hissed.

"I'm relieved the full spell doesn't activate until it hits the water. Otherwise, it would have sunk our boat," my father groaned.

They'd hired a witch to ensure I couldn't escape my death. Go figure the first time they put actual work into making something happen, it would be my death.

They hefted the weight over the side of the boat. Turning quickly, they grabbed me from the bottom of the boat and flung me over the side after it.

My body was airborne for a few long seconds before hitting the surface of the water and immediately being yanked downward.

The pressure changed, and my ears ached. Unable to clear them, the pressure continued to build until dizzying pain tore through both ears as my eardrums ruptured.

No! I couldn't pass out.

I needed to stay conscious if I hoped to escape this alive.

The boat overhead roared to life as my father and brother left me to a watery grave.

When the weight hit the seafloor, it sent a billowing cloud of sand into the water surrounding me.

The temperature had dropped, and combined with my blood loss, I struggled to keep my body heated.

If I were a full vampire, this wouldn't kill me. Very few things could kill a full-blooded vampire. I'd grow weak, but I wouldn't die. And if I caught a few large meals, I might have found the strength to break the chains. To be fair, catching anything without hands would have been next to impossible, but if a vampire stayed down long enough, it might happen.

But I was only half vampire, which meant I was half human. And pretty much everything could kill a human.

I could go without breathing longer than a human, but only if I slowed my thundering heart. Otherwise, I was going to burn through my air in less than five minutes.

Closing my eyes, I imagined Cerulean's arms were wrapped around me. Strong, reassuring, and full of love.

My heartbeat slowed until it was beating only once or twice per minute. The downside was my movements were now sluggish, but until I formed an actual plan, it was my only option.

For ten minutes, I worked the chains, desperately trying to bend the links or break the lock. It was useless. The chains were invincible and were probably going to be around at the apocalypse.

I was running out of time. Pulling myself down the chain, I felt for the screw that had to be anchoring me to the concrete. To my horror, the chain had been embedded through the concrete slab. There was no anchor or screw for me to pull loose.

My lungs screamed for air and tears of hopelessness leaked from my eyes to merge with the salty sea. This couldn't be how I died.

I'd just found Cerulean.

I'd just learned what love could be like.

Refusing to give up, I continued trying to pull my wrists

free. When my wrist cracked, I bit down on my lip to keep from screaming in agony. I couldn't afford to lose what little oxygen remained in my lungs.

Even with my wrist broken, I couldn't work it free.

Despite my determination to live, I was going to die.

And there was nothing I could do about it.

I closed my eyes as dizziness turned my vision black. My temperature had continued to drop thanks to my blood loss, and I couldn't feel my fingers or feet anymore. How long did I have? Two minutes? Three?

As I waited for death, I thought of all the things I wished I'd done differently. I'd lived an amazing life, but I'd gotten in my way of happiness at every turn.

My biggest regret was that I hadn't been brave enough to tell Cerulean how I felt.

The current shifted, and water surged into me. I would have been pushed away if not for the heavy concrete slab holding me down.

A pod of dolphins darted through the water around me, their smooth bodies looking like silver bullets. They were beautiful, and as my vision continued to darken, I was happy they would be the last thing I saw.

Suddenly, Cerulean materialized in front of me, his hands cupping my face and his terrified eyes searching my eyes. He thought I was already dead.

I blinked. The movement was slow, but it reassured him I was still among the living… or at least I was only half-undead.

His eyes and rings began to glow.

Breathe out.

How odd. I'd heard his voice, but his lips hadn't moved.

Beryl, trust me and breathe out.

I was too relieved to have him with me to question the sanity of hearing his voice in my head, or blowing out the last of my precious air.

Relaxing into his arms, I released the air from my lungs in a flurry of bubbles.

As the last of the bubbles left my cool lips, Cerulean's warm mouth sealed over them.

My lungs inflated with air.

Good girl.

My mind was still sluggish, and I wasn't entirely sure if he was a hallucination or if he was really there. I smiled at him.

He moved to wrap his tentacles around the cement block, testing its weight. My father had been right. The spell had worked, and it was unnaturally heavy.

Cerulean's tentacles moved to coil around the chains binding my wrists. Lapis appeared at Cerulean's side. Each shifter quickly attached his suckers along the chain, and with muscles straining, they swam away from each other.

The chain's groans were loud in the quiet of the sea, and I watched in shock as the links bent and stretched before finally snapping apart.

The chain from my wrists to the weight had been broken, but the chain around my ankles was still intact.

Cerulean moved in front of me a second time, his arms pulling my body into the heat of his.

Blow out again.

I didn't question him, and immediately blew the air from my burning lungs.

His mouth sealed on mine a second time, and air filled my aching lungs.

Unable to resist, I darted my tongue out to slide against his. I wasn't out of the woods yet, and if I was going to die, I wanted to do it with his taste in my mouth.

I love you, Cerulean.

Even if he couldn't hear me, I needed to say the words.

Cerulean's muscles went taut, and he held me, his body frozen.

Lapis moved behind him, a tentacle pulling him away from me. He motioned to the chain running from my ankles. Moving into position, he gripped the chain and waited for Cerulean to help him.

Cerulean eyes met mine.

Then he focused on the chain anchoring me. Wrapping his tentacles around the chain, he pulled against it.

I almost blew out my oxygen on a dreamy sigh while watching his gorgeous muscles flex.

Sure, I might be about to face a watery grave if his efforts failed, but I wasn't going to let that keep me from stopping to smell the roses... or, in my case, devouring my man's sinfully sexy body with my eyes.

The chain complained, fighting against the two powerful shifters, who were determined to rip it apart with brute force. Despite the chain's best efforts, it was no match for the brothers and, with a loud crack, it broke.

The moment it snapped, Cerulean's tentacles wrapped around me.

With my limp body tucked against his, he spun up toward the water's surface.

Chapter 19

BERYL

room 88

We burst through the water, and I sucked gulping breaths of air into my sore lungs.

Cerulean's mouth moved, but his words were soft. He continued speaking, but it was as though I were trying to hear him over the static of a TV.

"I can't hear you," I panted, still struggling to catch my breath. "Eardrums. Ruptured."

Under the water, I'd been able to hear the wrenching of metal, but only because it had been loud.

I'll kill them.

The words were in my mind, and this time I was confident that I hadn't imagined it.

I decided to test him.

Cerulean was holding me against him as he swam toward shore, so I focused on his face and thought, *if you can hear me, stop swimming.*

He stopped.

Huh. Maybe that had been a coincidence. And he'd stopped swimming because I had a weird look on my face?

I needed to confirm. *Stick out your tongue.*

Cerulean's tongue slid across his bottom lip before he stuck it out.

Kiss me.

The last wasn't a test, it was a plea.

And while we bobbed in the ocean, Cer cupped my face and kissed me until I was dizzy all over again.

I wanted to touch him, to feel his skin under my palms, but my hands were still chained behind my back.

We'll get them off once we reach land. I don't want to try ripping them off, for fear of breaking something.

Too late. My snort turned to a cough.

Cerulean stopped moving again. *What do you mean, too late? Did they break your bones?*

No. Well, yes. But only if you count the piece of my skull that is still fusing back together. I meant my wrist is broken, but I did that to myself when I tried to break free.

Cerulean's jaw clenched, and without another word, he surged forward.

My blood was warming as my heart pumped it through my body, but there was no way I could fully heal until I fed. That would have to wait.

My eyelids grew heavy. Trusting Cerulean to protect me, I fell asleep.

I AWOKE to Cerulean lowering me into a bathtub filled with hot water. I touched his stubbled jaw and then gasped.

Dark bruises still circled my wrists and ankles, but the chains were nowhere to be seen. "How?"

"Lapis beat us to shore since I was trying not to jostle you. He found the tool I needed and left it on our patio. You were so exhausted you didn't even wake up." Cerulean caught my less injured wrist and kissed it.

It was difficult, but I could hear his voice, although it sounded like he was whispering from across the room.

Cerulean washed my body with a tenderness that had my eyes blurring with unshed tears. I'd been on an emotional roller coaster over the past twenty-four hours.

My family had tried to kill me, and the man who'd just come into my life had saved me. I knew without a doubt I would not return to Boston as the same woman who'd left it less than a week before.

Cerulean lifted me from the tub and carried me to the bedroom. His hand brushed along my body, gathering the water droplets to him. By the time we reached the bed, I was completely dry.

Pulling back the covers, he settled me on the mattress before joining me. His strong arms wrapped around me, cuddling me against his chest.

I wished I could give in to my body's need for sleep, but there was something I needed more.

Feeling embarrassed, I cleared my throat. "Cerulean? Could you call room service and have them send several vampire blood bags here?"

Leaning his head back, Cerulean stared down at me, his brow creased in confusion.

"I'm a vampire. I lost a lot of blood when my skull cracked and burned through my reserves trying to stay alive," I tried to explain. "Until I get blood, I'm not going to be able to finish repairing the damage to my body."

"You could have fed while I swam. I'm sorry, I didn't realize." Cerulean looked devastated.

"Cer, you had no way to know. Drinking from you during sex is one thing. It's erotic. But I'm not going to use your body to feed."

"Why? I want to provide for all your needs, whether they are sexual, emotional, or physical. Plus, surely my blood is better for you since it is fresh."

I hesitated. It would be easy to drink from him... and so much more enjoyable. The thought of gagging down bagged blood made my bruised stomach ache.

"Where would be the easiest place for you to feed? My wrist? My neck?" Cerulean was already scooting down in the bed, lining my mouth up with his neck.

"Cer..." I whispered, still fighting the urge to accept what my mate was offering me.

"Please. I wasn't there when you needed me today and I'm struggling to deal with that. Let me take care of you."

Cerulean's voice cracked, and his eyes shimmered. "Let me feel needed."

I'd been so focused on what I'd gone through, I hadn't thought of what he'd experienced.

With a nod, I pressed my fangs to his neck and pierced his skin with surgical precision. I couldn't stop my moan of delight when his sweet, spiced blood poured into my mouth and ran down my throat.

While I fed, Cerulean rubbed soothing circles on my back. Snuggling deeper into the heat of his body, I closed my eyes and tried to commit every sensation, scent, and taste to memory.

As his blood mixed with mine, my body began to heal at a startling speed. The static in my ears quieted, and within a few minutes, it had disappeared. The throbbing fire in my broken wrist eased with each delicious gulp of Cer's blood.

I wasn't ready for the feeding to be over, but I didn't want to take too much from my mate. When the pain eased from my body, I slowed my sucking. Just enjoying being with my mate and taking the love, heat, and blood he was offering me.

Tears burned my eyes before sliding down my cheek to drop on his arm tucked under my head. I'd worked hard for every good thing in my life, but Cerulean had walked in and accepted me without question.

He hadn't made me earn his love.

He'd freely given it.

"Let it out. Crying is good for the soul," Cerulean rumbled.

Pulling my fangs from his neck, I licked the wounds to clot the blood. He held me close while I buried my face against his neck and sobbed.

I released all my pent-up anger, terror, and betrayal. My heart grieved for the family I no longer had, and the nightmare I'd just lived through.

Once I drained all the negative emotions, I clung to Cerulean and wept. I cried over his tenderness toward me even when I'd been cold. He'd come to the resort to fall in love, and I'd treated him like he was little more than arm-candy.

"I never asked your last name," I said between sobs.

"It wasn't important," Cerulean reassured me.

I leaned back so I could see his face, not caring that I was an ugly crier. "Cerulean, it should have been important to me. I should have asked your siblings' names and your favorite color, if you like music and if you have a hobby, but I was so focused on my needs, I couldn't be bothered. I was selfish."

"Stop being so hard on yourself. You are a survivor and have learned to take care of yourself. Beryl, you're strong, and that is nothing to be ashamed of! You knew what you needed from a partner and tried your hardest to be overly generous in return."

"But we claimed each other, and I still didn't know your name until Lapis said it in the restaurant!" I covered my face, filled with shame.

Cerulean chuckled. "Because I was keeping your body busy with things far more important than last names."

He wasn't wrong about that. I might not have known his last name, but I'd already figured out how to drive him wild with just a touch.

"And you arranged for my beautiful ring to be created." Cerulean held up his hand to admire his wedding band. Then his heated eyes locked with mine. "And you let me put my rings where I wanted them. You let me mark your body as mine."

I blushed, remembering how it had felt to be bound and bred... and wondering when we could do it again.

Cerulean stroked my cheek. "Beryl, I left the sea to find someone who wouldn't care what my family name was or the name of my company. I wanted someone to want me for me, not for my money or social standing. I never have to wonder what you wanted, because you claimed me as yours before you knew any of that."

I hooked my thigh over his hip, loving the feel of skin pressed against bare skin. "I love you."

Cerulean caught his breath. "I thought you said that out on the sea, but you were on the verge of passing out and I thought maybe you hadn't meant it or maybe I misheard."

"When I thought I was dying, it was my biggest regret that I hadn't told you. I don't want to waste any more time." I pressed a hand to either side of his face and pulled his lips to mine. "I love you, Cerulean."

"I love you, Beryl. I've loved you since the moment you opened those beautiful green eyes that very first night."

Our lips met in a kiss that had my blood and body burning with a different hunger. I wanted his body...

I'm yours. Take what you want, Cerulean's husky words brushed through my mind.

Curiosity temporarily distracted me from my lust. I'd wanted to ask him when we'd been in the ocean how the mind thing worked, but I'd been too exhausted.

"How can I hear your thoughts in my head?" I asked between placing kisses along his jawline.

"Octopus shifters have telepathic abilities that allow us to communicate underwater. We have to exchange blood, usually by cutting a tentacle and pressing them together, and the link isn't permanent." He pressed a kiss to the tip of my nose. "I didn't expect it to work with you, since it has never worked outside our species before."

"So exactly how long have you been able to hear my thoughts?" I asked, memories of his random coughs and barks of laughter flashing through my mind.

"Since you first tasted my blood. Your thoughts are adorable and made me feel closer to you, but I know I should have told you sooner." Cer's eyes looked every-where but at me. "Only some things slip through, so I haven't heard everything. And with time, I can teach you how to control what I can hear."

I should have been upset, but he couldn't control what he overheard. Maybe it was good he'd been able to pick up some of my inner thoughts since I'd struggled to open up to him about my feelings.

Which reminded me…

"Cer? Since we're confessing things… there is something

I need to tell you." I blurted out everything I'd suspected and had confirmed by the therapist.

"I'm not sure if you already know this, but vampires don't have fated mates—at least not by the traditional shifter standards. And by that, I mean there isn't one single fated soulmate out there that we need to find, and if we don't find them, we miss out on love."

Cerulean nodded, but his brow was creased as he tried to figure out where I was going with this.

"A vampire can claim anyone they want as a mate, but we also have a type of mate called a bloodmate. Sometimes, if a vampire shares blood with a partner, the blood will decide the match is good, and the vampire's instincts will be driven to complete the bond. When a vampire finds a bloodmate, they can choose to claim the mate, or they can fight their instincts and walk away. If a vampire walks away, it is possible they will find another bloodmate in the future."

"I've never heard of that. It's very interesting, but I'm not sure I understand what this has to do with us?"

"From what I understand, even though there may be two or three suitable bloodmates for every vampire, it is rare to actually find a bloodmate. It's almost unheard of to find a bloodmate outside the vampire species." Pushing him onto his back, I tossed my leg over his hips, straddling him.

"Cerulean." I rocked along his length.

"Hm?" he groaned.

"You're my bloodmate."

335

His eyes flashed open to lock with mine. "What?"

"I couldn't understand the odd hunger that you stirred in me. And frankly, my inability to be away from you was worrying me. So I spoke with an expert on vampiric nature and instincts today. She confirmed what I already suspected." Leaning down, I pressed a kiss to his mouth. "Not only are you my claimed mate, but you're my bloodmate. It gives us a unique connection. I think that's why your telepathy ability works with me."

"I was a perfect match for you?" Cerulean's voice was thick with emotion.

"Yes." I ground my hips against his length, causing us to moan in unison.

Our mouths met in a kiss filled with a passion we couldn't put into words.

Sliding my hand under the blanket and between our bodies, I wrapped my hand around his thick erection.

I lined him up with my entrance...

Only to freeze in horror at the masculine cough coming from our patio.

Chapter 20

BERYL

room 88

I turned my head to find Lapis and an unfamiliar woman standing on the patio. Two large duffel bags lay at their feet.

The blanket covered all my private bits, but from the smirk on Lapis's face and the grin on the female's... they knew exactly what was going on beneath the blanket.

"Seriously, bro? You couldn't have come back in thirty minutes?" Cerulean growled.

Sitting up, he pulled me onto his lap and tucked the blanket around me.

"We can come back." The female's voice held a lyrical quality that reminded me of a songbird.

"No, we need to take care of things." Lapis placed a weird emphasis on the words.

"Then let's at least give them a chance to dress in privacy." The woman stepped inside and pulled the curtain across the patio doors.

"Thank you, Azurea," Cerulean called.

"No problem, brother. Now get dressed so I can properly meet my new sister."

"She's your sister?" I whispered as I rushed from the bed and tried to find something to wear.

"Yes. Azurea is the nicest Thalassa sibling." Cerulean slid a hand across the curve of my butt as I bent to grab clean clothes from my suitcase.

"Stop that!" I hissed. "Or we'll never make it outside."

"Hey, Beryl?" Lapis called from the other side of the curtain. "How do you feel about your brother?"

"I have no brother. He's dead to me, and I hope he rots in hell," I snarled and viciously pulled my shorts over my hips.

"Perfect." Lapis's footsteps walked away from us.

There was a shout and a thud.

"Are they being attacked?" Pulling the shirt over my head, I followed Cerulean. We burst through the curtain to find Lapis standing on the patio with my brother motionless at his feet.

They hadn't brought duffel bags. They'd brought my father and brother.

"You killed him?" I yelped, staring in shock at my almost murderer.

"You said he was dead, and you wanted him to burn in hell…" Lapis scratched the back of his head, confused.

"You did say that." Azurea winced. "We thought you were serious and figured we'd just help tidy things up."

"He was almost dead anyway," Lapis offered, as though that made things better.

"How did you even find them?" I sagged into a chair and rubbed my forehead. I'd need to be very careful how I phrased things around octopus shifters in the future.

"We were with Cerulean when he smelled your blood. By the time we got to the bay where you'd been swimming, you were gone." Lapis rested his hand in the water, splashing it around.

"It was amazing, Beryl. You were bleeding so much in the boat that little drops were leaking into the water. It should have been too diluted for a shifter to follow, but Cerulean was able to scent it and the boat." Azurea sat on the edge of the pool, her feet gently splashing the water.

"How did you catch up?" I looked at Cerulean.

"He called the sea!" Azura grinned at me. "The dolphins answered his call, and the current bent to Cerulean's control over water. I knew he could do party tricks, but I've never seen an octopus shifter with that strong of an ability."

"You caused the current?" I asked, in awe of my mate's strength.

"Yes." Cerulean squatted beside my chair and caught my hands. "I have never been so scared or so angry in my life. I knew I needed to get to you fast. The dolphins were happy to pull us through the water faster than we could have gone ourselves, and I bent the current to push them forward faster."

"The dolphins are still chattering in the bay. You gave them the ride of a lifetime, Cerulean. I have a feeling they will follow you around for a while in hopes you will create another current to ride." Azurea laughed and turned to me. "Dolphins are such adrenaline junkies."

"Once we knew you were in the water, we split up. Azurea and several dolphins followed the boat, and I went to help Cerulean." A dark shape moved to bump Lapis's hand.

Was it one of the dolphins?

Lapis stood and grabbed my brother's arm. "After you were in Cerulean's arms, I rushed back to the resort to find the bolt cutter. Then I went to help Azurea with your family."

Lapis dragged my brother's limp body to the edge of the patio and toed him with his shoe. I watched in shock as my brother rolled into the ocean.

The dark shape smacked the water and then surged away from shore with my brother in its jaws.

"Did you just feed my brother to a shark?" I asked, incredulous.

"No muss, no fuss, no coconut butts." Lapis shrugged.

"At least his body didn't go to waste?" Azurea offered, trying to help me see the positive side of things.

Standing on shaking legs, I made my way to the other body.

"We knocked him over the head so he could see how it felt, so he's still out." Lapis scratched the back of his head.

Kneeling down, I rolled him over.

Inky black eyes met mine. My father lunged upward. His hands reached for my throat, and his fangs lengthened... a trick only full vampires could do.

I reacted on instinct. Grabbing his arm, I threw myself to the side and out of his way. My fangs sank into his arm, and it surprised me when my gums ached.

Cerulean flung him away from me as I gagged on the rotten vampire blood.

"What the—" Cerulean stood over my father's convulsing body.

A few moments later, he went still, his muscles unmoving.

Three sets of blue eyes turned to me.

"What are you looking at? What happened to him?" My chest tightened, and my heart pounded.

"I think you used venom on him," Lapis answered.

"I'm a vampire! We don't have venom, and if we did, my father would have been immune to it!"

"I don't know how you did it, but I think your body stored my venom and repurposed it. Many creatures adapt to have this ability. I think you did, too." Cerulean wrapped me in a hug.

"It would explain why her brother was so weak when we caught up with them. He was complaining she'd bit him. I'm guessing she gave him a lesser dose," Azurea answered, her voice thoughtful.

Lapis pretended to trip over my father, and suddenly, my father's body splashed into the water. A dark shape appeared, and with a splash, swam away.

"Oops." Lapis held up his hands as though he hadn't meant for that to happen.

"Really, Lapis?" Azurea scolded, but her mouth twitched upward.

"The crime took place in the water, so the ocean law stands. They attacked an ocean dweller's mate with the intent to kill. That is unacceptable, and they had to pay Poseidon's price."

Azurea stood and made her way to my side. Cerulean stepped back, and she wrapped me in a tight hug.

"I hope you will come and see us in Boston," I whispered.

They were all the family I had.

"We will!" Lapis gave me a tight bear hug. "Go home and finish your honeymoon... then we'll visit."

We watched them leave and then continued to watch the sun go down on the horizon. Tomorrow, we would leave this paradise.

It would be the beginning of a new chapter

"Cerulean?" I asked, my cheek resting on his chest and listening to the steady beat of his heart.

"Yes?"

"I've made some decisions, and I'd like to talk them over with you before I go through with them."

He placed a kiss on the top of my head. "I'm pretty sure that contract you had me sign said you would be making decisions for your life without my input unless it directly concerned me."

He was teasing, but my cheeks burned. "We are shredding that thing as soon as I get home."

"Are you kidding? I'm framing it. It's proof of my status as your sexy arm candy. Face it, I'm a kept man."

Why did the crazy man sound proud? I shifted positions and straddled his lap. "Cerulean! You're one of the wealthiest men on earth. I can't afford to keep you!"

"No take backs. The contract says so." His arms wrapped around me, and he rested his forehead against mine. "You're stuck with me."

I laughed at his ridiculousness, feeling lighter and happier than I'd felt since I'd been a carefree child.

I knew I should feel sadness about my father and brother, but I didn't. They'd broken our relationship years ago... and tried to kill me. It was a relief to no longer have to worry if they were lurking around.

"A friend from high school is a reporter for a national newspaper. That paper has tried to interview me for years, so I offered her the scoop on our marriage if she'd print it right away. If you are okay with it, she will interview us as soon as we get back."

Cerulean leaned back to study me. "I don't understand. Why would I care?"

"I wanted to do the interview because I wanted the gossipy investing community to know I'm happily married. Everyone is used to me being single and, therefore, available. I wanted to put a stop to that by making sure everyone knows." I paused. "Since few people on land know what you look like, we can just use your initials if you prefer people to not know your business."

Cerulean kissed me, slow and deep.

"What was that for?" I asked, my eyelids growing heavy.

"Because you want to shout from the proverbial rooftop that I'm yours, and it has nothing to do with my last name." Cerulean ran his fingers through my hair. "I love you, Beryl Thalassa."

Tears blurred my eyes.

"I know you wanted to keep—" he began.

I threw my arms around his neck. "My family was awful, and I don't want to be tied to them anymore. I want to be part of your family."

"You already are." His chest rumbled with laughter. "I wouldn't be surprised if my siblings haven't already bought the building next to yours in Boston. They're clingy, runs in the species."

"There's something else," I whispered into the crook of his neck.

He stayed quiet, his palm rubbing soothing circles on my back.

"I love my work, so I'm not ready to retire."

Cerulean started to laugh. "I kind of figured that out already."

Shushing him, I continued. "I'm going to speak with my assistant about taking over most of my day-to-day business. If your family does want to invest in land, I will oversee that. Otherwise, I will let my well-paid and well-trained staff do what I hired them to do. I'll spend my time considering potential acquisitions and then speaking with the owners. But my team will handle the details."

"But why? You made it very clear that your work is important to you." Cerulean was genuinely confused.

"It was. And Chiroptera still is." I absently brushed the backs of my fingers over his stubbled jaw. "But you are more important. By reducing my responsibilities, I should be able to work from home most days. Besides, I'm not sure I could stand to be away from you for ten hours a day while I work."

"I could go to work with you," Cerulean offered.

There was no stopping my laughter. "Cer! We can't be alone together for more than half an hour before we're breeding like bunnies."

"Which reminds me..." Cerulean rose to his feet and carried me toward the bedroom. "It's definitely been over thirty minutes since I last tasted you."

Butterflies took flight in my stomach, and my breathing hitched.

Maybe early retirement isn't such a bad idea...

ABOUT DARCI R. ACULA

Darci R. Acula is Sedona Ashe's not-so-secret pen name. Sedona's books tend to focus on Reverse Harem relationships, while Darci's books feature only MF relationships.

Darci (aka Sedona) doesn't reserve her sarcasm for her books; her poor husband can tell you that her wit, humor, and snarky attitude are just part of her daily life. While she loves writing paranormal shifter reverse harem novels, she's a sucker for true love, twisted situations, and wacky humor.

Darci lives in a small town at the base of the Great Smoky Mountains in Tennessee. She and her husband share their home with their three children, adorable pup, five cats, pet arctic fox, chickens, several crazy turkeys, two chubby frogs, and over a hundred other reptiles. When she isn't working, she enjoys getting away from the computer to hike, free dive, travel, study languages, and capture images of places and animals through her photography. Darci has a crazy goal of writing a million words in a year, and spending six months exploring Indonesia.

You can find more information about the author and her books here:

www.authorsedonaashe.com
www.instagram.com/sedonaashe
www.facebook.com/sedonaashe

SHIFTER PASSION

This recipe was created specifically for Last Shot at Love by Sedona's dear friend, and expert mixologist, José Aponté.

3oz of Sparkling Wine
1oz of Dragonberry Rum Flavor
2oz of Passion Fruit Juice
1/4oz of Grenadine

Shake and Stir Method

Combine the rum and the passion fruit in a shaker with ice and shake for 15 seconds. Strain into a glass Flute without the ice.
Pour in the sparkling wine and very slowly add the grenadine so it can sink to the bottom.
Cut the strawberry in a slice and if you're feeling extra romantic, use a cookie cutter to cut out a heart shape from the slice.

If the strawberry slice is small, drop it in the glass. If it's big, make a cut halfway through and slid it over the rim of the glass.

Enjoy!